PROVEN INNOCENCE

By

MARY J. ROCCO

Printed in the United States of America

Library of Congress Control Number: 2023923813
ISBN 979-8-9896871-0-7 (paperback)
ISBN 979-8-9896871-1-4 (hardcover)

For Everyone With Big Dreams:
It's never too late to pursue your passions.
The first step is believing in yourself.
Anything is possible.

CHAPTER ONE

My eyes are open, but there is no sight to see. Darkness remains. It is black—pitch black. I squint and shut my eyes to adjust to the darkness faster, but it does not help. No shadows lurk in the night for me to redirect my corneas upon. The darkness encloses me, encasing my body in its depth. My body is not upright. It is stretched horizontally across the ground. I am lying down. I try to stand, but my weak body forbids me. My left hand falls upon the surface I am lying on. The ground feels furry, almost carpet-like. I am not outside.

Where am I?

My best deduction indicates I am trapped in a restrictive box. My head has only four inches to move before hitting the top, and my legs are bent at the knees with my toes resting upon the opposite wall from my head. I look up and find a wall of darkness just inches above—pure darkness with no stars or moonlight.

Am I buried alive?

Every human's worst nightmare is to be mistaken for dead and lowered six feet underground where no one can hear the perilous cries for help. I try to scream, but no sound escapes from my vocal cords. Thoughts of Edgar Allen Poe's *Tell-Tale Heart* filter into my brain.

What if the people walking above can hear the faint beating of my heart from the depths below?

Get a hold of yourself!

I raise my right hand slowly to dislodge the top of my coffin. My arm shakes as it rises off the ground above my head. I am limp and exhausted. A sharp pain pulsates throughout my entire right side as I try to move. Electric shock waves run from my toes to the left side of my brain. It is not a comforting sensation, and I would rather not move ever again in my life than experience such agony once more. The only options are, however, shift my body to experience discomfort for a slight moment or lay still awaiting death.

My head is pounding from an obtrusive headache. It is as if a jackhammer is chiseling through the right side of my outer cranium. I wince in pain as I raise my hand to the right side of my head. An overbearing shockwave shoots out of my brain when I touch that area. The hair follicles are mushy, raw, and tender where they meet my skull. The hair is matted to my brain. A huge, painful lump has started to protrude underneath the skin. I am not sure how it got there. I am not sure how I got into the situation I am in at the present moment.

My fingers are sticky from whatever substance has glued my hair to my head. I try to smell them by placing my fingers underneath my nose, but I cannot ascertain the odor. I bring my index finger to my mouth to utilize one of my other senses. It is the last one available to unveil the mysterious substance. My saliva moistens my tongue to activate my taste buds. I recognize a fluid taste mixed with a hint of salt. It is blood––my own blood.

Why am I bleeding? How did this happen?

I am not in a coffin.

Why would they place a bleeding person in a coffin? A bleeding person would not be placed in a grave. That is way too quick of a turnaround for a wake and funeral. I have not been buried alive.

Though not completely fresh, the blood is still somewhat moist and cannot be over a few hours old. It explains why my head pounds and my body aches, though it does not explain where all this discomfort originated.

Then, in the silence, I hear it—the pounding of gravel against the pavement. I am not moving a muscle in my body, yet I am still moving. The low hum of an engine resonates through my eardrums. I feel around and notice a tire drum underneath me.

I am in the trunk of a car.

How did I get here? Where am I headed? Who would do such a thing to me?

There is no indication where I am headed. All I can hear is the low humming of the motor. If I strain, I can hear the faint beat of the radio, unable to recognize any distinguishable words. The only audible sound is muffled voices and murmurs.

Is the driver alone, or does he have a passenger with him?

By the speed, I assume we are on a major interstate. We are traveling pretty fast, and the car is not making any sharp or sudden turns. The ride is smooth without a change in speed to stop for traffic lights or stop signs. It is a straight path along the highway with an occasional lane change.

I have no idea if the person driving knows I am locked in their trunk, though I have a sneaking suspicion he is the person who placed me here. All I can do is lie in wait for the final destination. I am helpless, too weak to do anything drastic. No way to release myself from this dark pit.

My eyes remain open, afraid to drift back asleep. Alertness is a necessity upon arrival at the destination. I must devise a plan for when he takes me out of the trunk.

Should I pretend to be dead and wait until he has me over his shoulders, then initiate a surprise attack?

A problem arises if the person driving never plans to take me out of the trunk at all.

What if the plan is to leave me here until I die a slow and awful death? What if he thinks I am already a dead, lifeless corpse? What if the driver gets out, letting the emergency brake go, watching from the side of the road as the car, with me locked in the trunk, rolls forward into the depths of the nearest lake?

Too many possibilities. To concentrate on survival, I must assure myself that this person driving knows I am here and plans to release me from the dark layer upon reaching his destination.

Seconds seem like minutes, minutes like hours, leaving it nearly impossible to estimate how long I have been lying here. My best guess is about thirty minutes, not including how long I lay there unconscious in the sealed compartment. No sense of day or night. No idea if it is dark or light outside, what day it is, or where I am in the world. I keep straining to listen for faint conversation, but still no luck. The blood on my head is drying and forming the beginning of a thin, crusty layer on top of my skin. My head itches, but I will not move a muscle to scratch it as the pain has not been numbed.

Suddenly, I feel the car turn around a ramp. The curvy road throws my body to the back part of the trunk. Gravity and centrifugal force are not kind to my aching ailments as we exit the major highway. A series of turns are made after the exit, each a few minutes apart. I need to remember how many turns it takes to make a quick getaway back to the interstate, though, at this point, I have no foreseeable idea how that will happen. If my calculations are correct, the car proceeded off the highway as follows: it turned left at the end of the exit ramp; then it proceeded for about three minutes and made another left, a quick right, then another left. The ride begins to feel bumpier as the road beneath the wheels is no longer smooth pavement. From the sound of the gravel below, I deduce the road is not paved. The location is too remote for paved roads––not a good sign.

Everything slows to a stop, and the roar of the engine fades. We have arrived at our destination. Sheer panic ensues.

What am I going to do? Is it best to pretend as if I am still knocked out? This person obviously wants me alive, or he would have finished the job earlier.

Click.

The driver popped open the trunk. It is slightly ajar, just enough to let in a small beam of light but not enough for me to see outside. Muted sunlight breaks through the space between the trunk and the car.

Both the driver's side and the passenger's side doors slam shut simultaneously, causing me to rock back and forth slightly.

There are two people.

The conversation they carry on is too muffled to be deciphered. As I strain to listen, footsteps crunch the gravel below. Each step gets closer to the back of the car. My heart has now leaped out of my chest and onto the floor of the trunk.

This is it—the final moment of truth for destiny to take its course.

I hear a noise I doubt I have experienced before in person. I recognize it, nevertheless. The sound breaks the silence of the morning sky. Two gunshots. Two thunderous gunshots ring out within a close proximity of the trunk where I lie. I cringe and shut my eyes as the shots are fired. I think the gun is pointed at me.

I open my eyes and realize the trunk has never been opened. It remains unlocked, but I still cannot see out. Any person outside will never know I am here. The person who has made his way toward the trunk has not finished opening it. Everything outside is eerily silent. I hear nothing. No talking, no murmurs.

Are the people who abducted me shot dead?

Impossible.

Is the shooter still out there?

I pray he does not know I am lying here helpless. I can only do one thing: remain still for as long as possible. No unnecessary movement to alert this madman there is a woman lurking in the confines of the automobile of the two people he has just shot.

The noise of gravel crunching beneath shoes gets closer and closer to the trunk. The weight of the shoes upon the gravel indicates it is a different person from the original footsteps.

The killer is making his way toward the trunk.

With each step, my nerves tighten. The sound pounds my brain.

He is heading straight for me; I can do nothing about it.

He stops right in front of the trunk.

"Hey, Jimmy, help me load this body into the car."

It is a clear, distinct, deep, manly voice that would be perfect for radio. A voice permanently etched into the contours of my brain. A voice I will never forget.

By car, does he mean the one where I am lying? Even if he doesn't know I am on my death bed in the trunk, he is about to find out as he lifts the back to throw the warm body of the man he's just shot on top of me.

Another set of footsteps inch closer to me. This has to be Jimmy. The two men converse briefly, but the decibel has returned to inaudible levels. Then I hear the dragging. The two killers drag one of the dead bodies away from the trunk I am lying in. The sound of gravel falling to the ground, getting further and further away with each drag. It takes several minutes to get the body where they want.

A car door slams shut. Another set of footsteps heads toward me again.

Pure torture.

My heart is still pounding. Not knowing the precise moment they are to discover me is painful.

"Hey, uh, boss, what about Brandon over here?"

This new voice carries clearly. It is as if he is lying in the trunk with me.

Brandon? They know him. The person who's fired the gunshots knows the man he's killed. The killing was planned, cold-hearted murder.

I listen intently to see if I can make out more of the conversation.

The deep-sounding radio voice rings out, "Leave him there. He won't fit. We'll come back."

With that, the footsteps get further away from my hidden location. Two car doors slam shut, and an engine churns. The killer's vehicle pulls away down the gravel road. The hum of the car fades as it gets further and further away. I have no idea how long to wait, but I do. It already feels like an hour, but it is closer to two minutes. I know I should not wait too long because they will be back. Still helpless and defenseless, however, I cannot go on hiding in the trunk forever. Miraculously, I am granted life again. I must take action.

I slowly lift my arm and push the trunk open. As I quickly sit upright, I feel dizzy. Extreme pain rushes throughout my body. Normally, this would prevent me from going further, but I run on adrenaline. I do not care about the pain; I only care about survival.

Silence.

My eyes adjust to the bright light. I observe the surrounding landscape. It is impossible to take in the serene trees in the forest and the mountain in the backdrop when a corpse is on the ground right next to your car. I assume this was Brandon. He was a husky man who would have made a few bucks being a bouncer in one of those big fancy nightclubs. However, hopes of furthering that career are gone. He is dead——shot fatally in the head with a single bullet. I can only look for a few seconds at his body lying there, face up. It is too gruesome to witness. I imagine the body that was dragged away looked similar in body type.

Funny how Brandon is responsible for my present pain and suffering, yet now I feel a sort of remorse for his loss of life. It is a tragic loss of life, and the killer should be punished.

I gather my bearings and realize I have no idea where I am. All I can see are trees in the middle of secluded woodland. There is a long pebble driveway upon which the vehicle was parked. I proceed to make my way fully out of the trunk by placing both feet firmly on the ground and my left hand on the body of the car to keep myself from tumbling forward. My exhausted body does not want to remain upright. Slowly, I turn around and notice a log cabin set back so far into the woods that you would never know it was there if you were not looking for it. The surrounding oak trees and bushes camouflage the home as part of the natural woodland.

A sense of panic ensues once more.

Whoever killed these two men will be back. If caught here, I will surely be the next target practice victim.

Part of me wants to stay and investigate, but I know better. The only problem is I have no idea where to go as I have no idea where I am. Each second that passes is another second off my survival time. Action must be taken immediately.

I survey the landscape before me. Next to the cabin is a vast field with little coverage to hide. I need to get as far away from my current location as quickly as possible. The vehicle I just got out of is the best option. I jump into the driver's seat and search frantically for anything that would give me a clue where to go. I pull down each visor and check all the side seat pockets.

Nothing.

The glove box is my last bet.

Suddenly, I hear the familiar crunching of gravel on the ground outside. There is a presence at the driver's side window, I do not want to turn around to face it.

The killer has come back to clean up the rest of his mess.

I hear a faint tapping on the window, turn toward it, and scream. There, right in front of me, is a young fawn. I have never been so happy to see a deer in my life. As I scream, it runs the other way. I pause briefly to let my heart settle and go right back to my search of the glove compartment.

I find a map of the state of New York after having searched through a myriad of papers. A clue as to what part of the world I am in. Underneath the map, in the glove box, is a small black zip pouch. I pull it out and open the pouch to uncover the vehicle registration. It reads:

Cynthia Evans
34 Westwood Drive
Preston, NY 12241

This woman may hold the answers to what is happening in my life right now.

I open the map of New York and stretch it across the dashboard. A listing of the major streets in each county appears on the back of the map. There is a Westwood Drive listed in Orange County. No way to know for sure if it is the same Westwood Drive, where Cynthia Evans resides, but it is worth the drive. I scour the map and locate her street. There is a pen clipped to one of the sun visors. I circle the road and decide this is where I am headed——if I can get the car started.

No keys in sight.

As I sit in the driver's seat, trying to determine how to get the motor running, I feel something lightly brush my kneecap. Looking down underneath the steering wheel, I discover two frayed wires.

My last hope.

Taking a deep breath, I take the two wires in both hands. My body shakes as I gently press the two frayed wires together. Sweat is running down my face and dripping off my chin. I pray for it to work because it is my last chance to leave here alive.

Nothing.

Determined, I press the two wires together again. This time, sparks fly about, causing me to jump back. Still, the engine does nothing.

One last time.

It must work. I am out of options.

Taking the wires in my hands, I desperately press them together. Once again, sparks fly about. This time, the engine starts to roar. I press my foot on the gas pedal to reassure myself that I am not imagining the sound of the motor running. I jump excitedly as the car's engine churns, but this is no time to celebrate. The killers will be back any second to collect the second corpse lying on the driveway.

Checking the displays to make sure everything works, the engine revs as I back the car down the long gravel driveway. I try my best to remember how to get back to the major highway and eventually find the New York State Thruway. I arrive at the major road, pull over to the side, and write down all the turns I made. I have a feeling I will be returning to that cabin and at least I will be able to get there when the situation arises.

I study the map again. Westwood Drive is due south. On the map, it is only three inches away—one inch for every fifty miles. If my calculations are correct, it will take at least two hours. I put the car in drive and head to confront Cynthia Evans.

I drive the entire way in silence. No radio. Adrenaline pushing my drive.

This lady had better be able to provide me with answers.

Even after the exhausting early morning experience, I am determined to get answers. Any normal person would be exhausted after all I have been through, but I am determined to find out what happened to me. I begin to think about what I will say when I get there.

How is this woman related to the killer? Was it her husband I saw lying dead on the ground?

If so, I feel sorry for her as a widow. She probably has no idea what he is up to.

Or maybe her husband is the murderer. Maybe she knows every detail of his life and enjoys the thrill of being married to a murderer. Maybe she is in charge in that relationship and ordered a hit against me. Does this woman have some personal vendetta against me?

I will march right up to her and demand answers.

I am …… who am I?

For the first time, I realize I have no idea who I am. I do not know where I have been before waking up in the trunk. Memories from any of my prior encounters have vanished. As far as I am concerned, life began a few hours earlier when I woke up in a trunk, fearing for my life. I begin to cry uncontrollably, tears begin to stream down my face. It must look odd to cars passing by for a young woman, all beat up and dirty, to be clutching the wheel, sobbing out of control. A wave of sorrow, fear, and frustration comes over me simultaneously.

I have no identity.

I try hard to think about my life. I try remembering my parents, hometown, and childhood … but no memories form in my brain.

Should I contact the police? How can I explain to the cops what has happened to me when I don't even know who I am or was?

Cynthia Evans holds the answers I am seeking.

CHAPTER TWO

It is two hours later. I arrive at the suburban household address listed on the car registered to Cynthia Evans. Before me is a typical two-story, blue-painted suburban house with a two-car garage, a small front stoop, and a wooden fence that runs the length of the half-acre property. The front yard has nicely-cut green grass and two beautiful oak trees swaying in the morning breeze. The only a-typical thing about the house is that it is surrounded by yellow police tape, roped off like a murder scene from a thriller movie.

I pull the car to the curb in front of a house across the street, three houses away. I do not want to be seen. The engine comes to a stop, and I sit there for a moment to compose myself.

My search for answers only led me to more questions.

How is this woman related to the men who put me in the trunk of her car? Did they kill her, too? Is this where I was thrown into the trunk? How is this place related to what is happening to me? Are the police looking for me?

The home in front of me is swarming with police investigators and reporters. The scene indicates a serious mess. I do not know my name, let alone if or how this murder and chaos relate to me. I am convinced I am intertwined in the mystery before me, but that is where my knowledge of the situation ends. It does not take a Mensa genius to realize you are in serious trouble when presented with death, murder, and yellow police tape.

Once the madman on this killing spree figures out that I am alive, he will be looking for me. I need to lie low. Safety is a priority.

My gut tells me to contact the police, but I need to figure out who I am first.

No rash decisions until I get some answers. But for now, I will need to hide.

Sitting in a parked car three hundred feet from a police crime scene is not the best place to start hiding out, especially when you are unsure where you are or what you have been up to for the past couple of years. I restart the vehicle and drive. I have no destination in mind, just not Westwood Drive. Any place is better than my present location.

As I veer off Westwood, my brain starts to analyze the morning's events.

Did I really wake up in the trunk of this car just a few hours earlier?

I glance at the radio display next to the dashboard. It is a little after 8:30 a.m. My stomach rumbles as the adrenaline begins to wear off. Three miles down the main road on the right-hand side, I happen upon the Village Diner. It is the best option around to stop and figure things out. A quaint place with both 'I's in the neon sign lacking illumination.

I drive into a parking space toward the back of the diner. Before entering the restaurant, I know I have to be incognito. It is particularly hard to hide from someone when you do not know whom you are hiding from. I have no idea who is looking for me, but I have a suspicion he will not hesitate to make me his next victim. I will recognize that voice from miles away, but I will never see him coming if he is a silent stalker.

I scrounge around the car in hopes of something, anything that would hide me. Lying on the floor behind the passenger seat, I find an old Montreal Expos baseball cap—a perfect cover-up for my blood-scabbed head and dirty hair. I find a pair of sunglasses in the side panel of the driver's side door. Perfect.

I pull down the visor and look in the mirror to observe my disguise.

Not a total makeover, but it will have to do.

I reach for the handle to exit the vehicle and realize I have no money. No money means no food.

What will I do to afford a meal at the diner?

I open the glove box and dig around the mess of papers inside. Stuck to the very bottom, I find an envelope. It is a white sealed letter envelope with black block lettering on the outside reading 'FOR EMERGENCIES ONLY.'

I am hungry and on the run—sounds like an emergency to me.

Ripping open the envelope, I find ten twenty-dollar bills. Luck is with me. If ever there is a day to play the lottery, I am sure it is today. The lottery, however, will have to wait as my stomach growls in anticipation of the meal to come.

I get out of the car, leaving the door unlocked as I do not have the keys that belong to the vehicle. I close the door and walk up the ramp toward the entrance to the diner. Inside is a small joint. Five booths line the left side of the restaurant. In the back are a few tables for bigger parties. A counter with swivel stools runs along the right side of the restaurant. Two coffee pots sit on burners, fully brewing behind the counter, and hot food lies in the kitchen window, waiting to be picked up and delivered to hungry customers.

There are not many people inside, more employees now than actual customers. It is the type of diner in which you expect your waitress to be a curly, red-haired, gum-chewing, middle-aged lady named Alice and the chef, a toothpick-chewing, white undershirt-wearing, bald guy named Tony. Even though the only other customers in the establishment are a couple sitting at the front booth and an older man sitting at the counter drinking coffee, I still wait to be seated. Obviously, the hostess is not in a hurry to please the potential customers. She appears annoyed as she has to set down her cup of coffee and interrupt her story mid-sentence to provide me with a table. She does make eye contact as she guides me along the aisle to a booth in the back corner of the diner. I am thankful I am sitting in the back as I do not want to be recognized until I have figured out the mess I am in.

It is not easy to know if people recognize you or know who you are when you do not even recognize your own self in the mirror. I am banking on the fact that this was probably not my favorite place in my past life.

The menu is a typical novel-length diner menu that does not require reading, as they probably have every imaginable concoction one could create a craving for. Still, I try to read through some of the options in the breakfast section. The lighting above the booth is too dim, so I remove the sunglasses to read the food descriptions. My stomach fills with butterflies as I think more about the crime scene at the Evans' house than what I will eat for breakfast.

My appetite is not ravenous. I must eat something to prepare myself for the events that will undoubtedly unfold in the hours ahead. I have to keep my energy up to keep myself alert and moving. The menu lies open on the table before me, but I absorb no words. My mind races a mile a minute. It is hard to concentrate. I jump as the waitress asks me if I am ready to order. I have not noticed her standing over me with her notepad and pen.

Looking up, I find a pretty young blonde. She looks way too young and put together to work in a diner. My visions of diner waitresses include middle-aged, overweight, unattractive, divorced ladies. In my world, the typical diner waitress has had a hard life, evident from the lines and wrinkles on her face. Here before me is a fairly attractive woman in her middle twenties. She has a pleasant smile, and her hair is blown out straight, every strand in its perfect place. Not who I expected to be standing before me as I exit my trance.

"Sorry, I didn't mean to startle you," she says, staring at me with a puzzled expression.

"No, you didn't startle me," I reply, making it a point not to look at her or make eye contact.

"Can I take your order?" I must look confused, almost as if I have forgotten that I am in a diner and there to eat a meal. "Lady, are you alright? You look a little frazzled."

No time to panic, compose yourself, and make her mind her own business.

I look at her with half a smile, "It's been a long night. I'm not really in the mood for small talk." She is taken aback at my rudeness, but I am sure it is no ruder than she is accustomed to from her regular cheapskate customers: "I'll start with a cup of coffee, thanks."

Look down at the menu! Maybe she will get my cup of coffee without any further remarks.

The waitress lingers for another few seconds as if she is about to say something, but without so much as a peep, she turns around and heads behind the counter.

I pray she does not recognize me. It is possible to see how a person could be suspicious of me. I am filthy and acting shady.

Order a fast meal and get the hell out of the diner before you are recognized.

No more than two minutes later, the waitress returns with my coffee, placing it on the ad-filled placemat before me.

"Are you ready to order?" She has one knee cocked to the left, and her pen is upright, ready to jot down my culinary choices for breakfast.

I close the menu and push it to the edge of the table closest to the waitress. "An egg sandwich with cheese on an English muffin. Eggs over easy, please. Also, a side of home fries well-done." As I place my order, I wonder if I am still myself in many ways.

I order my eggs over easy, but is that how I really like them, or does the real me prefer scrambled eggs?

I have no way of knowing what the truth is, what parts of me are lost, and what parts of me remain.

Before the waitress leaves the table, I ask for a newspaper to read to distract my thoughts. She walks away and comes back with the early edition of the local *Daily News* dated today, September 12, 2007. The woman on the front page looks vaguely familiar, though I cannot grasp from where.

I read the headline: 'Search Is On For Cynthia Evans.'

I begin to shake as I read those six words.

It is her.

CHAPTER THREE

"It is her, I'm sure of it," Gabrielle told her coworker as she stood behind the counter, marrying the two coffee pots into one.

"You're crazy," her coworker assured her. "Why would Cynthia Evans stop in a diner … never mind the Village Diner, if she's on the run for murder? Besides, you are always looking for an adventure and a way to leave your boring life."

Her coworker may not believe her, but Gabrielle was sure of it. When she brought the newspaper over to her customer, she got a glimpse into the eyes of the lady sitting there. The green eyes gave it away. As she placed the newspaper on the table, Gabrielle compared the double sets of eyes between the woman before her and the paper's front cover. There was no denying the similarities.

Gabrielle had been fascinated with the headline story when she saw the newspaper cover that morning. It was the top story of the day, creating a media frenzy. Nothing of this stature has ever happened to the small town of Preston before. Cynthia Evans is thought to have gone off the deep end, a psychotic break, due to the pressures of her not-so-perfect marriage. The woman, whom her neighbors described as a 'quiet loner,' took a gun and killed her family. Her two young boys and her husband were found ruthlessly murdered in the home. A *Daily News* reporter interviewed the next-door neighbor, who openly stated she heard the gunshots, and when she went to look out the window, she saw Cynthia's car peel out of the driveway. The police put out a countywide search for the murderous wife; little did they know that here she sits in the Village Diner, awaiting an egg sandwich.

Any normal individual would be scared and run back, wanting to call the cops, but Gabrielle felt something different about Cynthia. She had a very calm demeanor, nothing at all like one would suspect of a heartless murderer. Gabrielle did not fear for her life. She does not fear death. The end is welcomed.

Gabrielle had been fantasizing more and more about how she would end it all. Three weeks ago, she scored an illegal prescription of sleeping pills, a black-market online purchase. The bottle was strong enough to sedate her into the afterlife. She was not sure what was holding her back. Each day after work, she goes home, sits on the couch, and grasps the bottle of pills in her hands. She just stares at the bottle. Her hands clam up, and sweat drips down her forehead, but that is as far as it goes.

"Today is the day," she tells herself. Yet, she never does it.

Two days ago, she managed to get the cap off the bottle, but the pills did not make it from her hands to her lips. Sometimes, she would sit on the couch for over an hour contemplating her death. Gabrielle knew it was cowardly, and she should be able to face her life, but why should she? There was nothing to live for, and not a soul would miss her, except maybe her coworker April, who would have to cover her extra shifts until a new server could be found. Not even her live-in boyfriend Hank would mourn her death. Really, the worst that could happen in befriending a murderer was no different than what she would face on her own when she returned to her apartment every day after work, the possibility of death.

Gabrielle did not fear the wrath of Cynthia Evans. Granted, the only interaction with this individual was her ordering an egg sandwich, but the vibe differed. Cynthia appeared helpless and lost. She was Gabrielle's ticket out of town, or at least a ticket out of depression. Opportunity came knocking, and Gabrielle would not let this fly away. She hated this town and needed a reason to leave——leave in both the physical and emotional sense.

Sure, Cynthia appeared frazzled and distraught, but she needed a friend and a place to run to. Gabrielle had nothing to lose in offering this to her.

"Gabby, I can see that look in your eyes. Please don't do anything stupid that you'll regret." She frowned at her overcautious coworker, April, and wondered where her sense of adventure was.

The cook peered from the back kitchen. "Hey, Gabrielle. Your food is sitting in the window. It's going to get cold."

The egg sandwich and home fries sat underneath the heat lamp above the counter. Gabrielle took the two plates in her hands and headed to the booth in the back corner of the restaurant where Cynthia was sitting. She placed the food in front of her customer and devised a way to start a casual conversation with the fugitive.

"Can I get you anything else?" she asked politely.

"No thanks," the mysterious customer said shyly without looking up from the newspaper before her.

This was getting nowhere.

As Gabrielle turned to walk away from the table, she decided to be brave and lay it all out, hoping for the best. She would be no worse off. The worst-case scenario would lead Gabrielle back to sitting on the couch after work, contemplating the end.

Gabrielle plopped down on the other side of the booth across from the unsuspecting murderer. "Listen, I know who you are."

Cynthia looked startled and amazed. "You do?"

"I can help you if you let me," Gabrielle pleaded. Cynthia stared back, expressionless. "I want to help you."

"I am sorry, but I don't need your help," she answered abruptly, trying to end the conversation.

"Well, you're not going to get very far without it. Listen, meet me outside around back when you are done eating. I'll take you to get cleaned up."

With that, Gabrielle got up from the table and left Cynthia alone to eat her breakfast. All she could do was pray that Cynthia would accept her offer of help and the two would be off on an adventure like Thelma and Louise. It was just the kind of excitement Gabrielle craved in her depressing and drab existence. She needed a reason to get away from her life. She was tired of being controlled by her abusive boyfriend, and this was the perfect opportunity to leave. It was a sign from God. She was sure of it.

CHAPTER FOUR

The waitress has just left. I sit here in the booth, now more puzzled than ever.

Does this woman really know who I am? Why is she so willing to help me? Maybe she has some answers about who I am and what is happening. Or is it a trap to lure me out of the restaurant to get me out back to finish the job that the madman didn't get to do in the early morning hours? Maybe she is the madman, a madwoman disguised as a diner waitress …

I am overanalyzing everything.

My instinct tells me not to trust anybody. But she is right; I will not be able to do this myself. If I have to trust somebody, she seems like the best bet. If she is an acquaintance of mine, she will be able to help. It is a risk I have to take, especially if I want answers. I know the two killers are of the male persuasion unless they are females with extremely deep voices. True, they could have a woman working with them to lure my trust, but the facts present before me today lead me to adduce that this woman is not working for them. Still, it is not to be ruled out completely.

I will go to the back of the restaurant and meet her, but not without my guard up.

I finish the last bite of my egg sandwich and leave some money on the table to cover my bill and tip. As I get up from the booth, I notice the butter knife resting across the dirty plate on the table. I slyly snag the knife and place it into my front pocket, anticipating the need for protection from the upcoming confrontation outside. I fold the newspaper under my arm and proceed toward the front door, out of the diner. Though the newspaper belongs to the restaurant, I take it so I can read the article on Cynthia Evans again. I need to understand who this woman is and how I am involved in her killing spree.

Once outside, I go to the car, start the engine, back it out of the parking spot, and pull it around to the back of the restaurant by the dumpsters, awaiting the waitress. Each second that passes feels like an eternity. I keep expecting a person with a gun to appear at my window, threatening me to get out of the car. I keep the motor running, the gears in drive, and my foot on the brake in case I need to make a quick getaway.

Panic ensues, and my heart races.

This woman is taking her sweet time.

The longer I wait, the less I think meeting this woman is a good idea. I envision being lured into a trap, surrounded by the swat team with megaphones telling me to 'come out with my hands up.' Engrossed in my horrific fantasy, I jump when the woman knocks on my window.

I roll down the driver's side window and let her talk first, making sure that the knife from the restaurant is in full view, ready to be used if necessary.

"I thought you were just going to take off. Thank you for waiting."

She is alone.

I stare at her, waiting for her to tell me what she wants. She shivers in her short-sleeved polo shirt as the crisp fall air blows fallen leaves in the wind.

"Listen, I can help you if you let me. Where are you headed? I want to come."

Is this woman out of her mind? "Do we know each other? Are we friends?"

The waitress looks perplexed. The longer she stands in the cold, the more I realize we are not friends. This confuses me more. Nevertheless, I will not survive alone, and need assistance. The problem is I have no idea whom to trust.

Tired of looking at her rubbing the goosebumps on her arms for warmth, I unlock the passenger side door and let her into the car. A giant step in trust.

"Let me help you, Cynthia."

Why is she calling me Cynthia?

"We can run away together and start a new life. We'll go to some remote state like Nebraska and start new lives where nobody knows about the life we have lived before."

I must set her straight. "I am sorry, but I think you confuse me with another person. I'm not Cynthia."

She looks perplexed and stunned. "You don't have to lie to me. I know it's you." She grabs the newspaper lying on the back seat of the car. It is the paper I stole from the diner. Pointing at the front page, she exclaims, "I'm not stupid. You mean you will blatantly lie and tell me that this person on the *Daily News* front page is not you?"

She goes on and on about how she does not care what horrendous crime I am being accused of and how it does not matter to her because all she wants to do is get away from her life and this small town. I do not process any of what she is saying. As the words spew from her mouth, I gaze at the unfamiliar picture on the paper's front cover. I do not recognize the face before me.

Surely, I would be able to recognize the contours of my face. Surely, I would be able to look into the eyes of the picture and see that it is me.

But I do not see me. All I see is this woman, who has a faint familiarity about her but not an inherent one for which I can shout, "Look, it's me on the front cover."

Surely, I would know myself and recognize a picture of myself even if I don't know my name.

The woman in the picture has straight brown hair and green piercing eyes, hardly the face of a relentless killer.

Why would this woman commit such atrocities against her family?

All I can do is stare in shock and disbelief at this waitress who thinks I am Cynthia Evans, the woman wanted for murder on the front page of the newspaper.

"I think you are mistaken. I'm not her." *Although I have no idea who I am, I am certain I would know if I am a heartless murderer.* "I am not her, but I'm looking for answers from her."

I am sure this statement confuses the waitress even more.

"Well, if you're not Cynthia Evans, who are you?" she asks.

I stare at her blankly, unable to answer. The woman stares back at me, awaiting some sort of response. The longer I remain silent, the more impatient she becomes. Finally, she breaks the silence and grabs the door handle to get out of the car. Tears form in the corners of her eyes.

"Well," she whimpers, "I'm sorry. I've made a terrible mistake here."

"Wait!" I instinctively grab her arm to keep her in the car. "Please. Don't go!" Something tells me I must trust her and let her help me. "I don't know who I am." I try to hold back the tears now forming in my eyes. "I can't remember who I am."

CHAPTER FIVE

Somehow, Gabrielle's convinced me to let her drive. It is better as she is familiar with the town, which is foreign to me. I am positive she is even more confused after walking around to the car's driver's side and getting in. Gabrielle pauses for a moment as if waiting for me to give her the key, but without saying a word, I lean over from the passenger seat to grab the frayed wires underneath the steering wheel. Sparks fly as I rub the frayed wires together to start the motor running.

Gabrielle does not ask me any questions. It is not clear if she is trying to figure out my story or if she hopes that as time passes, I will get more comfortable and eventually open up and tell her the truth about who I am.

The problem is, I do not know the truth. There is nothing to tell. My life story started five hours earlier as I arose from my grave and drove to the diner where she works. The rest is a mystery waiting to be unraveled. I am just as confused about why Cynthia would kill her family. How Cynthia's life is intertwined with mine is the number one question on my mind.

We drive for approximately fifteen minutes. I assume we are heading back to her humble abode. After that, I have no idea what the plan will be. I know I have to go to the police at some point to let them know a murderer is lurking in the countryside about two hours north. That may be the link they need to find out what really happened in the Evans' household the night before. It is still in my head. I know exactly how to return to that horrific spot in the wilderness. There, by the abandoned cabin, lies the answers to many questions, though all the questions have yet to be formulated.

Gabrielle pulls the car next to the curb and lets the engine roar to a stop. "We have arrived."

We are at a rundown apartment complex in a not-so-nice neighborhood, but there is no immediate sense of danger in the air. We leave the car and head toward an apartment on the first floor facing the busy street. Inside, it is charming, yet small. As you enter the front door, the kitchen is straight ahead. There is a tiny table against the far wall with enough chairs for two people to eat. Any greater number would not fit. The living room is to the right. There is a sofa bed, two end tables on each end of the sofa, and a flat-screen television. Toward the back of the TV room is a door——presumably, a bedroom. To the right of the door is the bathroom. The apartment is a nice enough size if you were single and did not require much space. It made me wonder where I live.

Do I live in a house or an apartment? Do I live alone, or would my roommate wonder why I haven't returned home the night before? How do I decorate my walls? What kind of stuff do I own? Do I like to cook?

There are way too many questions running through my mind at once. Before I can figure out the answers, I have to be able to find the answer to the most important question: *Who am I?*

Gabrielle gives me a clean towel and shows me the shower. It is exactly what I need. The blood and dirt are crusted to my body, holding on as if to form a new layer of skin on my being. It is the most orgasmic shower I have ever taken. I do not have to have any recollection of other showers in my life to know that it was the best shower of my lifetime. The jet streams from the showerhead rejuvenate my spirit. As I wash away the grime, I feel lifted and refreshed. The dead blood rushes off my body and down the drain. Every inch of my body gets a scrubbing with soap until I am positive the day's filth is vanquished. I must shampoo and rinse twice to make my hair soft and manageable. The cleansing process takes so long that my fingers wrinkle from the constant exposure to the water. Once done, I feel like a new person. A renewed, refreshed spirit emerges.

I turn off the water and step out of the shower. I wrap the towel around my torso and head toward the sink. The mirror above it is now foggy from the steamy water of the shower. I take my right hand, wipe away the condensation on the mirror, and squint at the sight before me. I raise my hands to my face, probing every line, pore, and structure in the reflection.

Could it be?

I stare at the image in the mirror in disbelief. I see a slight resemblance to the woman on the front page of the *Daily News*. My mind is definitely playing tricks on me. The features are undoubtedly similar. I have the brown hair and the green eyes, but there is no possible way I am Cynthia. However, it does irk me at how similar we look, especially after washing away all the grime. The clean version of me reflects an undistinguishable resemblance to the merciless murderer.

A man's voice, loud and distinctive, breaks my staring contest with the reflection in the mirror. Gabrielle is no longer alone. I dry myself off and slowly put on the fresh clothes she provided me. As I dress, I am attentive to the conversation outside the door. I have to be certain this person is familiar to Gabrielle and that we were not followed to her apartment. The voice is getting louder, and a screaming match ensues between the mystery man and Gabrielle.

CHAPTER SIX

Gabrielle sat on the couch while Cynthia showered. She was out of her mind. Only a mentally unstable person would befriend a wanted killer and invite them back to their house. Somehow, in her brain, she rationalized the saneness of her thoughts at the diner. She convinced herself it was appropriate and normal. She knew if she got caught with Cynthia, she could be an accomplice to murder. Locked up for the murder of people she never met a day in her life. Somehow, it all seemed worth it.

Gabrielle sat back and noticed the bottle of sleeping pills sitting on the table beside her. She still had options. She could end it all right then and not worry about spending the rest of her life behind bars, beating society to the punch.

She could avoid the consequences of her bad decision and end it all. Gabrielle grabbed the bottle of pills in her hand. She tossed it back and forth between her left and right hands as she contemplated ending it all. There she sat, right back in the very situation she thought she was escaping by meeting Cynthia. Thoughts of suicide weighed heavily on her brain.

In all honesty, what did she have to live for? This woman was a murderer, not to be trusted. She would not even admit to who she was. For all Gabrielle knew, she was in the shower planning her next unsuspecting attack. The newspaper made her out to be a horrific individual, incapable of compassion. Gabrielle did not see any remorse from this woman; she did not see any regrets in the contours of her face. Yet the label of a killer did not seem appropriate. None of the classic signs of brutality were present in Cynthia's persona. She did not appear agitated, mentally unstable, incapable of carrying on conversation, or short-fused. The opposite was true. Cynthia was grateful, polite, and soft-spoken. Regardless of what Gabrielle thought, the woman in her shower was still the number one suspect in the murder of Rick Evans.

This was not the answer she was looking for. There was no answer. Nobody would come to visit her as she rotted in jail. Nobody would write letters to her. Not even her boyfriend, Hank. Gabrielle never thought her life could get any worse. She thought she had reached rock bottom. Staring at the woman on the front page of the newspaper now resting on the couch beside her, Gabrielle realized her life had just gotten twenty times worse upon meeting Cynthia Evans. Tears streamed down her face. Her hands shook with a nervous tick. There was no way out. There was no place better. Even if Cynthia and she went off on an adventure, they would always be on the run, always on the lookout over their shoulders. That was no way to live. She did not want that life.

She did not want her current life.

Gabrielle grabbed the bottle of pills and tried to remove the cap. This was it; it was time to end it all. She finally made her decision, and there was no turning back. After several tries, the cap finally came off. Gabrielle turned the bottle upside down and emptied twenty pills into her hand. She was so caught up in her decision to take her own life that she did not hear the doorknob turn and the front door slam.

"What in hell do you think you are doing?"

Before Gabrielle could react to his presence, he flew his fist toward her sitting on the couch, hitting her hands and flinging the numerous pills onto the carpet. Gabrielle looked up at him, speechless. There was nothing to be said. Hank had just caught her about to kill herself, and this enraged him.

"I've asked you a question, bitch. What are you doing?" He stood over her. She could feel his heart pulsating from less than a foot away.

"That, quite frankly, is none of your business," Gabrielle snapped back.

As she spoke, she shoved him away so she could stand up from the couch. She needed to gain some leverage to defend herself from further attempted physical assault. As she stood, Hank took both hands and shoved Gabrielle's entire body onto the floor. Gabrielle knew she had made him mad, but she underestimated how furious he had become. Hank lifted his hand to continue the beating when he heard the shower turn off in the bathroom.

"Who is here?" Gabrielle did not answer, which only enraged him more. "I asked you who is here?"

CHAPTER SEVEN

"**Y**ou stupid fucking whore. Get up off the floor!"
The man's voice fills with rage. I huddle behind the bathroom door in fear, fully expecting him to break it down to get me. Shivers run up and down my spine, paralyzing me with the frightening thought that I have been discovered, and this is the end.

"This is my ticket out of here, away from you and your pathetic life," Gabrielle yells back.

There are evident tears in her voice. With those words, I realize the strange voice is a person Gabrielle knows. I wait in the bathroom, not wanting to reveal my presence in the apartment.

"You'll never leave me," he growls back at her.

"This time it is over." Her voice has a distinct fear as she utters those five words.

I prop myself closer to the door now that I know it is a fight between two familiar people. I stand next to the bathroom door as an eerie silence overcomes the apartment—the calm before the storm.

The beating starts. The wall shakes as a body slams into it on the other side of the apartment. Punches are being thrown— the sound of a fist smacking upon the skin of another. Gabrielle screams and whimpers in pain, each loud smack breaking the sound barrier. These are not love taps. There are perilous screams and cries begging him to stop.

I am unsure how long I have been hiding in the bathroom, but I finally muster the courage to intervene. Emerging from the bathroom, I find the strange man hovering over Gabrielle, curled on the floor next to the couch.

"Get the fuck off of her, you bastard!" I yell as I run toward him.

I reach for his fist before he lays another one on her. Instead of hitting her, he punches me straight in the stomach, knocking the wind out of me. I float in the air about a foot before landing on my side on the carpet. I crawl backward and away from him. I am hunched over, my left hand cradling my midriff. As I gasp for air, I finally get a good look at the son-of-a-bitch. At first glance, he does not seem all that intimidating. He is of average height and slender build. He has some muscular arms covered with tattoos——nothing in particular, but rather a cluster of objects and colors.

After that last swing at me, the madness has stopped. The batterer stands in the living room with Gabrielle to his right and me to his left. He is perplexed and does not know which of us to lunge at next.

Standing before the two of us, his breathing slows to a pant. I lie on the carpet, afraid to move for fear of another blow to the abdomen. The man stands there in a trance. He is taking in the events unfolding before him, his eyes focused on the couch. He peers over at the newspaper lying on the worn-out cushions. He slowly walks toward the couch. Gabrielle winces with each step he takes closer to where she lies. The man picks up the newspaper and peers intently at me. I can tell by the intensity of his stare, he, like Gabrielle, thinks I am the woman making headlines.

"You fucking bitches have no idea what's coming to you," he sneers at us. "You think you're so brave…justice will prevail." He takes one last long look around the apartment before heading into the bedroom and slamming the door behind him.

The coast is clear. I gather myself from the floor and limp over to Gabrielle, still crouched in the corner of the room. She is sobbing uncontrollably and covering her head with her hands. I do not say a word. I only wrap my arms around her body and give her a great big hug. Her body trembles as I console her. She peers up from her hands and lets out half a smile. I extend my arm to help her to her feet.

The damage is brutal. Black and blue marks are on her right arm and down her back. I guess it is from where he grabbed her and threw her against the wall. He has also given her a black eye and a swollen lip.

Who knows how extensive the damage could have been had I not intervened?

I look her square in the face and say, "Let's get the hell out of here!"

CHAPTER EIGHT

The two girls got in the car and drove with no specific destination in mind. They only knew they had to get far away from that apartment and Gabrielle's raging boyfriend.

Gabrielle had many questions—yet she did not want to know the answers. She did not want to know if this woman holding the steering wheel beside her could kill her family. It seemed impossible, especially after the compassion she displayed upon witnessing the wrath of Hank.

It was one of Gabrielle's worst episodes with Hank in a long time. Usually, he would yell a bit and smack her a few times across the face. Gabrielle would wind up with minor purple marks and a bruised lip. Maybe Hank sensed this time was different. This time, he could no longer control her. Countless times, she had threatened to leave him, yet she always came crawling back. Gabrielle even had him placed in the slammer several times because of the marks he left on her body. Still, she came back. Not because she was dumb, not because she was in love, not because she was weak … but because she had nowhere else to go. No matter how terrible things got between them, Hank always apologized and let her return to the apartment.

This time was different.

This time, she was through with him for good. It was the worst he had ever messed her up. It was almost as if he knew this time was different, and he was scared—scared of losing her. Hank loved her. She knew it. No matter how badly he beat her, Gabrielle knew he loved her and would always be there for her.

She had no friends or family. She did not make enough money to afford rent or food. It was a no-win situation. Either end it all or continue with a life of never-ending torment.

When Cynthia Evans walked into the diner that morning, it was Gabrielle's chance to run and get away. Befriending a criminal left her no worse off than if she took her life. If it got bad, ending it all is still on the table. How bad could it be living with a felon on the run? It definitely seemed better than coming home every night fearful it might be your last should your paramour decide to take one too many swings at you that evening. However, she did not expect to find such a kind and gentle individual. They had only been in each other's presence for a few hours, but there was no fear. Gabrielle did not fear for her life. She did not find Cynthia to be crazy and irrational. The exact opposite was true. Cynthia was displaying signs of compassion and consideration. The only perplexing part of the situation was Cynthia's denial that she was Cynthia.

Perhaps Gabrielle was mistaken, and the woman in the diner was not the 'Murderer from Preston.' Maybe Gabrielle had a case of mistaken identity. But the puzzling part was, earlier on, she told Gabrielle that she did not know who she was. When walking into the diner, Cynthia was clearly not well. She was trying to hide herself from the world. The cap and sunglasses were a poor attempt at an obvious disguise. There was more to this story. So many questions needed to be asked and answered, yet Gabrielle refrained. She was afraid. She did not want to know the truth. In the short hours they had known each other, a bond of friendship had formed.

Cynthia did not know it, but she saved Gabrielle. Without Cynthia, she would be sitting on the couch, contemplating suicide for the sixteenth time this month. Gabrielle did not have many people in her life she could trust. She did not have a lot of people in her life. Period. Her whole life had been that way. Growing up, her mother left upon birth, abandoning her in the nursery at the hospital. She spent her life jumping from foster home to foster home, unable to maintain close friendships as she rarely remained in a household long enough to complete half a school year in the same district. When Gabrielle turned eighteen, she aged out of the foster care system, and her foster mother threw her out on the street. All that woman cared about was the stipend she received and making room in her home for the next income-producing child. Alone on the streets with no real place to turn, she met Hank. Hank took her in and gave her a roof over her head.

It was not always this bad between her and Hank. At first, he was charming and sensitive. It took eight months into the relationship before he laid a hand on her. Even then, Gabrielle thought it was a simple mistake. He swore it would never happen again. She was never truly in love with him, but he was always there for her. She felt such an allegiance toward him, even when things were bad. He knew her better than any other person on the planet. He knew her well. He knew Gabrielle would jump at an opportunity to leave and never return. This was why he became so enraged when she told him she was leaving with Cynthia. He walked into that apartment and could smell the air was different. There was no "Hello, sweetheart." He had to let her know this was not acceptable behavior.

Gabrielle pulled down the sun visor above the passenger seat in the car. She opened the mirror and stared at her face. The bruising had already started to turn various shades of purple. She winced in pain as she brought her fingers to her eye to touch the swollen skin.

Cynthia looked over from the driver's side. "Painful, huh?"

Gabrielle looked over at her and nodded. "So where are we headed anyways?" Gabrielle asked.

"Do you have a few hours to kill?"

Gabrielle did not answer her. Even though the media had accused this woman of horrific crimes, Gabrielle was not afraid. She had complete trust in Cynthia wherever she decided to take her.

CHAPTER NINE

Iam not sure why I feel the need to share with Gabrielle the events in my life that unfolded earlier today. She seems trustworthy enough. She shared a horrific part of her life with me, and I should return the favor. It is foolish to return to the murder scene in the woods. I certainly was not going back alone. There is comfort in knowing another individual will be there with me. I have to assure myself I am not crazy. I have to assure myself I did, in fact, wake up earlier this morning in the trunk of the very car I am now driving. I need answers. The remote cabin in the woods is as far back as I can remember, and I cannot think of a better place to start and retrace my steps.

My stomach is starting to rumble. The egg sandwich at the break of dawn is all I have consumed today. It is time to refuel. A rest stop emerges right before the New York Thruway entrance. I pull the car off the exit ramp and head for the 'cars only' parking pavilion. It is a typical rest-stop area with a coffee shop, an ice cream place, an array of fast-food chains, and the ever-popular New York Thruway gift shop. The only evidence of civilization for the next fifty miles. We both leave the car and head into the junk food heaven. I am famished. All of the items on the greasy burger menu make me drool. I decide on the quarter-pound burger minus the cheese. Gabrielle opts for the fried chicken sandwich.

We eat in silence. I want to tell her my story, but the rest area, filled with people, is not the best place to unveil my tale. Too many people can overhear what I am saying. If the wrong person hears even a smidge of what I have to say, I could be in jeopardy. I decide to wait until we get back to the car.

After devouring our unwholesome meals, we head toward the car. I empty the remaining liquid from my soda cup into the garbage. I head to the self-serve soft drink dispensers. I fill the cup with ice to help ease Gabrielle's swelling. She is more than grateful for the gesture. As we exit the building into the parking lot, I spot the gift shop out of the corner of my eye. It is just what I need. Something deep in my stomach tells me it is essential for our journey.

CHAPTER TEN

Gabrielle turned around, and Cynthia was gone. She was sure she had been right behind her a second before. Could she have taken off and left Gabrielle stranded in the middle of nowhere? Maybe Cynthia was not the selfless, caring person she portrayed. Gabrielle's heart started racing, and panic began to ensue. She had nowhere to go if she was left here in the middle of the thruway. She had no home to return to and no person to call to come get her. After a minute and a half of daunting thoughts, Cynthia reappeared. She pushed open the building door and walked on the sidewalk toward Gabrielle.

"I thought you ran off without me," Gabrielle said with a sigh of relief.

"Now, why would I do that?" Cynthia stated as if that was the craziest thing she had ever heard. "Sorry, I didn't mean to leave you stranded outside here alone. I just noticed an essential item I had to pick up for our trip."

With those words, she handed Gabrielle a white plastic bag with an "I Love NY" logo. Gabrielle looked inside to find a disposable camera.

"This was your urgent purchase?" She was baffled——why was this necessary for where they were going?

"I'll explain on the ride."

The two adventurers got into the car and headed up into the mountains.

CHAPTER ELEVEN

I felt the urge to tell Gabrielle everything. She had to be in the know. She had to know I am not Cynthia and I am not crazy. I divulged everything to her. She just sat there in the passenger seat, passively listening. I could tell she was intrigued by my story, but she did not ask any questions. It was as if she was afraid to interrupt me, fearful I would clam up and not finish my statements. My story had to be surreal to her——it was surreal to me. As the words came out of my mouth about the trunk and the dead bodies, I found it hard to believe, and I was a firsthand witness to the entire gruesome scenario.

"So we're driving back up to the scene of a murder. What if they're still there?" Gabrielle had every right to question the insanity I was proposing.

"That's a risk I'm willing to take. It's not whether I want to return; I have nothing to lose. The question is whether or not you are willing to come with me. Remember, should you say yes, then there is no turning back. But if you are unwilling … I will turn this car around and return you to your old existence in Preston. The choice is yours."

Gabrielle sat silently in the passenger seat next to me for what seemed to be an eternity.

CHAPTER TWELVE

Gabrielle did not come this far to turn back. Cynthia did not realize that no matter how ludicrous and insane Cynthia's story was, Gabrielle could not go back. She had nothing to go back to. She thought to herself that Cynthia was truly a psychopath who kidnapped her and was taking her upstate to a secluded wooded area to kill her and dump her body alongside the thruway. There was, however, part of her that believed the crazy story. Cynthia's actions did not coincide with the allegations presented. The evidence before her showed that Cynthia was a kind, loving person. Maybe she was mentally unstable and had forgotten to take her medication. Maybe that is why she appeared to be delusional. The sad truth was anything, anyone, was better than the life awaiting her return in Preston. It was: stay with Cynthia or end it all. Gabrielle could not go back. She would not. Until Cynthia presented evidence that she wanted to harm Gabrielle, she would continue to help her.

As deranged as the story seemed, it was just as likely to be true. The way Cynthia looked in the diner that morning, how she did not know who she was, the frayed wires on the car, and countless other clues led Gabrielle to deduce Cynthia was speaking the coherent truth.

She turned to look at her newfound friend, gripping the steering wheel with a mission. With a half smile, Gabrielle uttered the words Cynthia was praying would come out of her mouth.

"Count me in!"

CHAPTER THIRTEEN

The car turns off the thruway and slows down to the speed of the surrounding curvy mountainside road.

"It should be about fifteen minutes from here." I pray I got the directions right when I scribbled them down on the map in the wee hours of the morning.

I can feel my heart pounding in my chest the closer we get to the secluded cabin in the woods. Gabrielle sits in the passenger seat, providing the perfect role of 'Shotgun Navigator.' She has the map with my notes on her lap. She guides each turn, telling me where to turn left and right. My hands become clammy. Sweat is pouring from my forehead. One last turn. I glance at Gabrielle. She appears as calm as ever.

How is that possible after all I told her? What if the madmen are there? What if they try to kill us both? Nobody will be around to help save us. Our screams will echo in the silent night for no one to hear except the wise old owls atop the towering oak trees. These thoughts enter my brain, and the air around me begins to feel heavy and cold.

It is hard to breathe. I am suffocating. No air is flowing into my lungs. My head feels light. Goosebumps run up and down my arms, legs, and spine. I must pull the car over to prevent it from crashing into the riverbanks below the winding mountain road.

"Are we here?" Gabrielle asks quizzically, looking around to find nothing but trees and forest.

I try to answer, but fear has consumed my entire being. Gabrielle stares at me. She must have noticed the sweat dripping from my forehead. I cannot speak. Gabrielle reaches out her hand and touches my right arm, which has a death grip on the steering wheel.

"It'll be okay."

She can say those words, but she cannot know if they are true. She does not know what we will encounter at the cabin. By now, the mad person knows somebody was in the car. When he returned to get rid of the second dead body, he was sure to notice the car was no longer there. He was sure to deduce he had not been alone that morning when he shot those two men dead. He was sure to be hunting for the person who could implicate him for murder.

It will not be okay!

"We can park here, hidden among the trees, and walk the rest of the way."

Is she crazy? Walk? How would we make a fast getaway?

When Gabrielle sees me not budging, she says, "We didn't come here to sit in the car. From the directions, the cabin appears to be just up that road there." She points to the dirt road directly to the left.

Gabrielle is right. I have to take her to the cabin. I cannot let my fear paralyze me. It is my only chance of figuring things out. I pull the car toward the trees to the right and drive underneath the shade, so our transportation is not visible from the street. We leave the automobile and walk silently up the paved side street to the cabin. No further than two hundred feet away from the car, and without warning, Gabrielle turns around and sprints down the pavement in the opposite direction.

She's changed her mind. She no longer wants part of this craziness.

Here I am in the middle of the road—no way am I going back there alone. I watch her run away, hoping she would turn around to say something, but she does not even look back. She disappears at the turn-off to the car.

Great, she is stealing my car and leaving me alone to face death.

As thoughts of my demise resurface, Gabrielle reappears. This time, she sprints up the road toward me, waving something in her hand that I cannot make out because of the distance between us. When she gets close, I notice the disposable camera

I purchased at the gift shop. My trepidation of returning to the scene where I experienced a brush with death caused me to forget it in the car.

"You made such a big deal about this at the rest stop; I figured it was important."

She is right. I want to document something, anything, that can help me figure out what is happening.

We walk another ten minutes and are now upon the gravel driveway.

"There it is," I whisper.

The cabin cannot be seen from the road. The driveway looks like a service road but is clearly marked 'Private Property' and leads back into the dark wooded area. Gabrielle does not wait for me to provide further directions and walks up the dreaded driveway. She is a good fifty feet ahead of me before I muster the courage to follow. I am in no hurry to race toward her. Part of me thinks returning to the scene was a bad idea. That is always how people get into trouble. People can never stay away from the crime scene. The police capture the most criminals when they stake out the places where the crime took place. My head fills with visions of the madman driving up the driveway and catching us standing there—the two of us paralyzed like deer in headlights, with no place to run—an image I do not want to see in real life.

"Look," Gabrielle points toward the ground at the gravel driveway. As she speaks, she takes a picture, rotates the wheel at the back of the camera, and shoots another photo.

"I don't see anything but gravel and dirt."

"No, look closer." I think she has X-ray goggles or possesses some Superman vision powers because all I see is dirt and gravel. "The tire tracks."

It is like looking at one of those paintings with the squiggly lines. Only the gifted people can see the dinosaur or shark popping out as a three-dimensional figure among the chaos of lines and shapes.

"There are three sets." She frantically points and clicks the camera.

"What are you going to do with pictures of tire tracks?" I wonder aloud.

"I dunno, but it can't hurt to take them."

True.

I glare at the ground, trying to use my best crime scene investigation skills to decipher the driveway beneath my feet. Then I see them. There are indeed three very pronounced sets of tire tracks——each vastly different.

"These are mine." I point to the tracks behind where I got out of the trunk this morning. "This set belongs to my car."

"These over here look like they have to belong to a big rig ... look at the double set of tracks." I am glad I have brought her with me. I need someone to see what I do not—someone who can look at this place with fresh eyes.

After examining the tracks, Gabrielle darts toward the cabin's front porch.

"Where are you going?" *Why is she headed deeper into the abyss of the unknown?*

"Well, we haven't driven all this way to hang out in the front yard."

She is crazy. There is no way I will step foot inside that cabin.

"That's trespassing." I know how ridiculous my rationale behind that statement is. After all, the mere presence of us on the driveway snooping around is already trespassing. I try to recover my poor judgment, "What if people are inside?"

"Don't you think they would've heard the racket we're making out front and come out here already." To mock me, Gabrielle knocks loudly on the wooden entrance to the cabin, asking in a loud, obnoxious voice, "Hello, yoo-hoo, anybody home?" Her sarcasm is not appreciated.

While speaking those words, Gabrielle's right hand twists the front doorknob. The unlocked door flies open.

"I guess that's your invitation." She is certifiably insane. I am not going anywhere near that cabin. "Come on, aren't you at least a little curious about what goes on here? The sun is setting soon. We don't want to waste any more time."

I have no choice in the matter. I am not about to stand alone in the open wooded area while she rummages inside the cabin. I sprint toward the front door when she disappears inside, I can no longer see her silhouette. She smirks as I appear before her, gasping for air.

We both turn around to notice the contents of the room before us. A huge room——no furniture, just open space. There are black curtains on the windows, drawn closed. There is a fireplace, but it is obvious it has never been used and is just for show. In the back corner is a bathroom. To the right of the front door, there is another room. The door is closed. I assume it is the bedroom, but that room is not piquing my interest at the current moment.

Before us in the empty open space are brick-sized silver rectangular packages——rows and rows of these packages. Stacks and stacks of them. They take up over three-quarters of the room. Feels like Christmas, except all the children are receiving the exact same presents.

"Heroin," Gabrielle whispers with absolutism.

I am shocked she even knows what it is. "Are you sure?"

"Haven't you seen the movie *Rough Riders*? They try to bust a heroin smuggler …"

"I can't even remember my name, and you expect me to remember if I have seen the movie *Rough Riders*?" She has a mental illness.

"Good point, but you should see it if you haven't, that Ethan Smith is a hottie …" she trails off and stops. She realizes this is not the time and the place to get into a discussion about who is who in Hollywood. Gabrielle takes out the camera and tries to snap a photo. "Damn, the flash wasn't set."

We hear rumbling. A truck. The engine roars as the wheels crush the gravel beneath them. We stare at each other in disbelief, realizing this is the end. If caught, our bodies will be tied to cinder blocks and dumped in the closest lake.

CHAPTER FOURTEEN

"Quick," Gabrielle grabs my hand and drags me to the door at the back of the heroin-filled room. We scurry across the floor and close the door behind us. We are in the bathroom. It is a small space with a stand-alone sink, a toilet, and a shower with a plain blue and white cloth shower curtain. Fate has to take its course. Hopefully, fate is on our side, and we will not be discovered.

The front door to the cabin creaks open, and several sets of footsteps enter the home. "Okay, boys." That voice——that indistinguishable voice I will never forget. "I have before me the list of who gets what and the drop-off points."

My hands feel sweaty. I cannot breathe. I cannot move. I am frozen with fear. We crouch at the bathroom door, listening to the pounding of feet on the floor. Obviously, they are taking their share of the stash of heroin stored in the room. An efficiently run operation.

The man with the voice is undoubtedly in charge of the undertaking. "I know we usually wait until the third Wednesday of the month, but it's a bit of an emergency. Somebody may be on to us, and until we know who that person is, we cannot leave the goods here." He is referring to me.

When Gabrielle hears these words, she turns to face me and whispers, "Did you see the heroin when you were here?"

I respond by placing my index finger to my lips, the universal sign language for 'shush.' This is not the time to discuss what could be left for the return trip to Preston should we be lucky enough to get out of this situation.

It does not appear the men involved in this drug ring know my identity. They do not know who took the car after the burlesque twins were shot dead. I must lie low. Hiding in the bathroom of a heroin trafficking cabin is not the most efficient way to lie low.

"Jimmy, take this list for me. I gotta run to the john."

Crap. Someone's coming our way. Not just someone, but *the* someone. The madman. We are about to be discovered.

Quick-thinking Gabrielle grabs my shoulder and shoves me into the shower. Here we are, the two of us huddled together a mere five feet from the person who would have killed me without hesitation had he known of my existence a mere twelve hours earlier. Curiosity is killing me. I have to get a glimpse of what this madman looks like. It is essential for my survival. I need to know what face to be aware of. I need to be able to see him coming from fifty miles away.

I peek around the curtain. There he is. His back faces the shower as he pees into the pure white toilet. All I can see are his perfectly polished black leather shoes. At least I would notice him coming if my head were down. The toilet flushes, and the water gurgles as it swirls into the manmade sewer deep below the ground. He does not stop to wash his hands.

"Alright, men, we're done here. Let's move out."

We wait at least twenty minutes before emerging from the shower. This is becoming a pattern in my new life. We do not say a word to each other. Gabrielle cautiously opens the bathroom door to find an empty room. The countless rows of heroin packages have disappeared. They are long gone to be distributed to their rightful owners.

It is dark. The moon is glowing with all its force and guides us through the pitch-black night back to the car.

CHAPTER FIFTEEN

They sat in silence for the first half of the return trip. Gabrielle convinced Cynthia to let her drive. Cynthia was in no shape to be behind the wheel as she was unmistakably shaken by the events that transpired at the cabin. Gabrielle was also slightly freaked out by the events, but it was more of a realization that the stories Cynthia told her were true. She believed her tales before, but any lingering notion that Cynthia was a ruthless murderer were gone.

"You know that man in the bathroom was him." These were the first words uttered out of Cynthia's mouth on the return trip. "I will never forget that voice. All I could see were his perfectly polished leather shoes. That bastard deserves whatever comes his way once I figure out what is happening."

Gabrielle just nodded in agreement. She knew the two of them were in way over their heads. They were dealing with a smart, conniving drug lord, and if the movies were an indication of their brutality to uphold their stash, there was plenty of danger headed their way. Even if Cynthia was not a murderer, her past life was somehow connected to drug trafficking. Not just a mere hash plant for pothead college students. Serious hardcore drugs. Heroin is no joking matter. Somehow, Cynthia's husband lost his life due to heroin; that was most apparent. The missing factor was how he was connected. This was more than a mere heroin user who failed to pay his dealer. These massive size operations do not take place simply because of a missed payment. Her husband had been involved way over his head, and it was clear these people killed him for that reason. Only problem is there was no proof. Neither Cynthia nor Gabrielle had seen any faces. The cabin remained deserted. Further investigation needed to be done, fast. Hard to do with no leads to guide them in any viable direction.

Before figuring out where to start, they needed a place to stay. Gabrielle knew she could not spend another night in Hank's apartment. It was over, and she would never go back there again. But she also knew she needed to gather her belongings, which she could not do alone. Hank worked the night shift. If she went there now, she could get into the apartment and collect her things unscathed by his wrath. She failed to consider how enraged she made Hank by leaving with Cynthia, and underestimated the lengths he would go to try and get her back. Gabrielle never imagined what he would do and was unprepared for the drama unfolding as she drove down the street toward the apartment complex. If she knew what was about to happen, she would have never gone back.

CHAPTER SIXTEEN

The red lights spun around like a disco ball into the front seat of the passenger car Cynthia and Gabrielle sat in. Gabrielle let the car run to a complete stop. She turned to Cynthia and mouthed, "I am so sorry."

The megaphone blared, "Get out of the car slowly with your hands above your head."

Hank called the cops. He told them everything. Gabrielle should have seen it coming since this was his only way to prevent her from leaving him for good. The girls opened the two front car doors and placed their hands above their heads. Officer Thomas walked over to them.

Gabrielle knew Officer Thomas quite well. He was the policeman who had come to the apartment and responded to her 9-1-1 phone calls after every single one of Hank's outbursts. He was a man in his early thirties with salt and pepper brown hair, a gentleman way out of her league. Still, she could not help but be mesmerized by his sincere smile and the dimples that formed at the corner of his mouth. Officer Thomas had always been sympathetic and offered her advice. Each time he would plead with her to leave and get away from the abusive relationship. If only he knew it was not that easy. It was not possible to get up and leave. She has a lot more to lose than just Hank. Hank was her entire life and giving him up meant giving up everything she knew. She had nowhere else to turn. This time was different, though. Hank crossed the line a step too far.

"Cuff that one over there; I'll handle this one." Officer Thomas was speaking to the other officer on the scene. He motioned for him to go and handcuff Cynthia Evans.

Gabrielle had never seen the other officer before. Officer Thomas usually arrived at the apartment by himself. Gabrielle thought this was the end for her. She turned around to face the car and placed her wrists behind her back to make it easier for Officer Thomas to place her under arrest.

"I'm not arresting you," Officer Thomas said as he grabbed Gabrielle's shoulder to turn her to face him.

"You're not?" she asked with complete shock and disbelief.

Gabrielle was positive she would be charged with aiding and abetting a known felon.

"Consider this your get-out-of-jail-free card." Gabrielle had no idea why Officer Thomas was so nice to her, but she was not about to question her freedom.

As Gabrielle turned to face the officer, he touched her face. His touch sent an electric shock throughout her body. Gabrielle was not expecting him to touch her.

"Did Hank do this to you?" he asked as he examined her black and blue eye. Gabrielle did not have an answer for him. Every time she met Officer Thomas, she was bruised and battered. "This is the worst yet." She could hear the anger in the Officer's voice as he examined the damage. "Gabrielle, you deserve so much better than this."

She knew he was right but had nothing to say.

"Gabrielle, promise me you're leaving. Promise me this is the end: you will not return to him; you cannot go back to him."

It was the same speech he gave every time they met. Gabrielle would nod each time but rationalize what happened between her and Hank. He drank too much, she overcooked the steak, she did not call to say she was working late, and on and on. There was always a reason why he hit her and why it was all right for her to return to the apartment. This time was different. As Officer

Thomas spoke, there was no rationalization for Hank's actions. Gabrielle agreed. She would not, could not go back to Hank.

Without saying a word, Officer Thomas sensed it, too. Somehow, he knew Gabrielle was stronger this time. He sensed this time, she was leaving.

"I'm risking my job here by letting you go free." Gabrielle knew this to be true without him saying so. "You have to promise me two things."

Anything for her freedom.

"You have to promise me that you will not go back to Hank, not tonight, not tomorrow, not ever." An easy promise to keep, as Gabrielle already made up her mind before Officer Thomas asked.

"What's the other thing?" Gabrielle questioned the handsome officer.

"You have to stay away from Cynthia Evans." This request was not as easy. "She is a murderer. I'm not clear how you got mixed up in all of this, but it has to stop tonight."

Gabrielle was unwilling to let her encounter with Cynthia end here, but she had to promise she would. Cynthia and Gabrielle had bonded. Cynthia was her friend, her only friend. Gabrielle was convinced she did not kill her family. How could she stand there and tell Officer Thomas she would stay away when she knew deep in her gut that this woman was a victim and not a murderer? Gabrielle also knew if both of them were placed behind bars, it would be impossible to uncover the truth.

"I promise I will stay away from Cynthia Evans." They were difficult words to say.

In a sense, she was not lying. All he asked of her was to stay away from Cynthia. This meant Gabrielle could not visit her at the jailhouse. However, Gabrielle did not promise to stop searching for answers into what really happened in the Evans' household. Without contacting Cynthia, the task would be more daunting, but she was a woman of her word. Gabrielle was strongly attracted to the officer. She respected him too much to risk him losing his job for her.

Gabrielle watched the police car pull away from the curb with her newfound friend sitting in solitude. She felt helpless. A smart individual would let it go. Only a fool would risk their freedom for a stranger they just met. Gabrielle had been lucky enough to escape danger and death. Eventually her luck would run out, and it was better to let Cynthia face her fate. The pit of her stomach told her differently. Her gut knew Cynthia was innocent.

Officer Thomas stuck around after his colleague left the scene. Gabrielle sat on the curb. She could feel the glare of Hank, who was standing outside the front door of their apartment. He stood there analyzing and watching her every move. His stare made the tiny hairs on her neck stand upright. She knew he was there watching without even turning around to face him. She did not want to look at him. She never wanted to see him ever again. The hurt and anger she felt was overbearing.

Officer Thomas saw Gabrielle sitting and made his way toward her.

"Do you have a place to go?" Gabrielle did not. "I can escort you inside to collect a few of your belongings and then drop you off at a motel if you like."

Gabrielle agreed to take the man up on his offer. She currently had no other options, and there was no way she was going into the apartment to face Hank alone.

Hank did not say a word to her when she walked past him through the front door of their apartment. He just stood there intently, watching every move she made. She grabbed a mid-sized duffel bag from underneath the bed and began to pack her essential belongings as quickly as possible. The eerie silence made her nervous. Chills ran through her body as she scurried around the apartment, looking for her personal effects. Officer Thomas stood in the middle of the living room. He did not say a word. He watched Hank to make sure he would not lay a finger on

Gabrielle. The tension between Officer Thomas and Hank was palpable. If it were any person other than a police officer, Hank would have started with, at the very least, an exchange of some not-so 'PG-13' words. Hank, however, knew better. He would rather let Gabrielle go than spend some time behind bars.

As soon as her bag was filled, Gabrielle walked past Hank again without saying a word and calmly walked to the squad car parked at the front of the apartment complex. Hank stood on the front stoop with the door wide open.

"Gabrielle!" Hank called out her name.

She did not turn around. She did not even acknowledge his voice. But he would not stop calling her. Each yell sounded increasingly pathetic. After several exasperated pleas to get her to turn around, Gabrielle paused to get one last look at the man she was leaving behind. She knew it would just be a sign to the jerk he still had a glimpse of control over her, but she could not help herself.

As she stood there, the length of a football field apart from the pitiful person who swore his love to her, a tear formed in her eye.

"I love you, Gabrielle!" Those words had once sounded sweet and innocent, but no longer.

One last plea for her to come back under his control. A yelp as if uttering those four words would create a magic spell, causing Gabrielle to drop her duffel bag and run, arms spread wide open into his. Those four words had the complete opposite effect on Gabrielle. They left a churning effect in the pit of her stomach. It was a weak attempt that maybe once in her past, she would have fallen for, but this time, she was stronger. She knew he was insincere. She wanted out of the vicious cycle she had been trapped in.

As she stood there facing Hank, Officer Thomas could sense Gabrielle's anguish. He placed his right arm around her shoulders, guiding her toward the car. That simple gesture validated she was strong enough to overcome Hank's spell and that she would be a better person for it. She was comforted. Officer Thomas's presence next to her consoled her. She knew he understood. Words were not necessary.

CHAPTER SEVENTEEN

I am sitting in the room in silence and solitude. I have no idea how long I have been in this room, but odds are I am being observed through the two-way mirror on the wall before me. They are the scientists, and I am the lab rat under the scrutiny of a microscope, my every action and breath being analyzed. The interrogation room is exactly as I have pictured: a blue room with a long rectangular table. There are two chairs, the one I am sitting in and one directly across from me, tucked in underneath the other side of the table. The only thing missing is the bright shining lamp, used to bring out the absolute truth when shone directly into the pupils of a suspected criminal.

I have used the alone time to think about what I will say to convince the officers I am not a murderer. A simple case of mistaken identity. Sure, I look a lot like Cynthia Evans, but I am not her.

If I am her, shouldn't I feel some loss for my family? Shouldn't I feel remorse for the death of the love of my life and my two offspring?

Herein lies the same problem I have encountered for the past twenty-four hours: *how do I convince people I am not Cynthia Evans when I do not know who I am?*

This case of mistaken identity will be resolved shortly. Upon being brought to the station, the officers had me fingerprinted.

Once they run a background check, they will see they have the wrong person. My fingerprints will not match, and they will have to let me go because they picked up the wrong person.

"Mrs. Evans, have you had enough time to consider your confession?" The officer is standing in the doorway.

This question throws me off. He is the same officer I saw with Gabrielle at the time of my arrest. Surely, Gabrielle told him what had happened. Surely, she convinced him of my innocence.

"Confession? I thought you were going to let me go." The expression on his face does not coincide with my statement.

"Now, why would I do that? You're a wanted killer."

He must be mistaken.

"I am certain you have the wrong person."

"That's what they all say," he snaps back, "but go ahead, being the kindhearted person I am, I'll give you the benefit of the doubt. Why is it you think I have the wrong person?" Convincing him of this would not be as easy as I thought.

The officer enters the room. He pulls the empty chair across from me away from the table. He turns the chair to face him and plops down in it, facing me, with his legs straddling the back of the chair. He rests his arms on the top of the chair and leans toward the table.

"Haven't you checked the fingerprints? Haven't you run a background check? If you have, you'll see I am not who you think I am. I am not Cynthia Evans."

The officer chuckles at my remarks. "I am sorry. If you are not Cynthia Evans, then who are you?"

That is the daunting question I cannot answer.

I sit back in my chair, folding my arms across my chest, unable to answer.

The officer slams his hand down on the table before me and speaks at me in a loud, intensive voice. "I can see the nice guy approach will not get me anywhere. I cannot even believe you would sit there across from me at this table and tell me with a bold face you are not Cynthia Evans. Let's cut to the chase. You are Cynthia Evans. There is no denying that fact. The fingerprints have produced a positive match. Now start talking, or I'll make your life miserable."

All I can do is stare back at him in disbelief. 'You are Cynthia Evans.' That statement plays like a broken record over and over in my head. *I am Cynthia Evans.*

"I am Cynthia Evans?" It is a question and a statement all at the same time.

"Now that we've got that out of the way, I have all the time in the world for you to start talking."

There is nothing to tell. In the physical sense, yes, I am Cynthia Evans, but I am not her in the emotional and mental sense. I am not a killer. I am not a deranged, unstable murderer. I sit silently, thoughts running through my brain at a million miles a second. There are so many unanswered questions.

How did the murder happen? Did I really kill them? Did I love my family? Was I unhappy? How did I get into the trunk? Am I a heroin addict? How does the drug ring from the cabin relate to me? Am I a horrible person incapable of emotion?

As these questions scroll through my mind, my body begins to shake. Tears stream down the front of my face. My eyes are open, but the room is a blur.

I killed my family. I think it, but I do not believe it for one second. There is no way I killed my family. I have no proof or memory otherwise, but I know I did not kill them.

"Mrs. Evans, get a hold of yourself, or this will be a very long night for both of us." He grabs a tissue from his pocket and hands it to me across the table, a sign that he is capable of some compassion.

"I don't know who I am," the sobbing continues.

"We've covered that already. I've just told you: you are Cynthia Evans."

The officer does not understand. I know I am Cynthia Evans, but that is just a name. I do not know who I am. I do not know my likes and dislikes. I do not know my hometown. I do not know my friends and family. I do not know me.

"Did you kill your husband and two young boys?" he asks.

God, I hope not.

"I don't know." That is the truth.

The officer does not like my answer. He gets up from his chair and paces the room's width back and forth before me.

"What is your alibi?" I look at him with a blank stare. I have no alibi. I do not remember where I was. My memories begin after the fact. "I will take the silence as there is no alibi. Why don't we start with what you do know."

Should I tell him everything? Should I tell him about the drugs in the cabin? Well, maybe not everything, but I should tell him I was beaten unconscious and placed in the trunk of a car, my car.

I start to speak. I speak about waking up in the car's trunk and being taken to the deserted cabin in the woods. I talk about the gunshots and the two dead bodies.

"This man, who shot the men dead in the woods, what does he look like?" he asks, questioning the plausibility of my story.

"I never saw his face."

"So, let me get this straight. You were beaten up, thrown in the trunk of a car, heard gunshots, saw a dead body, and never went to the police. You never once contacted the police to tell them what happened."

I have no response.

"Let's try this again. What happened the night you murdered your family?" This guy is making me angry.

I shout, "I did not murder my family!" Probably not the smartest move to yell at a police officer, but he is not listening to what I am saying.

"Okay," he stands up and says, "I can see we're done here." The officer heads toward the door to leave the room.

I plead with him, "Please, you have got to believe me. I am sure I loved my family and would never hurt them. Please, you have to help me."

My pleas are not successful. He does not want to hear any more. Before closing the door to the room, he turns around and looks me in the eyes.

"Save your tears for the jury. Maybe they will believe your lies."

CHAPTER EIGHTEEN

It had been a restless night. Gabrielle could not sleep on the lumpy mattress provided by the two-star motel at the edge of town. Most of the customers at the Preston Motel paid an hourly rate. It was the only place in town Gabrielle could afford. The lackluster room contained the essentials: a bed, a working bathroom, and a television. She rolled over and looked at the green light emanating from the digital clock on the nightstand next to where she lay: 7:14. Her work shift started at 8:00 a.m. The last place she wished to go, but it was all she had to hold onto until she figured out what to do with the mess she caused. As Gabrielle lay in bed thinking about the events that transpired the day before, she wondered if it was all a bad dream. She sat upright in bed and looked around at her motel room's brown seventies art deco——not quite the homiest of places, but it would do until she found a place to go. She placed her feet on the floor and stretched her hands to the sky above her head——trying to muster energy for the morning.

Gabrielle had left her car in the diner parking lot the previous day. It was likely still there, doubtful anybody would steal a 1989 Dodge Aries. The car was on its way to the junkyard; a key turn away from being left on the side of the road. Gabrielle could not complain, really; it served its function. She only needed the car to get her to and from work. Sure, the air conditioner was broken, the dial radio was stuck on light FM, and the engine roared louder than any audible conversation between the front two passengers. It was, however, the only car she ever owned, and with her salary, the only one she could afford for quite some time. Hank always gave her stickers for it to pass inspection. He worked two jobs, one being an assistant to an auto mechanic. She knew if she had to bring her car into the shop, it would never be legally allowed on the road again. Still, it got her to work. However, this morning, it was waiting for her at the diner, and Gabrielle would instead have to take a cab. Her trusty green hatchback would be waiting faithfully in the parking lot to return her to the motel after the workday ended. Calling a cab meant Gabrielle would be late for her morning shift. The least of her worries at this point in her life.

She looked in the bathroom mirror and pinched herself. Yep. This was real. The events that had transpired in the past twenty-four hours were reality.

She sifted through the duffel bag she quickly packed as Officer Thomas waited for her to gather some things and escort her to the motel. She prayed she remembered to pack her polo shirt and black pants for work. However, if not, there was no way she would go back to Hank's apartment to retrieve them. She never wanted to face him again.

As these thoughts filtered into her head, Gabrielle turned and noticed her reflection in the mirror. The shiner Hank had laid on her during his rage in the apartment had swelled into a beautiful array of purple and blue. No cover-up on earth was powerful enough to hide the damage to her face, but she was surely going to try to conceal it to the best of her abilities.

As she puttered around the unfamiliar motel room that she would have to call home for an unspecified amount of time, her thoughts shifted to her newfound friend. Sure, she had only met Cynthia the day before. Most would hardly call a mere twelve hours in one's lifetime a friendship. However, there was something different about Cynthia. Gabrielle could not place her finger on it exactly, but one thing was certain: she could not sit back and let the young woman rot in jail for a crime she did not commit. The only problem was proving she did not commit those murders. Even though Gabrielle had seen the cabin and the heroin, she could not piece together what happened only two nights before. How could a woman who appeared so innocent and naïve be involved in a sinister drug operation such as heroin smuggling? The pieces of the puzzle did not fit together. Granted, Gabrielle did not know much of the background story. She only knew the media's biased version of what happened. The skewed reporters had it all wrong. They made Cynthia out to be a cold-hearted, ruthless killer who hated her husband and her life. Even if Cynthia knew who she was, her demeanor did not lead Gabrielle to believe she could even kill a spider, let alone her family. There was more to the story.

Gabrielle strolled into work at 8:20 a.m., twenty minutes late for her shift. She hoped nobody would notice, and she could sneak in through the back kitchen door as if she had been there the entire time.

"Hola amiga, tú tienes muchos problemas." The cooks always heckled at her in Spanish.

Her Intro to Spanish course in high school gave her enough to understand about one in every ten words they uttered. She always felt she missed the picture because they would speak rapidly and giggle behind the stove. She did not mind. They were harmless, and Gabrielle figured what she did not understand could not bother her.

Gabrielle grabbed a clean apron from the rack in the back near the dishwasher and swung open the doors to the main dining area.

"You're late," her coworker stated the obvious. She stood there at the counter with the newspaper spread open and a fresh cup of coffee in her hand.

"Is Sheila here?" Sheila was the manager, and as long as Gabrielle made it to work before Sheila arrived, she was in the clear.

"No, she called and said that she was running late. We only have two customers, for now." April had been speaking to

Gabrielle as she perused the paper for the morning's latest head-lines. When she looked up from the newspaper to see Gabrielle's face, she noticed the damage Hank had done.

"Holy shit Gabrielle, what the heck happened to your face?"

"Is it that bad? I tried to cover it up with makeup."

The five minutes she allotted to this procedure had clearly not been enough. April reached for her purse underneath the counter and tried to cover up any evidence of Hank's rage as best as possible. Gabrielle had previously come to work with black eyes, but they were never uncoverable. This was the worst one. It was the last one.

Wednesdays were typically slow days at the Village Diner. This did not help Gabrielle in wanting to get off work. She made her money during the lunch rush, but by the time two o'clock rolled around, she was ready to leave. She needed a plan. All she could think about was Cynthia and what she was doing.

Gabrielle knew she could not visit her in the jailhouse. Officer Thomas did her a great service in not charging her as an accomplice to murder. Gabrielle knew he went out on a limb for her and that she should lie low until things were sorted out with the courts. Still, it was not her nature to hang back and wait for things to happen.

Since the diner was so slow, Gabrielle could read the newspa-per. Her friend Cynthia was, yet again, the *Daily News* cover sto-ry for the day. The lead article reported 'The Preston Murderer' was apprehended outside an apartment complex last night. "A young woman was with her during the arrest, but no charges were filed for now." That was Gabrielle. She was pleased her name was not mentioned in the paper. Gabrielle feared the en-tire town would find out she was helping an accused murderer. She would be threatened to be tarred and feathered until she left Preston for good.

The article then discussed the horrific tragedy of the Evans' household. It described Rick Evans and how he was a hard work-er. He worked for NATCO, which stands for North American

Trucking Company. He drove one of those obnoxious eighteen-wheel vehicles that come barreling down the highway after you as if they own the road. A prestigious job, but also a job that kept him away from his family for extended periods. There was an interview with Peter Lugo, owner of NATCO. He bought the company a mere twenty years ago and built it into the international powerhouse corporation it has become. The main headquarters are in Suffern, New York. The article also mentioned the organization having several other satellite locations, including Louisville, Kentucky; Sacramento, California; someplace right outside Montreal; and numerous other Midwestern towns Gabrielle had never heard of. Gabrielle knew the trucking industry in the United States was a huge operation. They are the bread of our country. Without them, the economy of one of the greatest nations on earth would cease to function. Peter Lugo talked about how sad he felt for the immediate family of his employee and how nobody should have to experience such a tragedy during one's lifetime. He is going to start a foundation for the Evans family. Peter Lugo's personal mission was to ensure that Cynthia Evans got the 'just dessert' for her crime.

As Gabrielle read this article, the bells went off in her head. This was the link to the heroin at the cabin. The trucks had come up to the cabin to drop off the heroin and disperse it to other people. Cynthia's husband was involved in a drug smuggling operation. She knew her first course of action was developing the roll of film from the cabin. The camera was still in the pocket of the pants she wore to the cabin with Cynthia. After the events last night, she had forgotten all about the pictures. That roll of film contained all the evidence she needed to prove Cynthia's innocence, or at the very least, show there was more to the Preston Murderer than mere disappointment in her marriage vows.

CHAPTER NINETEEN

At exactly eight o'clock the next morning, Gabrielle was outside the one-hour photo shop in town, patiently awaiting its opening. The store clerk was already three minutes late. Finally, the dark-haired middle-aged man in the store clicked open the lock from the inside. Gabrielle could barely contain herself from thrusting her body inside the store. The man inside was shocked to see a customer already standing at the counter before him.

"Well, good morning, young lady. I'm not accustomed to having such zealous customers at this early hour of the morning."

Gabrielle did not answer the man. She merely placed her disposable camera on the counter and asked him how long it would take him to develop the photos.

"Wow, these must be some pretty important photographs."

She was in no mood for chit-chat. "They're from an important trip I took."

"I see you still have many photos left here on the camera. Wouldn't you rather wait until you finished out the roll before you have it developed?"

"Who knows how long that would take? I rarely take photos." Gabrielle just wanted the pictures developed and now was fearful he would not let her have them.

"Well, suit yourself. Are you interested in a free CD-ROM with your photos so they are downloadable, and you can share them with your friends and family?"

This was taking way too long for Gabrielle.

"Sure … how long for the photos to be done?" she inquired of the talkative man

behind the counter.

"Come back in an hour."

With that, Gabrielle left the store only to be sure to return in exactly one hour on the nose. It was going to be the longest hour of her life. She needed these photos back as soon as possible. The faster she got them back, the faster she could begin her search for the real murderer of Rick Evans.

Gabrielle exited the photo shop and turned left onto Main Street. She needed to go someplace where she could take her mind off the photos. She headed to the Books and Nooks, three blocks up. The huge, multi-level bookstore took up the entire street corner. The residents of Preston protested the building of the store. They argued such a huge chain store would bring down the businesses of the small 'mom-and-pop' shops along Main Street. The exact opposite turned out to be true. The bookstore created more jobs, and people from the surrounding towns flocked to the store. A huge parking lot came with the store, providing ample parking for those who shopped all along Main Street. Revenue for the entire town went up.

Gabrielle pushed herself around the revolving door and rode the escalator to the bookstore's second floor. Gabrielle headed straight for the travel section. She frequented this place regularly. It was her chance to escape reality and experience exotic lands across the globe. Whenever Gabrielle was feeling down, she would come here to try and rejuvenate her spirit. In the past few months, she found herself here more often than not. She would pick a book off the shelf and get lost in the pictures. In the past few weeks, she had traveled to the pyramids of Egypt, the Great Barrier Reef of Australia, and the Mayan temples of South America. It was her only chance to see the world, as she knew she would never be able to afford such luxurious trips in her lifetime.

Gabrielle picked *Caribbean Beaches* off the shelf and sat on the floor with her legs crossed in front of her. She opened the book to the beaches of Aruba and tried to get lost in the pictures of the pure blue ocean water. Normally, she would imagine the warm breeze in her hair and the sand beneath her bare feet. Today, though, her thoughts drifted back to Cynthia. She imagined her sitting alone in her cold, dark cell. It would be a long fifty-three minutes until the photographs were done.

"Surely a pretty girl like you is not planning on traveling alone." Gabrielle was so lost in her thoughts she did not notice him standing over her.

It was Officer Thomas. She had never encountered him out and about in town. She almost did not recognize him in his street clothes. He wore dark, broken-in jeans and a gray t-shirt that fit snuggly in all the right places. What he was wearing, however, was not what struck her at that particular moment. It was the dimples that formed at the side of his mouth as he smiled. He extended his left hand toward Gabrielle to help her to her feet.

"So, do you frequent this place every Thursday morning?" he sarcastically asked her.

She looked at him coyly and replied, "No, do you?" From there, the conversation started flowing.

They stood in the bookstore chatting about nothing in particular as the minutes ticked away. If she did not know any better, Gabrielle swore she caught Officer Thomas staring into her eyes at various moments throughout the conversation. To Gabrielle, it was mere innocent flirting. She was sure he spoke this way with everyone he encountered in the town. Every guy she had ever been attracted to had been a complete and utter asshole, yet that was whom she fell for, and she fell hard. This was different. Officer Thomas was an upstanding citizen, one of the nation's finest. He was there to protect. There was no conceivable way he could ever be interested in her. He felt bad about her situation and wanted to ensure she was okay; the only plausible explanation.

"Do you want to grab a bite to eat at Annie's Café? It's my day off, and I was headed over there anyway."

Gabrielle took a huge breath. Without a doubt, he had just asked her out. Granted, it was an informal invitation, but still an invitation. As she contemplated what he really meant, Gabrielle caught a glimpse of her watch. She was fifteen minutes behind schedule. The evidence was at the photo shop waiting for her.

"As much as I would like to, I can't." As much as she wanted to go and be lost in the soothing voice of Officer Thomas, helping Cynthia was more important.

Gabrielle placed the Caribbean book back on the shelf and headed toward the stairs out of the building. Before she descended to the street level, she turned back to find Officer Thomas standing in the travel aisle, befuddled and confused.

She turned toward him and asked, "Can I have a rain check?"

He smiled brightly at her and replied, "You, my dear, can cash in on that rain check whenever you want."

It was an opportunity she knew she might regret passing up, but not helping her jail-housed friend regain her freedom was one she would regret more.

CHAPTER TWENTY

She walked into the photo shop. The suspense as to what the pictures would reveal was killing her emotionally. An Asian lady, who was not there before, was behind the counter. The man who had taken the camera to be developed was nowhere in sight.

"Can I help you with something?" Her accent was thick. She spoke in broken English.

"I dropped off some film first thing this morning to be developed an hour ago." To be precise, it was an hour and twenty-three minutes ago.

The woman started to root around the shelves underneath the counter. She first rummaged through three boxes but obviously did not find what she sought.

"What was the name?" This was not happening. These pictures were extremely important, and Gabrielle's only hope of helping Cynthia.

"Price, the last name is Price." She was having a tough time containing her annoyance. How could the store lose her film? How many people could have entered this store in the morning to drop off a disposable camera?

When the fiftieth attempt to find the photos was unsuccessful, the woman excused herself and headed to the back of the store. Gabrielle could hear a few muffled voices conversing in the background, though the exact conversation was inaudible. The man who had helped Gabrielle earlier must have been in the back because when the woman emerged to the front again, she made a beeline for a container hidden behind the printer.

"Here it is; sorry for the confusion." That woman had no idea of the minor heart failure she caused Gabrielle. Luckily, the crisis had been averted, and there was no need to call an ambulance. "Here is a club card. For every ten rolls you develop, you get one free."

Gabrielle was not interested. She just wanted to grab the photographs and get out of the store. She threw the money on the counter and headed out the front door.

Gabrielle could barely stop herself from ripping open the envelope and sifting through the photos immediately. She waited until getting into the front seat of her car, mindful of strangers passing by on the street so they could not view the evidence. As Gabrielle flipped through the pictures, she realized they were not all she had hoped them to be. There were fifteen photographs, most of which were too dark to determine what they were trying to show. Any outsider would have assumed the photos were from a simple relaxing excursion to the mountains. The first picture was the cabin. It was a shot taken from the end of the driveway. A great scenic image. It displayed the tranquility and peacefulness of the area to perfection. The perfect photograph for a real estate agent trying to sell this home to the highest bidder.

The pictures did not get any better from there. The next few snapshots were of the gravel driveway in front of the cabin. If you looked close enough, you could see a distinct set of tire tracks in each photograph. At a glance, it looked like they were mistakenly taken of the ground as the photographer walked along.

The final picture was a dark blob. If you squinted hard, you could see a blurry outline of the main room in the wooded cabin. It was the shot Gabrielle had tried to take of the heroin stash inside, but the lack of flash ruined it. This was the one picture Gabrielle was hoping to come out. Without a photograph of the drug stash, she had nothing. She had no evidence to take to the police. Gabrielle started to panic. She quickly flipped through the photos several times. Nothing.

Nothing was revealed in any of the photographs. Gabrielle's one chance of a clue, and there was nothing. She took the photos, messily placed them back into the paper sleeve they came in and tossed them onto the front passenger seat. She grabbed her head with both hands and tried to subdue the anger and disappointment she was experiencing.

"Excuse me," the voice emanated from the crack in the window on the driver's side of her car. Gabrielle did not see a person approach her, so it startled her a bit, and she jumped as the words were spoken.

She looked up. Officer Thomas was standing outside her window. He motioned with his hand for her to roll down the window, only the knob to roll it down had broken off, so she had to open the door to speak to him. He looked puzzled as he maneuvered away from the door to continue the conversation.

"Are you alright?" he asked.

"Yes, why?" she wondered how distraught she looked. Sure, she was extremely upset about the photographs, but she was not about to explain to the police officer she thought she had pictures of heroin and was mad the images did not develop.

"It's just that, well, you ran out of the bookstore in such a hurry, and then I find you here sitting in solitude in your car."

Gabrielle tried to explain her way out of her odd behavior. "I, um, realized I forgot to buy that book I wanted and was sitting here debating whether I felt like going back inside to get it or not." He was not buying it but knew better than to probe into Gabrielle's life further.

As she spoke the words, she glanced at her watch and noticed it was already 9:45; she had to be at the diner at 10:00 a.m. "I have to go. I'm late for work."

She closed the driver's side door and turned the key in the ignition to start her car. Officer Thomas stood there by the curb, watching her drive away. She waved goodbye to him in the rearview mirror and turned left onto Main Street toward the diner.

CHAPTER TWENTY-ONE

The young boy was hyperactive. He was three years old but had the energy of five men combined. He was running in circles around the young lady. She was busy folding laundry in the bedroom and was too tired to chase him all over the house. There was another young boy, about the age of five. He was playing with his fire truck, crawling all over the floor as he rolled the toy truck throughout the top floor of the suburban household. The woman had a stack of clean clothes piled in her arms and proceeded to exit the bedroom and into the hallway. The young, hyperactive child ran around her, trying to get her attention. The other young child was still crawling on the floor. Suddenly, a scream ran out. There was a huge thud, and the hyperactive child tumbled down twenty stairs. As he fell, his body cascaded down the steps in slow motion. He tripped over his brother, slipped on the fire truck, and stumbled downward. The woman could not grab him as her hands were filled with clean clothes. All she could do was gasp and pray that his heart was still beating as she hurried down the stairs toward the lifeless body lying face down at the bottom.

I awake with fright. It is only a nightmare—one of many since being locked up. For the last several days, I have been dreaming the most horrific nightmares. They are dreams of a family: a married couple and their two young boys. The dreams appear real as if I am living the family's life with them. This is the worst one yet. Such a small, fragile child facing death. I try to compose myself and sit on the edge of my cot. I have no concept of day or time. All I know is that I have been locked up here for fourteen days and counting.

I sit on the spring of the crusty prison mattress, with despair hovering like a pending storm cloud over my head, my thoughts reviewing the past two weeks' events.

How did this happen?

Luckily, I am placed without a cellmate because being in jail brings much to deal with, let alone any come-ons by a brooding detainee. The situation makes no sense to me. I do not feel like a relentless murderer, but how can I be so sure?

Maybe I am this ruthless, cold-hearted killer who hates life and the world surrounding it.

As ridiculous as it sounds, it is possible. My gut, however, tells me I am not a heartless killer; I do not have it in me. I have lost my memory but not my soul. My essence and core being are still the same and intact. My soul tells me I am, and have always been, caring and compassionate. Memory is but a small fraction of an inner human being. Loss of recognition is not a loss of total individual persona. A person is born with a certain disposition that stays with them throughout their lifetime. This Freudian way of thinking is the only way to get through this ordeal because if I believed that with my memory back I were a criminal capable of taking another person's life without remorse, there would be no reason to go on living.

Deep inside, I know with full certainty I did not do it. It is hard to convince others you did not do something when you cannot remember who you are or what you were doing. I am one hundred percent positive I did not commit murder. The problem is not convincing me, but rather, the rest of the world.

Sitting in a cold, solitary cell without access to the outside world is hard. I have one phone call but cannot remember whom I know. I could call Gabrielle, but I do not know her last name, let alone her phone number. Besides, Gabrielle is a stranger with her own problems and should not get involved with an alleged criminal. She already risked enough by driving me back to the cabin in the mountains where the real killers were.

"Hey!" snarls the prison guard. He bangs on the bars of the cell with his nightstick to get my attention. His brooding voice and the obnoxious clatter make me jump as he breaks through my deep, intense thoughts. "You have a visitor."

A visitor, who is here?

I did not tell anyone where I am. Maybe a friend or family member is trying to contact me to let me know everything will be okay. Maybe Gabrielle is here to offer some help. This is great news.

The keys jingle against the steel bars as the guard unlocks the cell. The gate swings open, and from the darkness appears a man. He is an older gentleman with light brown hair—male-pattern baldness on full display. He wears thin wireframe glasses hanging snugly on his face and a brown suit, not top-of-the-line, but he wears it well. Over his left shoulder, he is carrying a beat-up attaché case filled to the brim with folders and papers.

"Mrs. Evans." He stands about three feet in front of me. As he speaks, he extends his hand to say hello.

I do not move. I wait for this stranger to reveal more to see how he knows me. Instinct tells me not to trust anyone. I still do not know who my enemy is, but I am positive they are searching. When I do not respond, he smirks and drops his hand.

"I'm Mr. Phelps," his words linger off.

He stands there in complete silence until I say something in response.

"I am sorry, but do I know you?" I question him in a puzzling tone.

He responds, "I am your attorney."

Attorney? I did not hire an attorney.

"I work for the public defender's office."

I remain perplexed, uneasy, and unsure whether to trust him.

"Have we met before?" Maybe I needed an attorney in the past, and he heard I am in trouble and came on his own.

"No." He tells me the government assigned him to my case. He says this is a high-profile case, making national headlines, and there is no way I could get through this on my own. He has agreed to work the case on a pro bono basis.

That is great; use my falling for your personal gain to superstardom.

The more he talks, the more I begin to trust him. I realize I need him and I will not survive without his help. There are many things I do not understand.

"You have been arrested for the murder of your husband and two little boys." As he speaks these words, he pauses, waiting for my reaction.

This experience is overwhelmingly surreal. Feeling remorse for the dead is hard since I do not remember who they were.

When I fail to express sorrow, he keeps talking. "I am going to need you to tell me everything if we're going to have a shot at beating this thing."

He sits down on the cot against the wall across from me. He places his bag at his feet and pulls out a yellow legal pad, ready to take notes. I speak about my experiences, initially with hesitance, but this is my only chance toward regaining freedom. I decide to trust him. It is risky. He could be a decoy. The real killers are smart. Once they realize I am alive and in jail, they will be after me. My only friend right now is my instinct. I have learned to trust it. Something deep inside tells me this man is here to help. Taking a deep breath, I start talking, conveying my story while disregarding the prison guard standing watch outside my cell.

I talk about waking up in the trunk, the dead bodies on the gravel driveway, driving to the house and seeing the police tape, fleeing to the diner, that I do not know my identity or what is happening, but that I am sure the real killers will be after me once they realize I am alive. It is only a matter of time. Mr. Phelps nods at every detail I blurt and takes extensive notes. He fills an entire notepad.

I finish talking. Mr. Phelps places his hand on his receding hairline and sighs deeply. "This doesn't look good."

I stare at him in disbelief. This is my attorney; he is supposed to do whatever it takes to get me off scot-free.

"But I didn't do it. I am telling you everything that I know." I am agitated.

"Lady, your story sounds crazy, and every person in jail is innocent." Clearly, this guy has been jaded by his career of defending the worst society has to offer.

"But I am telling you the honest truth as I know it."

"I'm not saying I don't believe your story," he responds. "All I am saying is that you can't remember who you are, though I am positive you are Cynthia Evans, after the fingerprints they ran through at booking. You can't tell me where you were at the time of the murder other than you were locked in the trunk of a car. You fled the scene when you saw the police at your house … AND when you returned to this alleged cabin, it was filled with heroin, albeit there is no evidence as now it is deserted. There are no witnesses and no alibi. The jury is going to throw the book at you!"

"But I am telling you the truth; there has to be something else. What about that girl Gabrielle … she was with me when I got arrested?"

"Hmm, I don't think she would be a good witness. Let me tell you the background I have uncovered on Miss Price. She filed ten different petitions against her current live-in boyfriend for domestic abuse, yet she still lives with him. She was arrested for writing forged checks and possession of illegal narcotics. Also, she is the person who was hiding you from the police and can be charged with aiding and abetting a murder suspect. Let's just say we are in trouble if she is our most credible witness."

This does not look good.

"There has to be some other evidence," pleading with him as if he can work miracles.

"There is a lot of evidence stacked up against you. They have you placed at the murder scene. Your neighbor, Mrs. Williams *(the name did not set off any bells in my head)*, gave the police a statement that she saw you pull up in the driveway around 9:45 p.m. You got out of your car and went into the house. She heard a huge commotion coming from inside. There was a lot of yelling and screaming. Things were being thrown about. Five gunshots went off. Then silence. When she looked out the window at about 10:40 p.m., she saw your car backing out of the driveway and pulling down the street. According to the Coroner's Office, they place the time of death at approximately 10:27 p.m."

This is definitely not looking good.

"Did anybody ask her if she actually saw me pull the car out of the driveway or just saw the car leave? There has to be something." I speak this voice of desperation out loud, but more to me than to the man sitting before me.

"It is not favorable. Would you like me to tell you about the other evidence against you?" I sigh and nod in a slow yes as I hang my head between my hands, focusing my eyes on the floor. "They ran a background check on you and your marriage. They spoke to the people you associated with. Evidence shows you were unhappy with your marriage. Your husband worked long hours. His job had him away from home for weeks at a time. You were thinking of leaving him. Your doctor prescribed you Xanax for depression. The preschool teacher of your son Zachary described how he came to school one day with bruises all up and down the left side of his body. When she asked him about it, he said he had fallen down a flight of stairs. Although she was suspicious of it, she never reported it, and he never went to the hospital for his injuries. Because you are telling me that you cannot remember anything that happened before you were arrested, there is no way I can dispute any of this."

I look at him in desperation. "Is there any good news, positive evidence in our favor?"

He takes the glasses from his face and holds them in his hands. He leans slightly toward me, his client, and softly says, "I am afraid not."

CHAPTER TWENTY-TWO

"I have some bad news. I have to go away again. There is a huge shipment for ACME in Montreal, and my boss wants me to run it up there."

"You just got back. Can't he get somebody else to drive it up there? This is ridiculous. You were gone for two weeks, and now you are leaving again for another two weeks. I can't live like this. Do you know that I have been so depressed? Dr. Laurie prescribed me a sedative because I have horrible anxiety attacks."

"I am trying to leave, but getting up and leaving in this business is difficult. They don't have enough drivers. Besides, we would have no income if I just quit. I make good money. How would we support ourselves, our two boys, our family?"

"Not having a loving father in the household is not supporting a family."

"I AM DOING THE BEST I CAN HERE. WHAT MORE DO YOU WANT!"

"Please do not raise your voice at me. I am just frustrated, that's all … arrrghhh … okay, I need to calm down. Karate practice for the boys was canceled. I promised them that I would run out and get some ice cream. I need to cool off anyway. I'll be back in ten minutes."

The guard bangs his nightstick obnoxiously against the bars of my cell. I arise groggily from my cot.

"Ya ready, Evans? The van is here to take you to court." The guard sneers at me disrespectfully, but I don't take it personally. He has the same lack of respect for all the inmates. He is non-discriminate in his arrogant attitude.

"You're going to see the Judge," he tells me.

Is this really how I am going to live out the rest of my life?

Hardly seems fair. I do not even have the leisure of remembering all the great times from my life or childhood. The only memories I have are horrific memories of death and torture. Maybe it is a blessing in disguise. Maybe there are no happy memories from my childhood. Maybe these new memories are far less harsh than the ones I desire from my past.

When I meet my final fate, my death, will my soul remember my previous memories?

I am still the same person. Memory and soul are not connected. Memory is a mortal notion that people have on earth to help them deal with life. A soul is your essential being and does not change regardless of what you remember. I have faith that my soul is kind and gentle. In my life, I have done all I can to prepare for the great afterlife of eternal glory. I know I have. These horrific events are God's way of repentance for my sins. It is his way of allowing me to enter his kingdom without any gloom or sin over my head. I have to have faith. Faith is with me. It is the only thing with me. It is all I have.

The ride to the courthouse lasts about half an hour. The tight handcuffs around my wrists begin to cut off the circulation to the rest of my arm. Upon arrival, the correctional officer leads me to a holding cell at the back of the courthouse. Ten minutes later, my lawyer presents himself to me.

"How are you feeling?" he asks.

I hate this man. He does not care how I am feeling. Why even ask me that question if you truly do not care? It is not his fault; his profession leads him to be this heartless individual. He is overworked and underpaid. His representation of me is merely for notoriety as the attorney who represents the Preston Murderer. I shrug at his small talk and let him keep talking.

He explains what to expect when I enter the courtroom before the Judge. I am not a stranger to this courtroom. I had been in front of this Judge before, and he was a screaming lunatic.

About twenty-four hours after my arrest at Gabrielle's house, a mere thirty-eight days earlier, I was before the Honorable Booker. How fitting, I thought at the time, 'Book-Her.' Irony at its best—not a pleasant man then, and I am not expecting him to be any more understanding this time.

My lawyer is explaining to me the plan. I am entering a plea bargain. I am not fully sure what that entails. It means admitting I murdered my husband and children. A way to avoid being fried alive. My attorney is persistent this is the best available option. Otherwise, I will go to trial and be judged by a jury of twelve of my peers. Believe me, given the choice of ending this now or being harshly judged by my peers, I will choose the first. People are irrational and unforgiving. They will be sure to give me the death penalty two times over. Plus, a jury trial can last upward of a year or two. I want this hell to be over now. Anything to avoid further public humiliation.

Mr. Pro Bono sits before me and explains it all. I tune him out five seconds into his spiel. Not that I do not trust him with my life. I have no choice but to. Rather, I do not care what happens. This is the end, and the less painful, the better.

"They're ready for you." A man dressed in a police uniform pops his head into the holding cell.

"This is it." I take a deep breath and follow the officer down a back hallway and into the courtroom.

It is packed with people—cameramen and press line the back wall. I am about to be remembered for my worst moments, which is never good. I sit at the table before the Judge. The numerous bodies in the courtroom create a sauna of heat exacerbated by the lack of windows or vents for proper circulation. The Judge speaks, but it is too difficult to focus. I feel lightheaded and begin to drift out of consciousness.

I parked the car in the driveway and grabbed the ice cream from the front seat. I bought four different flavors at the grocery store. Zachary was in his picky eating phase and would only eat vanilla. Oliver had a sweet tooth for chocolate, and Rick loved his cookies and cream. I had a craving for coffee ice cream. As I walked up the driveway to the house, I noticed the upstairs bedroom light on in Ms. Williams' house next door. The window shade closed slightly as I turned my head toward her home. She meant well but was always snooping around, stirring contro-versy or conflict in the neighborhood. I walked up the stone walkway. Oddly, the front door was ajar. I was fairly sure I had fully closed it behind me. Maybe the wind had blown it open. A chill ran down my spine as I walked into the home.

Something was not right.

Then I saw them. The two burlesque men, present in my home. Rick was lying face up on the living room floor three feet from me.

Four deafening shots rang out. I was paralyzed in fear. My two young boys ran around in a circle, screaming my name. One of the ruth-less intruders stood there with his hand revolver, shooting twice at each of them. So young, so frail, they had so much to live for. All I could think was, kill me. Point the gun this way. Notice me standing here before you. I have nothing to live for. You murderers. You destroyed all I have to live for. Kill me, too. Then they noticed me standing there, still holding the brown paper bag containing four half-pints of ice cream.

"We have a visitor." I remained steadfast as he pointed the gun in my direction. I did not flinch as he pulled the trigger to unleash the fatal bullet toward my heart. I welcomed the end. I craved the end. Just when I thought my prayers were answered, nothing happened.

"I'm empty." They had run out of bullets. The chamber of the gun only held five. All five were used on the three slain bodies lying lifeless on the floor before me.

The man with the faulty gun charged at me. I held my ground. I did not move an inch. He held the gun upside down and raised it full force toward my head .... blackness, darkness, ...

"Mrs. Evans. I do not appreciate your non-responsiveness to me in this courtroom! This is a place of respect."

Have I been dreaming?

It took me a few seconds to realize where I was.

"Sorry," I whimper.

I am still floating, not fully aware of my surroundings.

"Now stand up." The court officer behind me forces me to my feet. "Your attorney says that you are willing to enter a plea bargain, and I need to ask you a few questions to ensure this decision is willingly and voluntarily made. Do you understand?"

"Yes," the words somehow managed to come out, but my brain is still in a dream state.

"Are you currently, meaning today, under the influence of any drugs or alcohol."

"No."

What is going on?

I am before the Judge.

Was this happening?

"Now, are you willing to withdraw your plea of not guilty and enter a guilty plea to the murder of your husband, Rick Evans and your two children, Zachary and Oliver Evans?"

"No." There is a rash of awws and sighs from the crowd gathered in the packed courtroom.

"Order, there will be order in my courtroom. Mr. Phelps, please explain to your client what is happening in these proceedings?" The Judge sounds rather agitated. My attorney tries to talk to me, but I am not listening.

I shout, "Your Honor, I am not guilty and do not admit to anything. I am not a murderer."

The crowd in the courtroom once again erupts.

"I will not allow such an outburst in my courtroom," the judge shouts as the gavel flails about in his hand. "Mrs. Evans, you will not speak unless spoken to, and I do not appreciate you wasting the court's time."

This enrages me.

I did not kill them. I am positive about it.

"I did not murder anybody!" I shout these enlightening words at the top of my lungs.

"Officer, remove her from my courtroom. Now! Set a date for trial!"

CHAPTER TWENTY-THREE

He sat in the back of the crowded courtroom, watching the hearing——not at all interested in what was happening procedurally. He only cared about the girl. How could they have been so stupid not to kill her off when they had the chance? Luckily, she had been knocked over the head so hard she suffered severe memory loss.

When his men pulled up to the drop-off, he shot them both before they could tell him what happened. He assumed the job went well. People in the mountains do not fear gunshots. They think a hunter is finding the game of the season. Unlike in populated urban cities, the cops do not appear instantly at the sound of a gun, even if it is merely the backfiring of an old car. He had to get rid of the bodies, so he dragged them to his car. Being a small two-seater, it is impossible to fit two dead bodies of bodyguard proportion. So he would take one at a time to the lake and dump them. The car would be stripped and left on the side of the freeway, a simple stolen, abandoned automobile. The plan was precise and infallible. Only he did not know she was lurking in the trunk. If he had, this whole mess would have been taken care of right then and there, and he would not be sitting in this courtroom today. His internal alarms sounded upon returning to collect the body he left behind. The car was gone and instantly he knew the entire operation was compromised. He could not fathom who it was. A quick decision was made to get the next shipment out early to avoid any detection.

Luckily, his informant at the jailhouse put the pieces together for him. She lost her memory. Cynthia had no recollection whatsoever of the events that took place in the night. She did not even know who she was until the fingerprints at booking confirmed it. She had been placed in the trunk and driven two hundred miles north. The alibi was missing and her place on the suspect list was solidified by the nosy neighbor. Evidence was stacked against her and without her memory, Cynthia had no proof otherwise. A best-case scenario for him. The detectives had a solid case and would never consider another possibility.

He was lucky, but still, he had to be extremely cautious. People who suffered from amnesia often started to remember things in waves. Memories come back to them in dreamlike sequences where they cannot remember if that really happened or if they were dreaming. If Cynthia started to recall even a little of what went on that night, it would jeopardize everything. There must never be a leak, which is why they had to get rid of Rick Evans in the first place.

It was supposed to be a cake job. His boys were supposed to go to the home and make it look like an innocent robbery. The kids were supposed to be on their way home from karate practice with their mom. If only he had known about Cynthia in the trunk of the car. He could have killed her himself, and this would all be over with. But he had to kill Brandon and his partner for fear that someday they would break down and confide what they had done. A risk far too great to take, no matter what.

Nobody would suspect or question why he was in court. It was perfectly acceptable, and he was not out of place among the media frenzy of cameramen and reporters. He feared her memory would return and Cynthia would reveal too much information. Something he could not risk. As it stood now, there was no chance she would be let go. She was doing the smart thing by entering a plea bargain with the District Attorney. Juries tend to sympathize with young kids and go against the mothers who kill them. There is no way she would avoid having the death penalty thrown at her. With the plea, she would get life with no possibility of parole, which at least spares her some time on this earth.

She is a lucky woman, an incredibly lucky woman—more than she knew. She is now escaping death twice, a mere improbability.

God must have a plan for her, but his plan cannot interfere with mine.

He chuckled at this thought as he lingered in the back of the courtroom, watching the events unfold.

Something very wrong began to happen. Cynthia was irrational. She was defiant to the Judge, refusing to enter the plea. To every other person in the courtroom, she appeared crazy and irrational, fitting the insane housewife label the media has portrayed. To him, however, it is apparent she has had a flash of memory. His most daunting fear come true. The way she stood up and shouted she did not murder them; she knew, she remembered what happened. This was a complete danger to his entire operation, his entire existence. He had to get to her first before she could talk to anyone.

As the court officer dragged Mrs. Evans out of the courtroom, he quietly slipped out the doors leading to the hallway, away from the media frenzy about to produce tomorrow's cover story. He hid in a back corner of a secluded corridor and flipped open his cell phone. Quickly he typed his text message. Making a phone call would have been faster but too risky. No one was to hear what he had to say.

"Our worst fear has come true. She remembers. Take care of it." The text was sent.

Ten seconds later, the response came back, "On it."

He knew there was no room for error. Cynthia had to be stopped. A man of his stature and power had connections in all aspects of life, including the criminal justice system. It is shocking how easily correctional officers could be bribed to commit the same atrocious crime the people they guard are behind bars for. In a few short hours, all his worries would be over. A little slip into her next meal, and Cynthia could not tell anyone what happened that fatal evening.

CHAPTER TWENTY-FOUR

I sit here in the confines of my drab, humid cell. The events in the courtroom happened in the blink of an eye. One moment, I was at home, watching my family being taken down in a bloodbath right before my very eyes, and the next, I am before the cynical Judge Booker, who is about to make me admit to being the perpetrator of the most disturbing events I am sure no human being ever wishes his worst enemy to bear witness to.

Could it be?

At first, I thought it was all a dream. A sequence I fabricated, but the more those scenes play out in my head, the more I realize it is not a dream. It is reality. My horrific reality. Two burlesque men gunned down my family. Somehow, I remained alive. I begin to sob uncontrollably. I am crying for many varied reasons. Part of me is crying because I am still alive, but I have nothing to live for. The rest of my life will be spent alone in prison with nothing to look forward to except writing another line on the wall to indicate how many days have passed. My only loves dead——gunned down. I vividly saw my husband lying face up in the center of the living room. The bullet was sent right through his forehead, penetrating his brain. His eyes were wide open, and his mouth left as if to shout 'No!' but life was taken out of him before his vocal cords formulated the sounds.

I saw my two young boys running frantically between the kitchen and the living room, trying to decipher what was happening. They were screaming for their mommy. I saw the man with the gun. The same man who would later meet his death in the wee hours of the morning to come. My only consolation is that he, too, met the same fate outside that cabin upstate.

I am weeping for their memories. Finally, I have a memory. Granted, it is not one I want to remember, but in that instance, I know what it is like to be me, Cynthia Evans. I loved my family, and they are gone. Nothing can bring them back. A sorrow too great for me to bear. I want it all to end; I do not want to feel this kind of grief anymore. Inside of me is empty—nothing but an empty pit of despair.

"Why, why am I here?" The words have just come out. As I speak them, they provide a cathartic relief. With each syllable, I feel a little better. Granted, it can take a lifetime of solitude to cope with the loss I experienced, but those few words help me gain some perspective. This is no time to grieve. I have to be strong and look at the bigger picture. At home, I prayed to be taken together with my family, but I was spared. I was left here on this earth to fulfill a bigger purpose. I am alive, and I need to be alive. I have to bring down the madman behind the murder. My short experience with him leads me to believe this is not the first and certainly not the last time he will commit such atrocities against other families.

I need to talk to someone and let them know I have my memory back——not my complete memory, but enough to know what happened. Enough to say with one hundred percent clarity I did not murder my family. Enough to know I am indeed who everyone thinks I am, Cynthia Evans. Only everybody else had it wrong. I am not Cynthia Evans, the Preston Murderer; I am Cynthia Evans, a loving mother and wife. Cynthia Evans who is not capable of laying a finger on her child for the mere purpose of punishment. Cynthia Evans who would do anything to help her husband, whatever his problems.

Where are all the people who know this side of me? Have they all abandoned me? Have they turned their back?

I need to talk to someone as soon as possible. I want to call Gabrielle. I do not know her phone number. She is the only person who will come forward to help me. The only other person I can contact is my lawyer, Mr. Phelps. He is no help. He took my case for self-gain. I ruined his game plan. I made him look like a fool standing before the Judge. It is an unbelievable story. I suddenly remember it all the moment before the Judge enters my guilty plea. Quite improbable, but true. Mr. Phelps will tell me I need to think this over again. He will advise me that even if I remember what happened, it was my words against theirs, and I have no witnesses. The only eyewitnesses are dead, including the actual trigger pullers themselves.

"Evans, time to eat." I hate that guard.

He slides the door to the cell open and the tray across the floor. He provides just enough force for it to come to a stop at the tips of my feet. I look down at the tray in disgust.

There is no way I am eating that filth.

I guess the guard sees the disdainful look on my face because he grunts in my direction, "You'd better eat that and enjoy it because that's all you're getting until tomorrow."

As much as I despise that uniform-wearing man, he is right. I need to keep my strength up. I want to be able to function and remember everything I can. I bend down, pick up the orange cafeteria tray, which I place on my lap, and try to consume the inedible morsels. There is a bowl of oatmeal that is completely mush. I pick up a spoon and scoop out some unappetizing slop. It is just as tasteless as it looks. I try to swallow the spoonful in one clump, not to let the mush linger any longer than necessary on the taste buds. I repeat this procedure half a dozen times until I find it completely unbearable. I have taken in as much as physically possible.

However, consuming this meal does not make me feel any better. It makes my stomach churn. I take the tray off my lap and place it at the foot of the cot I have been sitting on. I feel a little lightheaded from the events of the day. I need to pace to clear my thoughts, but now that I stand up, all the blood in my body has rushed to my head. I step backward on one foot to prevent myself from falling. The wooziness is persistent. My knees buckle as I reach for my forehead with my left hand. My body is floating in the air. I am falling toward the cement floor, and there is nothing to brace my fall. I am helpless.

CHAPTER TWENTY-FIVE

Gabrielle stood behind the counter in the diner with a coffee pot in her hand, half in a daze. It had been over a month since her encounter with Cynthia, but she had not been the same since. She could not believe Cynthia would admit guilt of murder before the Judge. She was innocent, yet she was throwing her life away, and there was nothing Gabrielle could do to stop her.

She followed the events of the Preston Murderer every step of the way. Each inch of her motel room was covered in newspaper articles. Every word from those articles scanned repeatedly. Individual words carefully scrutinized in the hope of uncovering a simple clue to lead Gabrielle in the right direction. So far, she discovered nothing, not one clue. The press was biased, frying Cynthia alive without a trial. The entire town was convinced she was guilty without justice. Well, not the entire town; Gabrielle was still convinced Cynthia was innocent.

"Sweetheart, are you just going to stand there looking pretty with the coffee pot or pour me a refill?"

Gabrielle was startled by the man at the counter. Her mind had wandered to thoughts of Cynthia. She slowly returned to the reality of the waitress job and found her favorite local, Mr. Crowley. He was a harmless man, constantly flirting with Gabrielle. An older man with white hair and a hefty build who thought of all the girls at the diner as his family. He came in every morning like clockwork, 8:15 a.m. on the dot. The other girls loathed serving him. He was a horrible tipper and talked incessantly. He also made harmless but inappropriate comments to whomever was his server. Usually, it was the normal "If only you were a few years older, and I a few years younger."

Whenever these words were spoken, Gabrielle would laugh lightly and tap him on the shoulder, thinking, *Not if you were the last man on the planet.*

Nevertheless, he was harmless, and she did not mind serving him. He was an easy customer, always ordering the same thing: two poached eggs, dry wheat toast, and half a grapefruit. He also had exactly two and a half cups of coffee. He liked to talk constantly. Gabrielle knew his entire story. He used to work for the DMV and retired five years ago. He said life at the DMV was not as horrible as people thought. The workers were not as disgruntled as people made them out to be. His wife passed away fifteen years ago. Gabrielle knew he was retired and lonely. His daily morning trip to the diner was the thing that got him out of bed.

"Sorry Bill, I was daydreaming. Coffee?" Gabrielle grimaced as she lifted the coffee pot above Mr. Crowley's mug before him.

"No, dear, I've had my fill. Sweetheart, I'm worried about you. You seem distracted. Is everything okay on the home front?"

She did not want to tell him anything. Although Mr. Crowley felt it was all right for him to divulge every last known secret of his life, she was not at liberty to share personal information with her customers.

"Me?" she said insincerely, "Oh, I am fine; just been having a little trouble sleeping."

"You know, whenever I have trouble sleeping, I get up and boil myself a nice warm glass of milk …" His anecdotes were sincere, but Gabrielle was not in the mood to listen to his babbling. The man could talk for hours about anything.

As she pretended to listen, she saw a special news broadcast flash on the television hanging in the corner of the diner. The prompter below the newscaster talked about the Preston Murderer, though Gabrielle could not hear the exact words. As she realized they were talking about Cynthia, she blurted across the restaurant, "April, would you turn up the volume on that television for me?"

April was standing beneath the television, attending to the table of businesspeople who, obviously, were taking some time off from the office for a quick coffee break. She looked at Gabrielle and ignored her request. Gabrielle was not about to miss what was being said by the anchorwoman on the television. She slammed the coffee pot on the counter and ran across the room. She threw a chair underneath the television and frantically searched for the volume button to create sound.

"Chaos ensued in the courthouse as Cynthia Evans, the now infamous Preston Murderer, made a mockery of the courtroom. She was prepared to enter a guilty plea for murdering her husband and children when she started acting bizarrely. She began to scream out her innocence. The Judge did not take kindly to her antics and set a date for jury trial proceedings. We turn to Kathleen Winston for more on this story … "

Suddenly, the television shut off. Gabrielle stood there horrified. She needed more information. She needed to know what happened. She turned around to find her manager standing beneath her with the television remote pointed at the sensor on the monitor.

"Gabrielle, get down from that chair. I will not tolerate this kind of behavior in my restaurant." It was one of the few times her manager had ever yelled at her. "Now, I don't know what is happening with you lately, but it affects your work here. Pay attention to your customers, or I will be forced to send you home."

Gabrielle had to get her act together. She needed this job. She had no other source of income. She got down and tucked the chair into the table before her. She knew she would have to be on her best behavior for the rest of the day. Still, not knowing what happened to Cynthia was destroying her. Cynthia must have remembered something. Gabrielle had to know what Cynthia knew. It was Cynthia's only chance for survival. She looked at the clock, a little after 9:30 a.m. The next six hours couldn't pass fast enough.

CHAPTER TWENTY-SIX

The end of her shift came, and Gabrielle hightailed it out of the diner. She headed to the Orange County Jail, which was half an hour north of Preston. Cynthia was being held there without bail, awaiting her trial. Gabrielle had to speak to her.

She had not visited her new friend since the arrest. Gabrielle feared Cynthia hated her for what Hank did. But the real reason she did not visit was the promise to Officer Thomas that she would stay away. She was a woman of her word. Officer Thomas risked his job by letting her go free, and she is still grateful. Gabrielle knew she had to keep her promises to the officer.

The first promise was easy. Gabrielle had not seen Hank since the incident at the apartment over a month ago. Sure, she thought about Hank. He was a big part of her life, but she had no desire to see him. She did not call him, drive by the apartment, or spend sleepless nights in the motel room wondering what he was doing. Gabrielle was sure the feeling was mutual, and that Hank did not waste one moment thinking about her. She chuckled at the thought of him already having a new live-in girlfriend to cook his meals. Hank was a coward and afraid of being alone. That is why Gabrielle stuck around for so long. He loved her, but she did not love him. She enjoyed his company and companionship but was never in love with him. He did not enrich her life or make her a better person. He provided a roof over her head and someone to talk to outside of work. Heartless, maybe, but Gabrielle experienced the low of the lowest points in her life with

Hank and became stuck. She had nobody else. He had nobody else. It was a mutual, symbiotic relationship.

Now, for the first time in Gabrielle's life, she had a purpose: finding out the truth about Cynthia. This mission was a distraction to the life she had been living just a month ago. Gabrielle has a renewed sense of self because of it. Thoughts of suicide were lifted off her broken spirit. Gabrielle knew it was selfish to think about ending it all when she was the only person who could help her friend. This is why her second promise to Officer Thomas had to be broken.

As much as it pained her, Gabrielle stayed away for over a month. Every night, after her shift at the diner, Gabrielle would go home and wonder about Cynthia in the county jail. She imagined Cynthia alone in her dark cell, crying, awaiting her fate. No way to live, regardless of guilt. Gabrielle was positive about Cynthia's innocence; it was now her life's mission to prove this in any way she could. Any newfound memories Cynthia had about her life would be important clues about what, in truth, had happened. The newscaster's account of what transpired in the courtroom indicated uncovered memories by her friend. Gabrielle had to know what Cynthia remembered. It was a matter of life and death. Cynthia's!

Gabrielle had no idea if Cynthia was even allowed visitors, but she would not take no for an answer. She had to find out what Cynthia remembered in the courtroom.

Thirty-seven minutes after her shift at the diner ended, Gabrielle pulled up to the security booth monitoring the visitors to the Orange County Jail. She opened the door of her rusty old car to converse with the man inside.

"Who are you here to see?" the man inquired. Gabrielle told him. He did a double take as she mentioned the name. "What is your relation?"

Gabrielle did not know how to respond to that question. She wanted to lie and say she was her sister, but she knew better than to lie to the police.

"I'm a good friend."

The Officer looked at a clipboard in front of him. Then, without saying a word to Gabrielle, he picked up the phone and spoke in a hushed voice to a person on the other end of the receiver. He scribbled down some jargon. After completing his mysterious conversation, he motioned for Gabrielle to close her car door. She obliged and awaited further instruction.

Initially, the officer was hesitant to lift the barricade blocking her car's entrance, but he eventually pressed the button that allowed her access to the parking lot. She parked her car and proceeded to make her way to the front entrance of the jailhouse. As she entered the double doors, she was met by yet another security measure: metal detectors. She had to empty her pockets and navigate the intrusive machines blocking the hallway. After setting off the buzzer and being scanned, the security officer directed her to the office down the hall to make her presence known.

"Are you the person to see Mrs. Evans?" the officer inquired. His voice had a weird tone, as if there was no plausible way a person who committed such heinous crimes against humanity could ever have a visitor.

"Yes," Gabrielle stated reluctantly as she felt the judgment resonate from the guards at the security machines.

"You will have to speak to one of the social workers in Room 113."

Gabrielle thought this was weird. Perhaps it was the procedure with such high-profile inmates. Without further questions or instructions, she went down the long, dreary corridor to find the designated room.

As she walked down the hallway, a familiar male voice called her name.

"Gabrielle?" At first, Gabrielle did not turn around. Who in this place would know her name? But the voice shouted her name a second time, and she could not help but turn around in response.

There he stood, six feet of beautiful masculinity. It was Officer Thomas. His presence made her heart flutter. She was shocked to see him. She also knew he would be angry as her presence at the jail broke their trust.

They both started to speak the same words simultaneously: "What are you doing …" and then paused in a moment of awkwardness.

Gabrielle did not know whether to tell him she was there to see Cynthia, though she was sure Officer Thomas had to know that was the only reason she could be standing in the County Jail. Still, she did not want to admit to a betrayal of his trust since he had been more than kind to let her go free without any charges.

Instead, Gabrielle quickly directed the conversation to his presence. "I didn't expect to run into you way up here. I thought you only worked at the local precinct."

"I had to assist in a transport here." He paused and then diverted the conversation back to where Gabrielle had tried to run from. "You really shouldn't be here. You should distance yourself from this thing until it blows over." As charming as he was, Gabrielle was not in the mood to be lectured by the police.

"Cynthia is my friend, and I need to see her."

"That's why I'm surprised to see you. You don't know?" She looked at him, trying to figure out what he was talking about. "From the look on your face, I take it that you don't know Cynthia was sent to the hospital this morning."

This was not happening. The color on her face disappeared as the news hit her hard.

"Is she alright? What hospital? I have to go see her." Gabrielle became flustered.

"I don't think she can have visitors." Every word he spoke revealed worse and worse news. "She is in a coma."

CHAPTER TWENTY-SEVEN

She stood there before Officer Thomas in shock. Cynthia is in a coma. Gabrielle did not want to believe those words. She wanted Officer Thomas to embrace her in his arms and hold her. She wished he would console her as he told her this horrible news. But he did not do anything of the sort. He just stood there before her, motionless. He did not flinch. This standoffish attitude made Gabrielle feel worse. Officer Thomas was obviously angry at her for attempting to see Cynthia.

He must have seen the look on her face because all he could muster up the courage to say was, "I'm sorry. I thought you knew."

But she did not know. How could she?

"Please don't hate me." The words flew out of Gabrielle's mouth without any prior thought process.

A slight smile peered out of the corner of Officer Thomas's mouth. His eyes went from emotionless to a slight hint of passion.

"I could never hate you, Gabrielle." His voice was soft and sweet.

She was relieved.

"So that rain check you offered me at the bookstore still stands?" she attempted to lighten the mood.

Officer Thomas reached into his pocket to pull out a piece of paper and a pen. He propped himself against the wall and wrote down his name and phone number. When he was finished, he turned and handed the piece of paper to Gabrielle.

"Here … anytime you need anything, anything at all." He paused to think about what he was going to say next. "Heck, even if you just want a good meal at a nice restaurant, do not hesitate to call this number."

Gabrielle's heart fluttered as she took the paper with the officer's phone number. She folded it and placed it in the front pocket of her khaki pants. This was a 180-degree change from the cold shoulder she received a mere ten minutes ago. She thought he was angry with her for trying to see Cynthia, and now he was giving her his phone number to call for a date. This trip to the Orange County Jail proved to be worthwhile even without getting to see her friend.

Still, Gabrielle wanted desperately to see Cynthia. She wanted to go to the hospital where she was taken, but even Gabrielle knew that would be too risky. Even without the risk factor, there was no way she would break her promise to Officer Thomas a second time.

This turn of events seemed too unlikely. The real murderer was an evil man. He was out to kill. This was no accident. Cynthia's coma was the result of foul play. If the real killer could orchestrate her friend's current medical condition, he could do things beyond Gabrielle's wildest imagination. She could not draw attention to herself. Gabrielle was now convinced more than ever that Cynthia was, in fact, innocent of all the heinous acts she had been accused of committing. Gabrielle's mission in life is to figure out what happened that chilly night in suburbia. She had to know who killed the Evans family. Who would be so heartless and ruthless to murder innocent young children and feel no remorse in blaming their loving mother? There was no turning back.

Gabrielle left the jailhouse with a mixed bag of emotions. Elated at the thought that Officer Thomas asked her on a date, yet her spirit remained crushed at the notion her friend was forced into a coma. Now determined more than ever to get to the root of what happened, Gabrielle spent the half-hour drive back to her motel mulling over what to do next. Hours and hours had already been spent reading article after article, searching for answers. To date, she had not produced anything. Nothing behind the words showed her what could have happened. That did not mean she was going to give up. This was now her calling. She knew it. Failure is not an option.

She walked into the motel room and threw herself onto the squeaky bed in the middle of the room. Exhaustion overtook her body. She turned on the television to let her mind relax. She needed to do something mindless before trying to conquer the impossible task before her. She reached to the nightstand and grabbed the remote control. There was a familiar movie playing on the television, but she could not recall the name.

It was hard to keep from drifting in and out of consciousness. Gabrielle was fighting slumber. She needed to start looking for answers. Her mind was saying one thing, yet her body was not moving. Her body was exhausted. It was the first time in several weeks Gabrielle could lie down and even think of sleeping. Her body was not about to give up on this valuable necessity. She fought it as best as she could but drifted into a state of dreams and unconscious thoughts.

When Gabrielle opened her eyes, she had no idea how long she had been asleep. She was in a deep state of sleep in which you did not even realize you were sleeping. Groggily, she rolled over to the side of the bed and placed her feet on the floor. The television flashed light sporadically into the dark room and caught her attention peripherally. Another movie was already in progress. Gabrielle recognized this movie immediately, *Mafia Uncle*, a true classic. Gabrielle thought Cameron Milano played such a great character in this movie. She was the future wife of your typical Italian New Yorker who had ties to the mob. She convinced her fiancée to help out her nephew, who had been wrongly accused of murder in Mississippi.

"How fitting," she chuckled as she watched the movie.

If only life were that easy. If only things worked out in favor of the good guy at all times. However, that was the movies, and real life was not that kind. In real life, the bad guy wins, and the good guy is screwed over, or in Cynthia's case, the good girl.

Gabrielle sat there and watched the movie in a trance. Cameron Milano's character entered the courtroom and was called to testify on the stand. She had big hair and a tight sequined dress. She testified as an expert in forensics. Her knowledge of crime scene investigations proved to be extensive and impressive. Milano's character, Ms. Genovese, was called to testify about tire tracks found in a picture she took outside a bank robbery. The prosecuting attorney, played flawlessly by the actor Philip Crowe, showed the witness the picture and asked, "Looking at this picture, isn't it true that the tire tracks can be traced back to the defendants?"

Ms. Genovese states the tire tracks were made by a 1960 Lincoln Continental and not the car that the defendants were driving.

"There is no conceivable way this can be determined by looking at a photo," the prosecutor states emphatically.

Ms. Genovese explains the tire marks and the function of a car. These things go way over the head of Gabrielle's base knowledge as to how a car works. The explanation was not important. It was not what Cameron Milano's character said that was important. It was the fact that such information could be lifted merely from a photograph of tire marks.

Gabrielle could not believe the movie. The answers were right in front of her.

"That's it!" she exclaimed out loud in pure excitement.

The answer to identifying the real murderer was right before her, played out in the fictional courtroom of the movie presented on the television.

The truth lay in the photographs taken at the cabin. Only two photographs. The developed camera roll lay on the nightstand in Gabrielle's motel room for the past few weeks. Since their development, she had been so disappointed that Gabrielle did not re-open the envelope to look at the pictures again. Gabrielle's search for answers focused on clues from the media. Gabrielle discounted the pictures taken at the cabin. When she watched Cameron Milano's character describe the tire tracks from the photo of the car, she knew where her answers lay. She just needed to find a person with enough knowledge to decipher the imprints for her.

Suddenly, Gabrielle's attention was again directed at the light flashing from the television. Divine intervention at work. On the television was a local business advertisement, an ad for Frank's Tire Shop on Route 20 in Preston. It was a B-level commercial with really bad actors pretending to be impromptu in the background, yet they were not fooling anyone with their fake conversations at the customer service desk. At the same time, a bald, middle-aged man was talking to the camera about the quality of service offered by Frank's Tires. This man was presumably Frank himself. The man talked about the new state-of-the-art technology used by the tire shop to ensure tires were functioning at their highest performance level.

It was a start. The search would have to wait until the morning, as it was now 4 a.m. and Gabrielle needed to catch up on some sleep.

CHAPTER TWENTY-EIGHT

Gabrielle bribed her coworker April with twenty dollars and a promise to cover any of her graveyard shifts in the future when she needed off, even if it meant working for twelve hours straight. Not a fair bargain, but Gabrielle needed the day to find answers. Too much time had passed, and Cynthia's life hung in the balance.

Gabrielle pulled her green Dodge into a lined parking space before Frank's Tire Shop. If she had wanted to go into the store in stealth mode, there was little chance of that happening as the roar of the engine alerted everyone within a twenty-mile radius of her arrival. Gabrielle sat in the car's front seat and looked at the two photographs she had taken. She had no idea if Frank could help answer her questions, but she was desperate. At this point, figuring out the missing link between the heroin operation and Cynthia was like looking for a needle in a football field full of haystacks; improbable but not impossible.

She placed the sleeve of photographs in her pocketbook and headed into the store. A pimple-faced teenage boy working behind the counter greeted Gabrielle.

"So much for this idea," a disheartened Gabrielle muttered as she approached the young lad.

Gabrielle feared this kid would have no idea how to help. Not that she was expecting to find the actual owner, Frank, the man from the commercial, but someone with a completed educational background was better than a clueless teenager.

The bells on the store door alerted the worker there was a new customer for him to help. When he saw Gabrielle, he smiled as if he had never seen a girl in his life.

"Great," Gabrielle whispered aloud to herself, "let's not let the raging hormones get in the way here, kid."

The teenage hormones, however, were working to her advantage. The young boy, whose name tag read Scott, was eager to please.

"Hi, how can I help you today?"

Gabrielle had not thought her trip to the tire shop fully through. She was not sure what she was going to say or how she would get the information she was seeking. Gabrielle just stared at Scott blankly. Again, he asked Gabrielle what she wanted. She had to think quickly on her feet, or the boy would think she was a lunatic and shut down any offer of help.

"Uhm, yes, I am here for a friend." He stared at her like she was nuts. "She has this car that runs … funny. She thinks maybe the tires are running unevenly." *Unevenly, what does that even mean?* "So, I told her I knew this great tire shop that might be able to help her out." Gabrielle did not even think the sounds emanating from her mouth were forming coherent words.

"Well, if you have her car, I can look at the tires for her."

"I don't have her car." He looked at her, dumbfounded. "You see, she lives deep in the countryside and dislikes driving." Gabrielle really needed to learn how to tell better lies. "You know those country bumpkin folk, the closest store is an hour away."

The boy just stared at her as if she were crazy. Gabrielle knew she would have to get to the point. She reached into her purse, pulled out two photographs, and placed them abruptly on the countertop.

"Here, she sent me these pictures." He still looked confused. "She thought maybe someone might be able to tell her what was wrong with her car if they looked at the tire tracks in the photo."

Cameron Milano's explanation of the tire tracks proved much more eloquent than Gabrielle's, but hopefully, the point still got across.

As ridiculous as the story she fabricated appeared, amazingly, Scott was still willing to help her. He took the photographs into his hands and squinted to find the tire tracks.

"You know there are three sets of tire tracks in these photographs. Do you know which one is hers?"

Okay, well, at least he appears to be somewhat intelligent.

Scott placed one of the photos on the counter in a position that he and Gabrielle could observe.

"See here." He pointed to the double set of tire tracks on the driveway. "These tracks belong to an eighteen-wheeler." Gabrielle just nodded in agreement. "The picture is a little fuzzy and small. I would need to scan the photo into our computer system. Then I may be able to blow it up to get a better read."

Gabrielle was not even sure what type of information she sought, but at this point, any information was better than none.

"The only problem is …" Oh no, this sounded like unwelcome news. "…our scanner is broken, so I have no way of getting this photograph onto our computers." This was not good. Gabrielle needed him to analyze whatever he could, to tell her whatever it was he could tell her.

Scott slid the pictures across the counter toward Gabrielle and told her the scanner might be fixed if she returned the following week. The following week was not good enough. Every day is precious when a person is rotting in jail. Every hour is essential in helping Cynthia regain her life. Gabrielle did not know what else to do, so she took the pictures off the counter and placed them back into her purse. As she peered into the bag, she noticed the CD-ROM that had come complimentary with the development of the photographs.

"Do you think that maybe this might help?" She held up the CD, hoping Scott was still interested in assisting her.

"That is perfect. I can load it onto the computer and play with the photo."

Gabrielle should have known the way to any teenage boy's heart is through electronics. Scott appeared giddy as he pushed the button to lead the CD into the disc drive of the store's computer.

"I love working with this new program we've just got. My boss is not so savvy with it, but it can tell you a lot about how a car runs. It can tell you how the tire treads are wearing, the type of tires, the type of car … all sorts of cool things. This program is totally hot." Gabrielle just made the highlight of Scott's day at work.

After fifteen minutes of pushing buttons on the keyboard and playing around with the mouse, Scott appeared to have discovered valuable information from the amateur photographs.

"See, there are three tire tracks. Like I said before, this is a double-axis truck. These tracks over here appear to belong to your normal run-of-the-mill American car. From the looks of the tire tracks, it seems it is a front-wheel car, most probably a Honda Accord. I assume this is your friend's car running a little low. It seems the air in the front two tires is much lower than the rear ones, thus causing a sense of being off-balance. You can tell where the tire treads are running and wearing down. You might want to tell her to get the tires rotated and check the air, but it is nothing to be alarmed about."

Scott was speaking as if he had solved all of Gabrielle's problems when, in fact, he had not told her any pertinent information. There had to be something more.

"Wait a second." Scott seemed overly amazed and excited. "Where is it that you said your friend lived?"

"Why do you ask?" Gabrielle had almost forgotten the fable she told the tire store employee.

"I'm just curious because this is a very weird group of tire tracks you got going on here. See, you have the normal run-of-the-mill suburban car, then you have an eighteen-wheeler, which one can say is a bit odd in the secluded woods, but not all that unexplainable … but then you see this other set of tire tracks."

Scott turned the computer monitor toward Gabrielle as if she could decipher anything that appeared on the screen.

"This set of tire tracks is very odd. They indicate that it is a rear-wheel drive car, which is only common in expensive sports cars." Scott paused. "Hold on a second." He ran to the back storeroom urgently as if he had just discovered hidden gold.

Gabrielle had enough. Quite frankly, cars bore her, and she had no interest in how they were made, run, or manufactured. As exciting as her trip to the tire shop had been, she was disappointed she could not obtain any vital information and was no further along in her investigation of the Evans' murder. Gabrielle was busy daydreaming about how she would get out of the store when Scott reappeared in front of her.

"See this magazine?" He showed her the latest car magazine with all the latest, most expensive hot rods. She was not at all impressed. "This is the new model of the Python 3600. There are only a few of these car manufacturers in the entire world. Only five stores, to be exact, one in Los Angeles, one in London, one in Berlin, one in New York, and one in Milan." Gabrielle was hoping he would get to the point faster. "In this magazine, they did an entire spread on the car and all its special features. They show the tire tracks … look here." Gabrielle peered into the magazine. "Now, look closely at the third set of tire tracks in the picture you gave me. It appears as if they are the same tracks. These highly specialized cars come with specially made parts, including specially designed tires." Gabrielle was not interested in the history of the latest specialty car. She started to zone out when she heard, "There are only 5,000 of these cars in the entire world."

"You mean to tell me those third tire tracks belong to an extremely rare car?" Gabrielle was not buying it.

"Not only a rare car, a car worth half a million dollars!" Scott's voice rose louder as his excitement level rose.

"Okay, thanks for your help, but I have to get going." Gabrielle motioned for her CD rom back so she could leave the store. Scott proceeded to shut down the computer program and retrieve her disc.

As he handed it back to her, his curiosity got the better of him. "Where is your friend living in the country that there is a Python in her driveway?"

Gabrielle shrugged and said, "Her neighbor is a wealthy farmer." With that statement, she knew she had overstayed her welcome in the tire store. It was time to leave.

CHAPTER TWENTY-NINE

Gabrielle walked out of the tire shop, assessing the events that had transpired. The newfound knowledge swirled about her mind. She learned Cynthia drove a Honda Accord, which she already knew as that was the car in which she first met Cynthia. That exact car took the two women up to the cabin, where they witnessed the heroin operation unfold before their eyes. Identifying the big rig tire tracks was also not useful or new information. A roaring truck appeared at the cabin to retrieve the stacks of heroin stored in the otherwise abandoned wilderness. The Python 3600 … now that was interesting information.

Gabrielle did not know a thing about cars. She only knew that for a car to run smoothly, she had to change the oil every 3,000 miles, which she was lucky to do every 7,000. A diner patron once showed her how to check the oil underneath the hood by sticking and probing some long rod, but she had never attempted to do it herself. Color was the most exciting question she asked anyone who mentioned purchasing a new ride. The boy's monologue about this car made her think this was particularly valuable information she was glossing over. The Python 3600 is expensive, and only a person with an extreme amount of money could afford such a luxury. No surprise in dealing with a drug ring that this would be a car of choice. The lure of such dangerous operations is the power of money. Anyone who participates in such an endeavor probably enjoys extravagance and extreme wealth. If it is true there are only five dealerships worldwide, then Gabrielle should be able to find out who owns such a car. New

York City is only a three-and-a-half-hour drive away. The owner likely purchased the car at that dealership. If only a handful of people owned this car nationwide, then only a handful would be on a list, and she would be that much closer to figuring out who the killer is. Gabrielle had no other clues, so this information was as good as any.

Gabrielle drove away from the tire shop mindlessly and found herself turning onto Main Street in the downtown shopping district of Preston. She parked the car in the bookstore parking lot and calculated her next move. First and foremost, Gabrielle had to find out the exact location of the Python dealership in New York City. The town of Preston was too many miles from the city for it to be listed in the phone book, so she would have to resort to other means than the yellow pages. As she peered out through the front windshield, the landscape in front of her faced the sidewalk and the street. There, on the corner of Main and 3rd Streets, was a pay phone. In this era of modern technology, it is hard to imagine the pay phone still exists. Everyone these days is connected wirelessly. Every citizen has a personalized mobile phone number, which is more common than a personal social security number—the age of instant connectivity. That is everyone except Gabrielle. She does not own a cell phone and prefers it that way. She did not feel the need to be able to air all of her grievances in public at any moment of any second of the day. Nothing annoys her more than the restaurant patron who gabs away throughout their entire meal, disturbing the peaceful dining experience of those surrounding them. So, the pay phone on the corner was just the item she was looking for.

Before exiting the car, she searched under the front seat, the passenger seat, and in the cup holder. Her search revealed two dollars and twenty-five cents in quarters. Enough for the phone call she had to make. Gabrielle also searched for a pen and a piece of paper. Once gathering all the needed items, Gabrielle left the car and headed to the corner phone.

The air outside was brisk and cool. Gabrielle hoped the phone call would not take long as she was dressed inappropriately for the weather. She had on a short-sleeved t-shirt underneath an oversized green sweater. The wind cut through the small stitches in the yarn, causing the tiny hairs on her arms to stand upright.

She placed a quarter in the designated slot, picked up the receiver, and dialed 4-1-1. The tone on the other end disconnected and told her to deposit ninety cents. She pressed her index finger on the receiver knob and listened for a new dial tone. The phone did not give her back the quarter she had deposited for the first attempted phone call. Good thing she found extra change lying around the floor of the Aries. This time, she deposited the correct amount and redialed the number for information.

"What city and state?" the automated voice on the other end questioned.

"New York, New York." As she spoke, a truck barreled down the road, honking its horn obnoxiously.

"I am sorry, I did not hear your response. What city and state?"

"New York, New York," Gabrielle repeated.

"I am sorry we do not have a listing for that city; please try again. What city and state?" No listing for New York City! Gabrielle was getting frustrated with the machine—a testament to why she hated the digital era.

"Manhattan, New York."

"I am having a hard time understanding. Please hold." The attempt to make things easier was actually causing rage. After ten seconds, the automated system transferred to a live operator. Gabrielle wondered how automation was supposed to make things easier when, in the end, you wound up with a live person, the very place where you should have started and thus could have remained in a happy place.

"Hi, what listing are you looking for?" Gabrielle told her she was looking for the Python dealership in New York City. After some keyboard sounds, the woman said, "I don't see a listing for a Python dealership in New York City. The only Python dealership listed is in Manhasset, New York." Gabrielle figured that had to be the correct listing.

"Can I have the address and phone number, please?"

Before the call went any further, an automated voice told Gabrielle that she had to deposit seventy cents or her call would end. She frantically grabbed three quarters and slid them into the slot on the phone. Luckily, the operator on the other line was still there.

"1357 Route 25A, Manhasset, New York ... phone number 516-555-2300." Gabrielle jotted down the information as quickly as possible. There was an offer to connect to the number for an additional charge, but she declined with only one quarter left in her stash.

Gabrielle hung up the phone and contemplated her next move. She knew that Manhasset was a city on Long Island. She had never been there before but remembered it being mentioned in a random after-hours television movie.

She headed back to the car and searched underneath the front seat. She found her *McNulty United States Road Atlas*, dated 1997, and flipped it open to New York State. There was a blown-up map of Long Island with the town of Manhasset listed in bold typeface. Route 25A appeared to be a major highway. It was listed as one of the roads running through the entire length of the island. Gabrielle figured that it would not be too difficult to find.

Although she successfully obtained the car dealership location, Gabrielle knew she needed additional information about this exotic car before heading to Manhasset in order to keep up with the car salesman. She closed the door to her car and ensured the door lock was in the down position.

Gabrielle had not been back to the bookstore since she turned down Officer Thomas's invitation for a bite to eat. She wanted so much to go on the date, but that day was the start of her quest for the truth about Cynthia. Gabrielle made a mental note to call Officer Thomas. His phone number lay on the nightstand next to her bed but she had yet to take him up on the offer for dinner. She knew she should call, but something inside her caused her to hang up the phone before he answered every time she dialed the numbers. Gabrielle was extremely attracted to the Officer, but she did not see how it would work out with her strong convictions about her friend's innocence—he could not see past the media bias. This realization saddened her but did not deter her from her mission. She would have to long for him from afar, for now.

Gabrielle's usual ritual into the store involved heading to the travel section upstairs at the top of the escalator, but her mission differed today. Instead of going up, she remained on the bottom floor, perusing the three rows of magazines in the back left-hand corner. All the other women in the section were crowded around the first aisle filled with fashion and wedding magazines. Even on a normal reading day, she would have no interest in reading about the latest issues of what not to wear. Gabrielle thought those magazines were deceitful. The writers and editors proclaimed to be for women's liberation and independence but then filled the pages with articles about how to succumb to men and the necessity to be perfect in every way to be a meaningful person in society. The woman reader is told to accept every inch of their body for what it is but then is bombarded with images of anorexic beauty. It is no wonder over sixty percent of the United States's female population has serious body image issues. This was not appealing to Gabrielle. She had many more important things to worry about than whether or not she was using the best face moisturizer for her skin type.

Gabrielle kept walking and found herself among the numerous car and motorcycle periodicals. Oddly enough, five other men were also browsing these magazines, each fitting the part of the testosterone-producing alpha male. One man was wearing a leather jacket and jeans and holding his purple motorcycle helmet as he searched for the latest edition of his favorite motorcycle magazine. The other men appeared to be searching for their favorites as well. Unsurprisingly, these magazines were in the aisle right next to the cabaret selection of periodicals—those with scantily clad women gracing the covers. The only difference between these two reading genres was that the automotive magazines had a scantily clad woman on the front cover with articles of cars and bikes inside, while the other magazines had the women both on the cover and inside. Gabrielle proceeded to search for *Automotive Monthly*, the magazine the giddy teen brought from the back of the tire shop. She figured she had better read up on the Python in case she needed this information. She sifted through the various car magazines and came across the article. The magazine did a full spread on the specific features of the Python, comparing it to all the other expensive cars on the market. Apparently it has the roomiest trunk space in the sports car market, enough to hold up to three large suitcases. She glanced through the article quickly and proceeded to the register to make her purchase.

Gabrielle was now equipped with the necessary tools to visit the dealership in Manhasset. It was a trip, however, that would have to wait for three days due to work constraints. She was unsure what to expect, but at the very least, if she could obtain a list of Python owners, she could mull through it and search for anyone remotely related to the Evans' murder. It is grasping at straws, but those straws were all she had at the moment.

CHAPTER THIRTY

Although Gabrielle would not risk going to the hospital to visit her friend, she did call the nurse's station daily to get an update on Cynthia's condition. Each day was the same.

The nurse would tell her calmly and gently, "She is stabilized, but there is no indication she will come out of the coma soon."

Gabrielle pictured Cynthia lying alone in her cold hospital bed, motionless and barely breathing, hooked up to a ventilator provided by the hospital. Sadly, nobody was at Cynthia's side, day or night, to hold her hand until she awoke from the coma. No person to gaze her eyes upon when she traveled back into this realm. No voice from beyond reading to her daily, encouraging Cynthia to return to her life. There was nothing for that woman to live for, nothing for her to come back to. Her husband and two children had been murdered. Her family and friends had abandoned her. She is framed for murder and will be given a death sentence once she breathes again. Gabrielle thought it was strange Cynthia was still hanging on despite all the horrors and struggles she had recently endured. She was clinging on to her life and not giving in. Despite all that had happened, there was still something to live for, something for her to return to and greet in the world. Gabrielle could not imagine what that glimmer of hope could be for Cynthia, but she was glad that it was there deep in Cynthia's unconscious thoughts. It was strong enough for her to hang in there and not give up on life.

The last three days were the longest period of Gabrielle's life. She wanted more than anything to leave earlier for the dealership in Manhasset, but she could not afford the days off. Time appeared to stand still and motionless as Gabrielle served a plethora of customers coffee and burgers. Finally, Tuesday arrived, her scheduled rest day. It was time to make the three-hour drive.

The dealership was not in the middle of Manhattan but rather a forty-five-minute drive outside of the city to the North Shore of Long Island, appropriately named 'Miracle Mile.' This is a stretch of land worth more in wealth than most of the third-world countries in Africa. Some of the most famous stores and designers have shops and boutiques located here. Also within the city limits, among the Porsche, Hummer, Ferrari, and Lamborghini dealers, is the Python dealership.

Gabrielle pulled her noisy deathtrap into the parking lot and turned off the engine. She walked toward the pristine entrance to the spotless automobile gallery. Inside, there was not an ounce of dust. An impossible feat unless a housekeeper was hired to walk around full-time cleaning the viewing area. A total of five cars were on display. There were tiny two-door sports cars that could fit the driver if he were a slim 5'9 or smaller. Two of the cars had four doors, but those extra two doors were a sham, as they did not appear to provide any more access or room for the sporty vehicle. Each car had its allocated salesman in a crisp Armani suit standing in front of it, waiting to snag the commission of a sale. The room was bright and surrounded by windows stretching from the floor to the ceiling. Gabrielle felt out of place in the presence of such money and snobbery. She wore faded jeans and a cute purple t-shirt with a Chiquita banana logo across the chest. Not your typical luxury car purchasing attire.

As soon as she opened the front door to the showroom, Gabrille could feel the judgments and piercing looks being thrown her way. Immediately, a gentleman in a flawless suit approached her. He was on her like a vulture circling roadkill, waiting for the clear to dive in a take a bite. Gabrielle did not want to spend any more time than necessary in this atmosphere and hoped it would be as painless as possible. Still, she knew she needed to obtain the information she sought.

"Yes, ummm … I am interested in the Python 3600." The man stared her up and down as she spoke these words. He appeared shocked that she knew what kind of car she wanted.

"Certainly. We have a floor model right this way." Although Gabrielle could feel his obnoxious demeanor, he was still working on commission and had a duty to be nice to all customers who entered the premises.

Currently the only patrons were Gabrielle and a middle-aged man wearing a polo shirt tucked into khakis. She was the floorwalker's only shot at obtaining some kickbacks that day. Gabrielle walked with the young money-hungry wannabe toward the blue-floor model in the back of the store. It was a sea-blue sports model with two doors. Gabrielle stared at the tires. She could not spot the difference from the tires on her trusty Dodge Aries.

"These appear to be specially made tires. Could you tell me what they are designed for?" The salesman proceeded to describe all of the special features that the car had to offer.

Gabrielle was not paying the slightest attention to what he had to say. She was not interested in a new car, and she squashed any glimmer of an unrealistic hope when she glanced at the sticker price attached to the rear passenger side window. At first, she thought she had misread it or that it was a misprint. She nearly choked on her own saliva, realizing that never in her lifetime would she make half of the going price for the Python 3600. She knew she was wasting this poor salesman's time and was also nauseous about the unnecessary materialism she was currently surrounded by. She had to end the facade and leave the showroom immediately.

Gabrielle decided just to be upfront and tell him what she wanted.

"Listen …" She glanced at the name tag on the man before her. "… Chad." He stared at her as if he had no idea what she would say next. "I'll be straightforward with you. I can't afford any of these floor models."

Gabrielle swore she heard the man say under his breath, "Apparently, by the junk you drive."

She ignored the rude comment and kept talking without skipping a beat. "However, I am interested in the Python 3600, albeit not the brand-new floor model you offer me here. I know it's an extremely rare car, and I was hoping you could give me a list of current owners within, say, a three-hundred-mile radius so that I can contact them directly to …"

"Seriously!" The man interrupted her and raised his voice with each word. "Seriously, lady. You're wasting my time here."

Gabrielle looked around the showroom and noticed she was now the only customer present.

"You come in here pretending to be interested in this car and then have the audacity to tell me you don't want a car and want to see if I can give you a list." Well, when he put it that way, the idea also sounded a bit ludicrous to Gabrielle. "I'm not at liberty to divulge information about our customers. That information is private and confidential. And even if I were allowed to pass that information along, there is no way I would give it to you."

It was obvious to Gabrielle this man had some serious anger issues. Instead of listening to him berate her further, Gabrielle switched her thoughts to possible underlying causes of his extreme hostility. She imagined it stemmed from his low self-esteem, a Napoleon complex, as the man standing before her was merely 5'5". Or, she concluded, he grew up a poor orphan desperate to make his mark on wealthy society but was stuck working in this wretched car dealership. She decided that it was a little bit of both.

"If you're not interested in purchasing a car today, you will have to leave the premises." Not that Gabrielle wanted to stay any longer. She had already overstayed her welcome and was quite happy to leave. She headed out the door without saying a word.

As Gabrielle approached her green Dodge she started to laugh. Any other human being on the planet would have been mortified at how she had been treated by the Python dealership. Her picture would be hung at the front desk, forbidding her from ever entering the showroom again during her lifetime. Any other customer would have started to shed a tear and demanded to speak to the manager, but Gabrielle just began to chuckle at the absurdness of the events that had transpired over the last twenty minutes.

What on this earth made me think that I could waltz into a car dealership and get the names of all the owners of the cars they sold? This thought made her giggle more.

This was not just any dealership, but a dealership of some of the most expensive cars in the world. She did not even look the part. Her plan was absurd. Gabrielle was unphased at the fact that she could not obtain the list of the names she wanted, as the entire plan was ridiculous. She made a mental note to watch less television, especially those amateur detective shows in syndication on cable. They were messing with her head and distorting her perceptions of reality. The only sad and frustrating part of the day was she was no better off with information to help Cynthia than earlier that morning. She still needed that list of people, but now she had no idea how to obtain it, and without it, Cynthia was guilty until proven innocent.

CHAPTER THIRTY-ONE

"Honey, you haven't been yourself these past few weeks." Gabrielle was not in the mood for small talk with Mr. Crowley. Most days, he did not bother her with his mundane and pointless conversations, but lately, she was worn out. She was distracted and had other things on her mind. Cynthia Evans was one of those things.

A chance encounter can change your life and very existence. It was an unintended meeting right here in this very diner, just a few months ago, that transformed Gabrielle's entire existence. Since that moment when the dreaded 'Preston Murderer' wandered into the Village Diner, Gabrielle's life had been transformed. She knew that Cynthia's, too, would never be the same. The only life Cynthia knows is the one that she has had for the past few months, the one of an accused killer spending time behind bars, awaiting day after day for a glimpse of something better. Only she may not even get that. She is now someplace between life on earth and the afterlife, with her mortal body lying in Lincoln Memorial Hospital. Gabrielle hoped Cynthia was free and happy wherever her subconscious had taken her because, at this moment, any place was better than reality.

"You know you have dark circles underneath your gorgeous eyes." Mr. Crowley meant well, but his tact left much to be desired. "Honey, you need a vacation."

For once, you have it right, Mr. Crowley. Gabrielle quietly laughed to herself as she refilled the older man's cup of coffee on the counter.

"You have that same look in your eyes I saw when I worked in the DMV. As soon as a person's eyes started to glaze over, you could tell that it was time they took a vacation. That's what you need: a sunny beach vacation to a tropical paradise. You know Hawaii is especially beautiful." Gabrielle heard one word in his statement: DMV. It was the only word that made coherent sense to her. It was exactly what she needed—a contact at the DMV. The Department of Motor Vehicles kept records of registrations, and surely they could print out a list of people who have registered a Python 3600 in the area. This was the help that she was looking for.

"Mr. Crowley, how long did you say you worked at the DMV?" She was blatantly changing the conversation topic from his last experience drinking frozen daiquiris on the beaches of Maui to one of excitement involving his mundane government job.

He did not even seem to skip a beat. The fact that Gabrielle was interested in what he had to say rather than simply pretending to listen to his incessant babble threw him off pleasantly.

"I worked there thirty-three years. I still work part-time when people are sick or out on vacation." Her ears perked up a little more. The man still had access to the motor vehicle databases.

"So, do any interesting, famous people come into the DMV? I mean, everybody has to come there to renew their licenses and register their cars." She was stretching this conversation, but he was eating it right up. As she spoke, she leaned in over the man. Her elbows were perched on the counter directly across from his body. "So, what's the most impressive car you've had to deal with at the DMV?"

"Well, you'd be surprised how many people have Ferraris and Hummers."

"Any Python 3600s?" This was a stretch.

"Gabrielle, I did not know you were a female car junkie. You don't fit the part." If fitting the part meant an overall-wearing, oil-changing, big-haired female, then no, she did not fit that part, but she was willing to be whoever in order to obtain the information she needed to save Cynthia's life. "Where is this sudden interest in automobiles coming from?"

"My brother ..." She knew she had to make it a good lie. "My brother just came into some money after a terrible accident a few years ago. Horrible tragedy, really. They thought he wasn't going to make it. He was camping in the woods in the Adirondacks with a group of poor children from the inner city when he saved one of the little girls from being attacked by a grizzly bear. He lost sight in his one eye as a result ..." She wanted to stop, but the words just kept flowing out of her mouth. She knew she had to tie this story back to her brother. "His lifelong dream was always to own a Python 3600, only they are too expensive to buy off the lot. If we could contact a local owner, he may be willing to sell his Python for a deal, or at least let my brother have a test drive."

Mr. Crowley was stunned. He looked at her like she had four sets of eyes. So, instead of letting the fish tale settle, she kept talking, trying as little as possible to maintain eye contact with him.

"I went to the closest Python dealer outside of town, but they turned me away without even a 'hello.' Must have been the waitress uniform. I guess they figured I don't dress the part ..."

"Honey..." Mr. Crowley paused for a few seconds. Gabrielle cringed as she feared he was about to scold her like her foster father did when she was five years old for eating the last chocolate chip cookie in the cupboard and denying it as the crumbs spilled out of her mouth and onto the floor. "Gosh. Dang ..." he continued, "that is the sweetest, most endearing story I have ever heard. You know I might be able to get you a printout of Python owners. Let me see what I can do."

He pointed his index finger toward Gabrielle and motioned for her to come closer to him. She tried not to wince as the stale smell of his coffee breath blew right into her face.

Then, in a low, whispered voice, he said, "But don't tell no-one, as that's probably something I can lose my pension over. However, if your brother is half as sweet as you are, he deserves all the good things that come his way." He winked and lifted the freshly filled cup of coffee to his mouth to take a sip.

Gabrielle turned around and replaced the coffee pot on the warmer behind the counter. With her back facing Mr. Crowley, she simpered. She could not believe what had just transpired.

Let's just hope the old man follows through on his promise.

CHAPTER THIRTY-TWO

"I'm sorry Mrs. Evans is still in critical condition in the ICU. There has been no notable change in her state."

Gabrielle hung up the phone. Cynthia was still at the hospital, in a coma. Gabrielle called there once a day religiously. Each day, it was the same. Cynthia remained in stable condition with no progress toward recovery. Gabrielle wished for her friend to recover from the vegetative state quickly, but also knew if Cynthia remained that way until she could solve this mess, it would be better. Still, Gabrielle had to know how her friend was doing. She dialed the number enough that it was implanted permanently into her brain. The nurse on duty recognized her voice when she called. Of course, Gabrielle wanted more than anything to visit her friend, but it was much too risky. Besides the fact that there was a security guard stationed right outside the hospital room, Gabrielle knew it was much smarter to lie low than to draw too much attention to herself. Not even the safety of being locked behind bars could help protect Cynthia, and Gabrielle did not want to alert the madmen to be on the lookout for her as well.

After hanging up the phone, Gabrielle turned to the array of newspapers sprawled across the bed in front of her. Every night, she studied these articles. She knew each word by heart, yet she was still searching as if this last read-through would reveal something she had overlooked hundreds of other times. Each perusal, there was nothing. She had to be missing something. Without that list from the DMV, she was at a standstill.

In reading all the headlines, she gathered a lot of information about her friend. Things they did not discuss during their brief encounter. She learned Cynthia was a housewife. She moved to Preston recently from a small one-stoplight town in Idaho. Her parents died in a tragic fire when she was eighteen, and she was an only child with no other kin to be accounted for. Her husband seemed like an upstanding person, having recently received an award from the community for helping preserve the natural reserves in the county's western end.

Cynthia volunteered part-time at the Preston Library. The workers there were very shocked to learn of the murders. They described Cynthia as a 'sweet girl who kept to herself.' She was a 'private individual who did not like to divulge too much information about her personal life.'

Gabrielle knew whoever was reading that article was thinking to themselves, *It is always the quiet ones, the ones you least expect.* However, in this case, it was not her. She was wrongly accused.

There was another article. It was about Rick Evans. He was described as a 'hardworking, upstanding individual who loved his family very much.' He worked for North American Trucking Corp., lugging cargo back and forth across the country and sometimes even internationally to Canada. The owner of the corporation was Mr. Peter Lugo. He appeared to know each of his truckers personally and spoke highly of Mr. Evans throughout the article. He stated his company's mission was to ensure the happiness of his truckers, as he knows how difficult it can be when away from their families for long, extended periods. Each of his truckers was provided with a home in the surrounding suburbs of Winston Township, New York, as that is the major shipping port where most of the cargo originates.

The man must have some business savvy as he is a multi-millionaire, Gabrielle thought as she glanced at the picture of Mr. Lugo in the *Daily Times.*

Her skin crawled when she looked at him. Something about that man did not sit right with her. Somehow, NATCO was involved, though she was unsure how all the puzzle pieces fit together. She was getting close. It was just a matter of time before all the clues led to the real murderer. Gabrielle would not stop searching until it did.

CHAPTER THIRTY-THREE

"Two poached eggs and wheat toast, dry."

Gabrielle put her best face forward but did not want to be at work that day or any day after. Her sole purpose was to help Cynthia, and serving people food was not getting her any closer to accomplishing that goal. It did, however, provide her with a sense of normalcy, without which, she would be locked up in her motel room foaming at the mouth, unshowered, and memorizing every single article mentioning the now infamous 'Preston Murderer.' She was at work physically, but her mind was elsewhere, and she did not hide it well—evident in the small tips and countless messed-up orders to the cook. Still, she needed to work. It was her only source of income.

Two weeks passed, and no additional clues. Each night, she would stop at the convenience store to buy every edition of the newspaper. Then, she would head back to the motel and mull over the words written on the pages before her. Gabrielle was unsure what she was searching for but knew it would jump off the page at her when she saw it. There had to be a piece of evidence she was missing. Gabrielle was getting discouraged and losing hope, but something deep inside told her not to give up. Firmness of purpose pushed her to keep searching with patience and perseverance. She would find what she was looking for.

"Honey, my cup has been empty for ten minutes; I need a refill over here." Mr. Crowley's crackly old voice startled Gabrielle's pensive stare.

"Lucky you're good-looking, or I would hold this against you and give you less tip this time." Gabrielle managed to let out half a smile and grabbed the coffee pot to refill the older man's cup on the counter.

"I almost forgot to tell you; I have that list you were looking for."

Gabrielle paused for a moment; she had forgotten what list he was talking about. A puzzled look must have appeared on her face because Mr. Crowley kept on talking, "You know … the Python list."

She had abandoned hope in Mr. Crowley obtaining the DMV list. Gabrielle pushed the idea to the back of her mind and lost faith in his empty promises. Since their original conversation, Mr. Crowley visited the diner daily and never mentioned it. She figured he was talking big talk and had no access to any list. So, Gabrielle did not mention it again for fear of being too pushy and revealing the truth that such a list did not, in fact, exist.

Mr. Crowley took a packet of about ten pages, stapled together, and placed them on the counter. With his greasy pointer finger, he slid the packet across the counter toward Gabrielle.

"Remember, this is not to be mentioned to anybody, as I can get in a lot of trouble."

Gabrielle just stared at the packet in disbelief. She could not believe the information was right on the counter in front of her. It appeared before her like a mirage in the desert. Gabrielle did not want to grab it and have it disappear.

"Go on, don't you want to look at it?" Mr. Crowley urged as he slid the packet further in Gabrielle's direction until it hung half off the back of the diner counter.

"Sure." Gabrielle picked up the list and pretended to flip through it.

"Your brother is going to be thrilled. I hope he gets what he's looking for." Gabrielle looked at Mr. Crowley, "My brother?"

"You know, the one in the accident with the bear while he was hiking."

She really had to learn to be a better liar. The number one rule is to remember your lies, so they do not reappear to bite you in the back.

"Yes, yes, he'll be thrilled. I can't wait to show him." She quickly pretended she needed some supplies in the back kitchen and exited the counter area to avoid any other conversation.

Gabrielle pushed the swinging doors back in toward the kitchen and walked through them. She could not believe she scored a list of people who owned a Python 3600. She exercised fierce restraint, stopping herself from leaving work early and immediately continuing her investigation. Instead, she went to the back locker and placed the list in her purse. She would have to wait until her duties at the diner were completed.

Three hours later, her shift ended. Gabrielle did her routine stop at the convenience store for the newspapers. She fought every urge to bypass all stops and speed down the highway back to the motel. She was excited about the DMV list, but it was not a given it would contain what she was looking for——a familiar name leading her to the actual murderer. She did not want to waste her energy and excitement on something that may not even be there. However, it was hard to fight natural instinct and women's intuition. Her gut told her this was it. It had to be. If this list from the DMV did not contain the name she sought, her search was at a dead end with no turnaround. Gabrielle was close to exhausting her resources. This list was her last hope——Cynthia's last hope.

The Dodge Aries came to a halt in the lined parking space right outside her motel door. She turned the key in the ignition toward her to stop the car engine from running. Gabrielle did not reach for the handle to open the door immediately. This hesitation confused her. It was exciting, yet something deep in her stomach felt queasy. Once she knew the killer's identity, she would be in over her head. She would not be able to turn back. Reading newspaper articles and pretending to be a detective kept her busy. No different than reading the latest *New York Times* bestselling thriller to figure out 'whodunnit' before reaching the last page. This was no novel. This was real. Once a name was revealed to her, Gabrielle could not put the book down and walk away. She would have to do something, whatever that something may be, to help bring him to justice. These scary thoughts caused hesitation. She was committed to her friend. Even if she was not ready, she had no choice.

Gabrielle sighed deeply and walked to the door of her motel room. She turned the key in the lock and proceeded inside.

The moment of truth has arrived.

Although she was not one to attend religious services or even sit back and think of God daily, she silently said a prayer, asking for the name to reveal itself. She prayed not for herself, rather for the injustice to Cynthia.

Without taking off her jacket and apron, she sat on the edge of the bed closest to the door, the DMV list in her hands. She started to read. The stapled packet was ten pages—each page containing eight names. The search box at the top of the page revealed it was a list of every person who owned a Python within a thousand-mile radius of Preston, New York. The list contained each person's name and revealed their mailing address, car insurance information, VIN to the Python, license plate number, color of the car, and the person's state tax identification number.

Gabrielle realized how much Mr. Crowley went out on a limb to get this list to her. If he got caught printing it out, he could have been charged with attempting to steal information for possible identity theft. Once you obtain a person's name, address, and state tax identification number, she imagined it was pretty easy to access their personal information. Gabrielle was not interested in stealing anyone's identity. Through this list, she was helping to regain one. All she needed was the name and the fact they owned a Python.

As she read through the names, none seemed familiar. Mostly boring business-type names––Walter Abrams, Bradly Daniels, Edward Malkovich.

Suddenly, there it was. The name jumped out at her as if it was the only bold-faced, all-caps word on the page.

PETER LUGO

Gabrielle took her hand and rubbed her eyes in disbelief, making sure she read the name correctly.

"Could it be?" she said out loud in shock and dismay.

No need to look through the DMV list any further.

Gabrielle had to ensure she was reading the name correctly and not confuse it with another person. She placed the DMV list on the bed and headed over to the dresser, where she left numerous articles about the Preston Murderer sprawled open. She was not sure exactly where she left the article she was looking for, but she was certain she had seen that name. She had to be one hundred percent sure about it. Gabrielle frantically looked through the old newspapers, discarding the useless ones on the floor and moving on to the next without skipping a beat. Finally, she found it. An article published in the *Preston Gazette* ten days after the brutal killing of Rick Evans. Gabrielle scanned the article and found what she was looking for.

"'Rick Evans was a hard worker, a loving father, and a devoted husband,' stated Peter Lugo, founder and CEO of NATCO, the national trucking company through which Rick Evans was employed as a truck driver.'"

Gabrielle paused and read those words out loud to herself fifteen times in a row.

He was the man responsible for the murder of Rick Evans. Gabrielle was certain.

CHAPTER THIRTY-FOUR

"**I** know who murdered Rick Evans."

Officer Thomas looked up from his desk and found Gabrielle Price standing before him. She had to tell him about her discovery. With this information, he would re-open the case and let Cynthia Evans off scot-free.

He stared at her in disbelief, not at the words she spoke, but more of a disbelief that she was actually standing there before him. This took Gabrielle by surprise. His silent smile sent butterflies through her every time she saw him. She almost forgot why she went to the precinct to find him in the first place.

"Did you hear me?" Gabrielle questioned him.

"I'm sorry, but your mere presence threw me off guard." At least the man was honest and forthwith in what he was thinking.

"I know who murdered Rick Evans." She said it again, waving the DMV list in her right hand.

Officer Thomas looked around the open area as she spoke those words. His colleagues were starting to stare. Not only were they intrigued by a young female coming into the testosterone-filled room; they were curious about what she was saying to him.

"Why don't we go someplace a little more private?" He took Gabrielle's hand and led her to a room, obviously used to interrogate suspected criminals and deviants. It was a blue room with a rectangular table and three chairs. "Sit." He pointed to the chair across from him at the table.

"Did you hear what I said?"

He smiled at her before he answered and took a deep breath. "Of course, but it's not something I wish to discuss in the open air of the precinct."

"Fair enough." No matter how enraged or crazy Gabrielle became, every time she saw Officer Thomas, he had the unique ability to calm her down.

"Now, what makes you think Cynthia Evans is not the murderer?"

Gabrielle proceeded to show Officer Thomas the Python list from the DMV with Peter Lugo's name highlighted and circled. "That man killed the young boys and their father, I am certain."

"Peter Lugo, the CEO of NATCO?" Officer Thomas uttered those words as if there was no way he would ever buy Gabrielle's accusations.

"I know. I was shocked when I thought about it, but it makes perfect sense."

Before Gabrielle could spit out another word, Officer Thomas interrupted her. "Listen, Gabrielle, I know you have some sort of bond with Cynthia Evans, apparent from the fact that I found you two together when she was arrested, but you must stop this snooping around. It's not going to get you anywhere." Gabrielle sat back in her chair with her arms folded across her chest, frustrated he would not help her. "I don't want to see you waste your time on a wild goose chase or get involved in something over your head. You have no idea how important it is to lie low until Cynthia's case dies down. I let you off, but if it comes out that you were helping her at the time of her arrest, you could be charged as well. I suggest you stop."

Each word he spoke enraged her. Sure, she knew he risked his badge for her, but he was not seeing the big picture, Cynthia did not commit those murders and was, in fact, innocent.

"This list, I'm not sure how you got it."

"I had a friend help me," Gabrielle muttered.

"Well, at any rate, all it shows me is that Peter Lugo owns a Python. You are accusing Peter Lugo, a multi-millionaire and head of a major US trucking company … you are accusing him of owning a Python … it's not all that uncommon. I'm afraid without any other evidence, there's nothing I can do."

Gabrielle made one last attempt to plead with the handsome cop. "I saw the stacks of heroin in the cabin, and there are pictures of tire tracks, one set being a Python …"

He cut her off, clearly not listening to the words she spoke. "Gabrielle, you have no concrete proof. Cynthia is on trial in the court system. There is nothing I can do. Let justice take its course. It's a shut case already. Please, you have to let it go."

Gabrielle was furious. "That's easy for you to say, especially when you're not the one in a coma facing murder charges for a crime you know deep down you didn't commit."

Officer Thomas had nothing to say in response. Gabrielle just stared at him.

Despite their different convictions and stubbornness about Cynthia, there was a sexual tension in the room that could be cut with a knife. The fact that Officer Thomas remained resolute in his beliefs did not change Gabrielle's attraction toward him.

Even though he did not believe her, Gabrielle would not hold it against him. Deep down inside, she knew he was right. There was no corroborating evidence. If only the picture of the heroin from the cabin had developed properly, but it did not. Gabrielle would have to keep searching and prove to him she was right. Officer Thomas wanted to believe her, but in his duty as a cop, he could not do so. She did not want to jeopardize his friendship any further.

"Thank you for listening to me."

This meeting did not ruin her chances with the officer, but she was now more determined than ever to seek out the truth and convince him of Cynthia's innocence.

CHAPTER THIRTY-FIVE

Gabrielle sat in her car in the parking lot of the precinct. She did not know what to do next. She was convinced once she presented the list to Officer Thomas, he would indict Peter Lugo and let Cynthia go free. That dream could not have been further from the reality of what actually happened when she walked in there. In a nutshell—he told her Cynthia was guilty, and nothing could convince him otherwise. Still, Gabrielle would not let this stop her. The only problem was that, yet again, she hit a brick wall. There was no next move. She knew who the killer was, but she had no proof. Until that proof existed, Cynthia would not be a free woman.

"Think Gabrielle, think. Where do you go from here?" She was sitting in her car talking to herself. Gabrielle found this to be the case more and more lately; she would sit in solitude, talking. Though, Gabrielle was not concerned. Only when people start to answer themselves out loud can they be diagnosed as certifiably insane.

As Gabrielle sat there, she felt a presence outside her car. A shadow appeared across the front windshield and the steering wheel. Gabrielle looked up from her solo conversation and saw Officer Thomas standing outside the driver's side window. She opened the car door to speak to him.

"Everything okay?" he inquired. A legitimate question as Gabrielle left him just twenty minutes earlier, and now he found her, once again, in her car talking to herself.

"Sure, why do you ask?" She replied as if talking to herself was an everyday occurrence that should not be a cause of concern.

"I just got off duty. Do you want to grab something to eat at Malloy's up the street?"

If there had been any doubt about him asking her out before, there was no uncertainty now. She wanted to go with him more than anything, but her free time is valuable. Every available second would now be devoted to ensuring Peter Lugo is implicated in murder.

"I can't go." Those words were stated, but not the ones she wanted to say.

Officer Thomas took those three words and inhaled them into his chest. He looked shocked the offer was declined and wanted more than anything for her to have said yes. "Gabrielle, I'm sorry I can't help you, but that is no reason for you to turn me down."

Gabrielle attempted to quash what he felt, "No hard feelings, really. I would love to grab a bite with you, but …" She paused to think of a reason. However, as time passed, the more it looked like she had no excuse. Each second that went by without a reason to go to Malloy's felt like an eternity, but in reality, it was only five seconds.

Officer Thomas broke the awkward silence. "I understand." He bowed his head and attempted to close the car door to end the conversation.

Gabrielle put her hand out to stop the door from shutting in her face. "I really want to go. It's just that I can't." She did not know what else to say.

He looked at her. "Don't expect another offer like this to come your way."

Those words haunted Gabrielle. She blew her chance, but now was not the time to go on a date with Officer Thomas. He shut the door, turned around, and went to the other side of the parking lot. This was one of the worst days of her life.

Gabrielle put her head in her hands and proceeded to sob. Some of the tears were in response to the events that transpired with Officer Thomas. She thought about Officer Thomas and how he caught her attention the very first time he came to Hank's apartment. From the initial encounter, she was drawn to his personal magnetism.

If only the situation were different.

A majority of these streamlined tears, however, were a cathartic release in response to the past few months. Life was flying by at warp speed, and Gabrielle had no time to stop and process what was happening. Her life completely changed, and she had never paused to take it all in.

Without Cynthia, the situation would not be any different. Gabrielle would still reside with Hank, clinging to him, fearful of being alone. She would put up with his anger and occasional beating. Life would be okay. Life would be okay, not great.

As bleak as it looked at this particular moment, life was great, with the potential to be outstanding. Life with Hank was stagnant. It stood still with no hope of moving forward. To Gabrielle, she would take the hurt and humiliation she felt right now over a stationary existence.

It was the first time since arriving at the motel that Gabrielle thought about Hank. She wondered how he was doing. She wondered if he even thought about her. Sure, even though she did not love him, she still cared for him. They spent years together, and he knew her better than anyone else. She longed for companionship and friendship but did not long for it with Hank. That chapter in her life was closed, and reopening was unnecessary.

"You always remember the good times." Her coworker April told her this time and time again.

Whenever Gabrielle came into the diner with bruises in various stages of black and blue, April would always ask Gabrielle why she returned to Hank. It was true; no matter how bad the situation got, when she stepped away from it, she always remembered the good times with him, and there were plenty. Hank could be caring, but he was also harsh. Gabrielle, however, was no fool and knew the bad times far outweighed the good ones. The past few months strengthened her, and she had Cynthia to thank for that. Cynthia, lying comatose in a hospital bed, has affected Gabrielle's life more than anyone else. She saved her life. Cynthia saved Gabrielle's soul. Since their meeting, Gabrielle found purpose. She found a reason to go on living. That thought made her smile and forget why she was upset. She remembered why she was determined to help her friend.

As Gabrielle wiped the tears away from her eyes with the sleeve of her shirt, she looked in the rearview mirror to see if she could spot Officer Thomas walking away. Of course, she did not find him as twenty-five minutes had passed since he closed the car door in her face. What she did find in the mirror, however, was the starting point in her quest to implicate Peter Lugo in murder.

CHAPTER THIRTY-SIX

It was so simple. Gabrielle was shocked she did not think of it before. Mr. Crowley had given more information than she thought she would need on the DMV list, but as it turned out, extra information proved vital to her investigation.

There, behind her in the parking lot, was the Preston Library. Ironically, it was the same local library where Cynthia Evans spent several hours a week volunteering. Although it was a short distance behind the precinct, Gabrielle decided to drive to the main parking lot. She did not want Officer Thomas to return to the police station to find her car still sitting there.

Gabrielle walked up the ramp to the building, and the doors automatically slid open to let her inside. From the outside, the building appeared to be built in the pre-war era. The interior, however, was immaculate and modern. Upon entering the front doors, one was greeted with a huge circulation desk. Behind that desk was the card catalog. A non-tech-savvy person could look up books using the old Dewey Decimal System, but the majority of the book browsers appeared to prefer the computers stationed on top of the card catalogs, enabling book lookups using a simple search for author, title, or genre.

A wave of sadness came over Gabrielle as she thought about Cynthia coming to work at this very building. Gabrielle was expecting to find a shrine or a mention of Cynthia, however, it was quite the opposite. Almost as if they had written her off completely and wanted to forget she ever set foot in the building. Gabrielle looked around to observe the prejudgers who worked in such a stuffy establishment. The woman behind the counter was at least seventy years old—an old granny quality about her. She wore a crocheted sweater and a long floral skirt revealing no more skin than her ankles. Toward the back of the first floor was a young girl who appeared to be in her late teens. She pushed a cart full of books that needed to be re-shelved. She did not enjoy the tedious task of placing the books back on the shelf in their assigned home. In the back corner sat a lady, whom Gabrielle immediately dubbed in her head 'The Dictator.' She was a scary lady; bifocals hung around her neck and she wore a bun wound so tight it most likely restricted her brain. Her sole purpose was sneering at the library workers and criticizing them when they did a bad job.

As Gabrielle observed the workers, she realized the environment she was in. It did not appear any of the workers liked their job. They did not seem to like each other. None of them interacted. None of them smiled at each other as they passed by among the rows of books. Upon observation, Gabrielle concluded Cynthia did not enjoy her job here. She was too strong of a woman to succumb to such snobbishness. The thought made Gabrielle appreciate her job as a waitress.

"I can't even imagine how Cynthia worked here," Gabrielle whispered the comment to herself. Cynthia appeared so nice and innocent. She must have had an extreme love for books or no other options.

Gabrielle felt the need to ask someone who worked there about Cynthia. She was curious what the coworkers thought. She had to know if the Cynthia she knew, who did not remember a thing about herself, was the same Cynthia who checked out books and organized them on the shelves according to their assigned decimal number. Gabrielle contemplated asking the elderly lady behind the circulation desk but then vetoed it as she was probably hard of hearing, and shouting was not a subtle way to obtain information in a place that forbid talking. She ruled out speaking to the drill sergeant with the Amish hairdo for fear of German obscenities being yelled at her and then being made to drop to the floor to perform twenty pushups as punishment for asking such absurd questions.

A final surveillance revealed the best option; the teenager re-shelving books. That girl was now lost among the countless rows of non-fiction periodicals in the back right of the first floor. Gabrielle pretended to be interested in the War of 1812 and stalked the poor girl, currently replacing books on the Spanish-American Revolution. The hard part was how to bring Cynthia Evans into the conversation casually.

"Excuse me." Gabrielle had to say it again for the young girl to realize she was being addressed. "Excuse me, is this the only section on the War of 1812, or is there another place in the library where I can find information?"

It was a start but did not open the door to questions about a former employee who murdered her family.

"You may be able to find some information on the microfilm downstairs." The girl continued what she was doing as if that was the end of the conversation between the two strangers.

"Thanks. Have you worked here for a long time? Because you seem to know the library well. I always come here to do research, and I've never seen you." *Great, now the girl will think I am hitting on her.*

The girl gave her a blank stare, not quite sure how to comment on that last remark.

"It's just that I used to have that woman Cynthia help me with all my research, so it's been difficult for me to find the things I need for my thesis, since she no longer works here." The girl kept staring at her, wondering why Gabrielle was still trying to engage her in conversation. "You know it's such a tragedy what happened to her. Did you ever suspect she would be capable of such a tragedy?" If the girl did not take the bait with this comment and start talking, it was a lost cause, and Gabrielle decided she would abandon further conversation.

"She was quiet. I didn't often work with her, but she seemed nice enough. I was very shocked when I heard about it. But, you know, it's always the quiet ones."

"So, you believe that she committed the crime?" Gabrielle probed.

"Not sure. Everyone else who works here seems to think so. Mrs. Evans used to keep to herself, but occasionally, she would complain that her husband was gone for weeks and never home. The month before the murder, she became very withdrawn and depressed. She was not herself. We all think she snapped and went crazy."

That was all Gabrielle needed to hear. She thanked the girl for her help and walked back to the open area of the library.

These comments did not shock Gabrielle. Life experience taught her that most people are predictable. They will be with you to celebrate the good times, but as soon as something bad happens, you are left to your own devices.

What's the old saying? 'Laugh and the world laughs with you, cry and you cry alone.'

All the articles Gabrielle studied led her to believe Cynthia was, in fact, depressed. Not surprising for a mom with two young boys and a husband who was never home. Cynthia did not have a support system. Her parents died, her coworkers kept to themselves, and she was left to survive alone. Gabrielle knew firsthand how difficult life could be, especially with nobody to turn to.

Even with what the young girl said, she was not convinced Cynthia committed the crime. She knew the real killer, and that person was still functioning freely in society. It was her mission to bring him to justice.

Gabrielle remembered the reason she came to the library in the first place. She wanted to find as much information on Peter Lugo as possible. These days, all libraries have free internet access, and since it was the only place Gabrielle could surf the web, it was a good place to conduct research. The sign over the staircase directed her to the computer lab in the basement.

On the bottom floor, Gabrielle found a room with approximately fifteen computers. There were only three other people in the computer lab. One person was checking his e-mail, and the other two were typing a college paper. Gabrielle chose the computer furthest away from the others. She needed as much privacy as possible. She sat before the monitor and moved the mouse to make the computer turn out of sleep mode.

When she clicked the icon for the internet, the Preston Library home page appeared. In the top box, Gabrielle went to Google and typed 'Peter Lugo.' There were over 300,000 hits to peruse. She was unprepared for the task at hand as she had nothing to help her write notes. Gabrielle got up from the computer and stole some paper from the drawer on the printer at the back of the room. She then interrupted one of the computer lab patrons for an extra pen. After acquiring the necessary material, she again sat at the computer and compiled a file on Peter Lugo, the multi-millionaire founder of NATCO.

Four hours later, it was 8:30 p.m., and the library flashed its lights for the half-hour warning that the doors would be closing. The last thing Gabrielle wanted was to be locked inside the eerie building filled with dusty books and periodicals. There was something scary about being in the library. She was not sure if it was the quietness of the building or the visions of haunting souls floating around the card catalogs in the opening scene of a scary movie she saw as a young child. Most likely, a combination of both.

Gabrielle closed out of the internet browser and gathered the six pages of notes she scribbled about Mr. Lugo. Nothing in those pages was overtly incriminating, but it was a start in the right direction. She could have spent several more hours on research, but it had gotten to the point where she was duplicating information she already had. Plus, the library was closing, so her time at the computer ended.

When Gabrielle returned to the motel, she sifted through her newfound knowledge and compiled a background file on Mr.

Lugo. He was born an only child on July 28, 1957, in Wethersfield, Connecticut. From what Gabrielle could tell, Wethersfield was a small suburban town comprised of more affluent citizens than not. When Mr. Lugo was ten years old, he won first place in a county fair tap-dancing competition. Not that the last tidbit of information would be pertinent to her task, but it did amuse her that a murderer could also be a great tap dancer. When Mr. Lugo was a teen, he had a lot of trouble with the law. He was arrested as a juvenile for shoplifting, graffiti, possession of marijuana, possession of cocaine with intent to sell, and petty theft of a bicycle——not to mention the three assaults on other teenagers his age. Lucky for Mr. Lugo, all of these incidents happened before he turned sixteen, so he was never tried as an adult, and the charges were never held against him.

In high school, he was a star of the varsity wrestling team's middleweight class, losing the state championship title after being pinned to the mat in the second round. Given his delinquent background, it is remarkable he turned his life around from crime to head a million-dollar trucking corporation. Gabrielle, having the inside information on heroin trafficking, did not deem this feat as remarkable as others had made it out to be. He did not become less of a criminal, just a smarter one.

The most interesting information Gabrielle uncovered was that the death of Rick Evans was not the first loss of an employee at NATCO. Since Lugo took over as CEO fifteen years ago, two other men, besides Rick Evans, faced death. Peter Lugo was never formally charged with their deaths, and not once was NATCO ever suspected of wrong dealings, but Gabrielle surmised there was more to these stories.

The first one was seven years earlier. A man in his late twenties, named Justin Enrel, lost his life when the brakes on the big rig he was driving failed to work. The truck went barreling full speed into an overpass on Interstate 90, causing Justin to die instantaneously. Medical examiners concluded it was a freak accident, and no charges were ever sought for the death of the young man.

Then, two years after the first death, a man named Earl Peterman lost his life. He was a gentleman in his late fifties who had no family and kept to himself. An unidentified criminal broke into his small apartment when he was home. Earl suffered a single bullet to the head. The apartment was ransacked. The burglars made a mess of the living room and bedroom. The television was smashed and thrown on the floor. All the dresser drawers in the bedroom were thrown open, and the mattress was torn open with a knife.

Something about this account of robbery did not sit right with Gabrielle. The facts, as told in the local paper of Earl's hometown, did not appear to be consistent with a simple apartment break-in. Earl had no family or friends come forward, so the police were not able to determine what, if anything, was stolen from the apartment. The police report concluded they took all of Earl's money. The man had a bit of a gambling problem and owed some serious dough to a ruthless bookie, though no investigation ever followed through on that theory. Eventually, enough time passed, and the police closed the Peterman investigation without any charges regarding his murder. The case was deemed unsolvable.

The more Gabrielle read about each of these three cases, the more she wanted just dessert for that heartless Peter Lugo. She obtained the address where he grew up and the name of his old high school. Although, on the surface, this information did not appear useful, it was a starting point in her further investigation. Gabrielle knew she would have to visit Wethersfield, Connecticut, to learn more.

CHAPTER THIRTY-SEVEN

Gabrielle begged April to cover her shift at the diner on Monday. April was not pleased, as this was one of several requests in the past few weeks.

"I promise it's the last time," she assured her coworker. What she really meant was 'she would do her best.' The way life had transpired lately this was not a guarantee.

April did not know the real reason Gabrielle needed the day off. If she told her coworker it was to go on an evidentiary expedition for a supposed murderer, there is no way she would agree. Instead, she told her she had to attend a funeral for a friend who resided out of state. It did not matter if April believed this fabrication, only that she agreed to the coverage. Gabrielle's concern for Cynthia outweighed her remorse for lying to April. Peter Lugo is a murderer, and until Gabrielle can gather concrete proof, every minute he is left free in society is dangerous.

The trip to Wethersfield, Connecticut, would take four hours, one way. Gabrielle had no idea what she was looking for, but she would figure it out once she arrived. She could observe the environment Mr. Lugo grew up in and gather insight into his psyche.

Wethersfield is a small Connecticut town located in the middle of the state. As she drove down the main town drag, the green welcoming sign read, "Welcome to Wethersfield, established 1737, population 24,633."

"Quaint, yet not too small," Gabrielle thought out loud to herself.

Her research unveiled numerous accolades for Mr. Lugo from his high school years. This seemed like a good place to start her evidence gathering. While she waited at a stoplight in town, a yellow school bus passed by her. The school bus driver would know the location of the town's high school. Gabrielle attempted to flag down the driver from her car. Just as she contemplated her next move to catch the bus driver's attention, the yellow vehicle pulled over to the side of the road to take a short break. Sure enough, the door to the curb opened up, and an unkempt lady walked down the steps. The disheveled driver immediately searched her pocket for a lighter. Her hand reached for a cigarette tucked behind her right ear and stuck it between her lips. Gabrielle pulled up to the curb just as she was about to inhale.

"Excuse me, where is Wethersfield High School?"

The woman was less than thrilled that a stranger was speaking to her but was able to provide the needed guidance.

Ten minutes later, Gabrielle pulled into the parking lot of what looked more like a jail than a school. A handful of students were hanging outside the front doors. It was the middle of a class period, and most students were expected to be in their assigned seats, ready to learn. Gabrielle was hopeful there was some record of the infamous Peter Lugo from his years of passing through the hallways of Wethersfield High School. Although he graduated over twenty years ago, she was banking on there being at least one remaining staff member who could remember the troubled teenage boy.

Gabrielle went through the main entrance and made a left toward the principal's office. Her stomach churned as she entered the claustrophobic hallway. It brought back memories of her own high school career. Gabrielle was teased and tortured by the most popular girls in the school and ignored by most others. Teachers did not care one way or another for her. In fact, on most days, she felt invisible. Gabrielle did not see a point in going to school. It was a babysitting mechanism to keep kids busy while their parents worked to keep food on the table and a roof overhead. She had neither a mother nor a father whom she cared to go home to, so Gabrielle dropped out of high school as early as possible. It had been a long time since she set foot inside the walls of a secondary school. The smell made her dizzy. This would have to be a quick trip to avoid being in the learning facility longer than necessary.

Gabrielle walked into the office and found an elderly lady with gray hair. The woman wore an unflattering two-piece skirt suit that hugged her curves in all the wrong places.

"Can I help you?"

Gabrielle had her entire car trip to Connecticut to come up with an answer to this simple question, yet she was unable to provide one. The woman stared at her and would continue to do so until something was said. "I'm here to see the principal."

"What's this in regard to?"

"Peter Lugo." *Why, why would I say that?*

"Is he a student here? I'm not sure the name sounds familiar."

Before Gabrielle could speak another ill-conceived statement, the secretary left the main area and headed down a hallway out of sight. Gabrielle sat in the front and waited for the principal's arrival. She had never been sent to the principal's office once, but she imagined this seat was meant for troubled children who did not know how to behave in their respective classrooms. The wait was torture.

"Hi there, I understand you're here to see me regarding Peter Lugo." Standing there before her was a woman in her late forties. She had short blonde hair and a well-fitting tan pan suit. "I'm sorry, my admin, Gloria, did not catch your name."

Gabrielle stood to greet the woman and extended her hand. "Miss Price, Gabrielle Price."

The woman did not waste any time getting down to business. The principal looked at her quizzically. "Is Peter Lugo a student here? That name is not ringing a bell."

"No, well, sort of. Peter Lugo was a student here some time ago." The school administrator waited for the much-needed clarification.

"Peter Lugo is a graduate of Wethersfield High. He graduated maybe twenty years ago. He's a successful entrepreneur in New York. I'm writing a human-interest piece on him and his life. It's quite a story. The man started from nothing to the multi-millionaire he is now."

"I'm not sure how much help I can be. I started at this school ten years ago, which was still some time after Mr. Lugo graduated." Gabrielle knew she was too optimistic to think she could walk into a public high school and gather whatever information she sought. "The only staff member I can think of that has been here that long is Mr. Waverly. He's a language arts teacher here at Wethersfield High. I can introduce you to him. He may have lunch during seventh period, so he should be in the teacher's lounge. If you follow me, we can try and track him down."

Gabrielle was shocked and amazed at the principal's trust. The two women walked down the hallway and through a door to the faculty room. It was a large room with some tables and couches. There was a television in the corner, a fridge, and a coffee pot on the other side of the room. On the couch sat a man in his late sixties. He was a little heavy-set and had wild gray curly hair. He sat there eating a salad and reading the local newspaper. When the door opened, he looked up to see who was entering the room.

"Ms. Barrington, what brings you to this area of the school grounds?"

"Mr. Waverly, this is Gabrielle Price. She's writing an article on a graduate of ours, named Peter Lugo. He graduated quite some time ago. Not sure if you remember him, but I thought if anybody knew him, it'd be you."

"Yes, I remember him quite well," he looked intriguingly at Gabrielle as he reminisced about the former student. Ms.

Barrington left Mr. Waverly and Gabrielle alone to discuss the former pupil.

"Peter Lugo was an interesting young lad. I can't say I have fond memories of him. He was abrasive, and most teachers in this school feared him."

"Feared him?"

"Did I stutter? He had every teacher in this building conned and wrapped around his finger, everyone except me."

Gabrielle knew she had found the right person to talk to. She spent the next forty-five minutes conversing with Mr. Waverly about what appeared to be his least favorite student during his entire career at Wethersfield High School. Not once did he question Gabrielle as to why she was there on the school grounds, but she felt the need throughout their conversation to interject that she was writing a human-interest piece on Peter because he managed to make himself a successful businessman.

Mr. Waverly was not impressed. "That young man was a con artist." The disdain for Lugo was apparent. "He would blackmail teachers into giving him grades for assignments he never completed and marking him present in class on days he wasn't there."

"Blackmail? Come on now, how could a 16-year-old blackmail a teacher?"

"Easily, very easily. He knew things, things that none of us ever figured out how he knew. He forced the math teacher, Ms. Smalls, to give him an A average. Somehow, he found out she was having an affair with the assistant principal and threatened to make it public knowledge."

Gabrielle was astounded. Nothing to say in reply.

Mr. Waverly got up from his seat on the couch and headed over to the bookshelf in the back part of the teacher's lounge. He searched through some books on the middle shelf and appeared to find what he was looking for.

"If I remember correctly, this is the year he graduated." He took the book he pulled off the shelf and showed it to Gabrielle.

It was the school yearbook from the same graduation year as the infamous Peter Lugo.

"Never before in my career had I been so happy to see a student leave these hallways."

Gabrielle took the book and flipped through the pages. She turned to the Seniors and quickly scanned for the L's. There was a young Peter. He looked the same as the newspaper photo, just younger, with a baby face. His eyes pierced the camera, jumping out of the picture and into her soul. It made her hair stand on end. Underneath his picture was his name. There were no quotes, no idols, no clubs, no honorable recognitions, just his name.

"How boring." Gabrielle did not realize that she had said those two words out loud.

"He was a star wrestler for the school. Though, if you ask me, he also bribed his way to the state championship."

Gabrielle had gathered all the information she needed from the high school. Her next step was to visit the home in which he grew up. All part of her master plan to uncover further information on the real Peter Lugo.

CHAPTER THIRTY-EIGHT

It was not at all as Gabrielle expected—the home listed for the Lugo family appeared very normal. Normal like the Waltons. There was no sense of eeriness. Nothing forbode of a young lad who would grow up to be a killer. Gabrielle sat in her car and surveyed the property in front of her. She found a two-story home with pruned shrubbery and cleanly cut grass. She wanted to find an abandoned mansion with rusted gates and an old broken-down pickup truck in the driveway.

Gabrielle parked her car and got out. It was time to see how the other half lived and who really resided behind the front door of this suburban household. She walked up the driveway and waited patiently on the front porch as the doorbell chimed the first four chords to Pachelbel's *Canon.*

A brunette-haired lady poked her head through the curtain to the right of the entrance and unlocked two locks before cracking the door just enough to make one eyeball visible.

"Can I help you?" she asked cautiously.

"I'm writing a human-interest piece on the person who owns this home."

"Are you sure you have the right place?"

"Is this 22 Chestnut Drive?"

The woman paused as if she forgot the address of the home she was standing in. "This is 22 Chestnut Drive, but I am not sure you have the right place."

"I'm trying to find some information about a man who used to live here, Peter Lugo."

"There's nobody with that name who resides in this home."

"Peter Lugo, he was not your son?"

"No, sorry, I don't have a son, only daughters."

There were only a few ways this was plausible. Either the woman was a liar, she was senile, or she truly did not have a son named Peter Lugo.

"He grew up here in this home, and I'm trying to reach him."

"My husband and I moved into this house about ten years ago. I don't know much about the family who lived here before us."

Gabrielle could see this was not going to get her anywhere.

The woman saw the disappointment in the news she gave and she grasped at straws to provide some useful information. "Two houses down, they've lived in this neighborhood for at least thirty years. They may be familiar with the Lugo family. You should try there."

Before Gabrielle could utter a thank you, the door shut in her face, and the window curtain looking outward was drawn to a quick shut.

Gabrielle stood there for a few seconds, trying to gather her composure and figure out her next move. Clearly, the residents of 22 Chestnut Drive did not know the Lugos nor care to know anything about them. The woman seemed quite content living in the home she bought without ever learning the identity of the prior owners.

Gabrielle was still intent on finding out more. She spent half the day in Connecticut and was not any closer to obtaining pertinent information about the life of Peter Lugo. The residents of the house two doors down would be her last stop on this trip. Gabrielle did not want to leave Wethersfield without something to further her quest. Although it was only a football field length away, Gabrielle still got into the green Dodge and drove the short distance.

All of the houses on the block looked the same. They had that suburban cookie-cutter appearance with a front door, two bay windows on either side and an upstairs floor. In the middle of the triangular peak on the roof was a window to the second floor.

Although the house two doors down was similar to every other house, it had a different look and personality. It lacked a sense of homeliness. This house, 26 Chestnut Drive, was painted a faded green color, and the trees were overgrown in the front yard, leaving the home in an overabundance of shade. So much shade that the grass in the front yard refused to grow in several patches.

It did not appear anybody was home, but Gabrielle did not come this far to assume the residents were not there. She parked her car in the driveway and walked up the stone walkway to the front of the home. Gabrielle rang the doorbell and listened patiently for movement inside. She heard a thump down some stairs, and a young man in his mid to late thirties answered the door. He did not say a word when he opened the entranceway. He just stood there staring at Gabrielle uncomfortably until she finally broke the tension.

"Hi there." He said nothing, and Gabrielle knew she would have to say more to break the ice. It would not be an easy task to illicit information from him. "I'm writing a human-interest piece on a man named Peter Lugo, and I was told the people in this house may have some information as …."

"Peter Lugo, huh?" He raised his eyebrows as he spoke the name.

Gabrielle was startled as she was abruptly interrupted. "Do you know him?"

"Yes. I know him." Gabrielle was in luck. She cheered silently.

"Who are you?" His tone was unfriendly.

"I am writing a human-interest piece on his life and was trying to gather some background information on the man," she told him again.

"The best person to talk to would be him, then. Wouldn't it?"

Gabrielle had to think fast on her feet. "I agree, and I have. Only, for a good article, a reporter needs to gather as much information from as many different sources as possible." It was impossible from the man's demeanor to ascertain whether or not he believed the tale.

"I hardly know the man. Best I can tell you is he used to live in that house two doors down, but not anymore. He no longer visits this area, and I haven't spoken to him in years." Gabrielle did not believe him. His body language became shifty, and his eyes darted about as he spoke these words.

"Any information you have would be helpful."

"What paper did you say you write for?"

"The *Preston Gazette*."

"Never heard of it."

"It's a local newspaper in New York near where Mr. Lugo now resides."

"Human interest? Tell me, Miss … I am sorry, I didn't catch your name."

Gabrielle knew she did not give it and was not about to. "Katie Jones, it's Ms. Jones."

"Okay, Ms. Jones, what, might I ask, is so interesting about Mr. Lugo that would create human interest?"

"Well, I haven't gathered all the information yet, but he does have an interesting background, coming from a suburban household and growing into the multimillionaire he is today."

"I guess that's interesting," he stated out loud to himself rather than to Gabrielle.

"Sorry, I didn't catch **your** name."

"I didn't give it." With that, the stranger closed the front door in Gabrielle's face without warning, leaving her alone on the front porch, dumbfounded.

Gabrielle did not know whether she should ring the doorbell to try and talk to him again or turn around and go home. Although this man did not provide any insight into Peter Lugo, she was sure he had more information than he was willing to convey. As soon as Gabrielle mentioned the name Peter Lugo, the man took a defensive stance and closed off the possibility of any further conversation.

It was clear Gabrielle would not elicit any further information from the town of Wethersfield, and it was time to return home.

CHAPTER THIRTY-NINE

He stood by the front door and watched the young female as she left down the walkway away from his home. He did not know her name. She told him her name was Katie Jones, but it was clearly a fictitious handle. He knew full well no human-interest piece was being written about Peter Lugo. He was not positive, but he would even bet money there was not a *Preston Gazette* in circulation in Preston, New York.

This woman wanted information about Peter Lugo, but for what purpose? What information did she need? What information did she know?

He observed the young woman get into the Dodge Aries parked in his driveway. The car was parked close enough to the home for him to record the license plate number. She may have given a false name, but one run through the computer system, and her true identity would be revealed.

After the car turned down the street, he pulled his cell phone out of his pocket to place an important call.

"Hello, boss. It's Jimmy. We have a serious problem."

CHAPTER FORTY

Peter Lugo did not like what he heard on the other end of his cell phone. Jimmy was the one person whom Peter trusted with his life. He was the only person Peter had complete confidence in and could rely on until his dying day.

Trust did not come to Peter Lugo easily. Jimmy, born James Pickard, had met Peter at the age of sixteen. At that time, Jimmy was four years old. An adorable four-year-old, full of life and questions. At first, Peter found him to be annoying rather than cute. But the kid lived two doors down and looked up to the teenaged Lugo. He was always around, underneath his feet and lurking in his shadow.

Jimmy longed to be loved. His parents passed away before he could remember, and he lived with his grandmother until she died when he was eighteen. When Peter discovered this horrific tragedy, he vowed to take Jimmy under his wing for life. He unconditionally loved the kid, and Peter knew no matter what happened in life, he would be there to take care of Jimmy like family.

When Peter started the trucking company, Jimmy was by his side. Not the brightest bulb, but he was the most loyal. Never questioned anything Peter asked him to do. Blindly obliging. Although Jimmy worked in New York as Peter's sidekick, he still lived in the same house where he grew up. It was a present from Peter. The least Peter could do, as Jimmy always had his back. A perfect sidekick.

When the phone rang, Peter sensed the urgency. Jimmy called him constantly, but intuition took over when he saw the number flash on the small screen. Peter knew before hearing the voice on the other end there was a serious problem.

"Who was she?" Peter asked his friend.

"No idea, but I have her license plate number, so it'll be easy to find out."

"Run a check immediately."

CHAPTER FORTY-ONE

Gabrielle went to put the motel key into the slot provided. A swift chill ran up and down her spine as she glanced at the door. Something was not right; she could feel it in her bones. The lock had been jimmied, and the door was slightly ajar. As exhausted as she was from working a double shift the day following her adventures in Wethersfield, Gabrielle was certain she shut the motel door tightly upon leaving for work that morning. She paused at the entrance, debating whether to head inside. She strained to listen for any movement from the room, but no sound was heard. She took a deep breath, placed her hand in a protective stance in front of her face, and kicked the door open with a swift movement of her right leg. Not the smartest move. Whoever was on the other side of the door to face her could be staring back with a revolver pointed. She braced herself for the gunshot but found an empty room when the door flew open. Nobody presented themselves on the other side.

Gabrielle quietly approached the end of the bed and headed toward the bathroom. She threw the door open to the toilet chamber, only to be face-to-face with her reflection in the mirror above the sink. There, in plain English, smeared across the glass in her favorite mauve lipstick:

I KNOW WHERE YOU ARE. YOU CAN'T HIDE!

She stared at those words, frozen in fright and unable to move. The merciless killer was on to her, out to get rid of her, too.

She turned around and headed into the main part of her motel room. It was a nightmare. The room had been completely trashed. When she first entered the room full of adrenaline, she failed to notice the destruction.

The television had been smashed and thrown on the floor. The lamp on the dresser had been knocked over and also thrown on the floor. The sheets were ripped off the bed and torn in half. The comforter strewn across the other side of the room. The garbage rooted through. The articles regarding the Preston Murderer torn into a thousand little pieces with no hope of being restored.

Gabrielle gasped in shock. Horrible things could have happened to her had she been back in time to face the criminal who destroyed her living quarters. She was now, officially, in over her head. This made it real to her, not that it was fake before, but before she was still on the outskirts of the action.

Prior to tonight, she was sifting through clues, trying to get answers to what happened. She was merely a sideline contender, but now she was a player. Peter Lugo now knows who she is. She is no longer an anonymous observer on the outside looking in.

Gabrielle did not know everything about that fateful night in the Evans' household. But she knew Cynthia did not pull the trigger. She knew it was the work of a ruthless drug lord who would risk anything to have it all. She was close to blowing his cover, and he knew it. Gabrielle was no longer safe. She needed protection.

She walked toward the nightstand next to the once made-up bed. Gabrielle leaned to the floor, picked up the phone, and placed the bottom half back on the nightstand where it was intended. She reached deep into the pocket of her down coat and pulled out a folded piece of paper. When she received that note, she never thought she would have to use it.

She placed her hand on the plastic piece of the phone that resonated with a dial tone. Once she heard sound on the other end, she carefully entered the seven-digit number written legibly on the paper in her left hand. It rang several times before a groggy voice on the other end answered.

Gabrielle paused before speaking, trying to hide her quavering voice. "Hello, Officer Thomas, this is Gabrielle … Gabrielle

Price." Even though she could not see him on the other end of the phone, through the use of his words and his tone, she could tell he was startled to hear from her. "I'm sorry to bother you so late, but there's a bit of a crisis here at the motel." Without hesitation, he told her he would be right there and hung up the phone.

The fifteen minutes it took him to arrive at her motel felt like an eternity. There was nothing Gabrielle could do to make the time go by faster. She was afraid to leave the room because she did not know what the crazed person who trashed it looked like. He could lurk down the street, waiting for her to appear out of the darkness. She would never see him coming, but he would see her. She was also anxious sitting in her motel room alone. The culprit could come back at any moment. Gabrielle prayed that Officer Thomas sensed her urgency and made it there in record time. She was disappointed in herself for calling him. She planned to call him to ask him out to dinner, not to be rescued.

Since Officer Thomas had blown her off when she went to the precinct with the list of car owners, it was clear he was not on her side regarding Cynthia's innocence. She did not hold that against him. In his mind, he had the proof that Cynthia had murdered her husband. It was a logical explanation. Looking at the facts objectively, they all pointed in her direction. Gabrielle had inside information, but no proof. Sure, she saw the heroin in the cabin, but Cynthia herself could have been involved in the drug dealings. It was possible, but Cynthia's demeanor left a different impression upon Gabrielle.

The red light swooped through the drawn curtains into her motel room. Officer Thomas attempted to knock on the door but immediately noticed that the lock on the door had been tampered with. He slowly opened the door and peered into the trashed room to find Gabrielle sitting in solitude on the bed.

"Gabrielle, are you okay?"

"Sorry I called you, but I had nobody else."

He looked at her as if to say she was being ridiculous and she should always feel free to call him no matter what time of day or night. "This is definitely a reason to call. I'm glad to see you are alright. What happened?"

She explained how she had returned from work and found the room vandalized. He proceeded with his investigatory skills, asking questions designed to elicit a step-by-step detailed analysis of what had happened. It was the basic, 'who,' 'what,' 'where,' and 'when'—the 'why' caused her to hesitate. She had no problems divulging information to Officer Thomas regarding when she came home, who was there, and what she found when she mustered the courage to open the hotel room and enter. While explaining the events that evening, she even got up from the bed and led him to the bathroom to reveal the message scrawled across the mirror. It was the next question she had trouble divulging the answer to.

"Why would somebody do this to you?" An innocent question, but she did not want to tell him that she was the next target on a drug lord's hit list. She avoided any comment at all. "Well, whoever it is, it's clear to me you are in danger and cannot stay here any longer."

"Where am I going to go? I can't run from motel to motel." Gabrielle knew she would never be safe, no matter where she went. They would find her.

"Pack your things. You're coming home with me."

Twenty minutes later, Gabrielle pulled her Dodge in front of Officer Thomas's ranch house. She turned the car off and inhaled deeply. She would stay at the officer's house. Gabrielle was certainly fond of the man, if not deeply attracted to him, but their relationship was not one where she should be spending the night at his residence.

Officer Thomas approached the driver's side and opened her car door. "Are you going to come inside, or would you rather spend the night out here?" He extended his right hand to help Gabrielle out of the car. "Don't worry. I promise I don't bite."

She looked up at him and was mesmerized for a second by his eyes. Every time she looked into them, they melted her heart.

This is going to be an interesting adventure.

When Gabrielle had left work that evening, she did not plan on seeing Officer Thomas, let alone spending the night in his home.

She grabbed her bag out of the trunk and followed the officer. He unlocked the front door and turned his body toward Gabrielle, invading her personal space. His face a mere three inches away. His lips even with hers as they stood on the front porch.

"You know, I'd prefer it if you didn't call me Officer Thomas; it's way too formal and impersonal. Call me Mike."

Gabrielle grinned. She never realized she was addressing him as Officer Thomas. Even in all of their previous encounters, it never occurred to her that he might have a first name.

They crossed the threshold into the front door of the home. He was a gracious host and quickly gave Gabrielle a tour. A ranch home with the makings of a bachelor pad. The hallway at the front door opened into the living room. There was a leather couch and an expensive high-tech entertainment center with surround sound and an XBOX gaming system. To the back of the living room was another hallway. The bathroom and a bedroom branched off from there. Across from the bedroom was another room converted into an office space. There was a desk with a computer and two bookshelves filled with many paperback novels. The kitchen was across from the living room, on the other side. It was decent-sized, with plenty of cabinets and counter area. An island in the middle of the kitchen allowed space for an extra sink and a cutting board. Behind the kitchen was a smaller room, big enough to hold a dinette set with four chairs. Beyond the table was a sliding door leading out to the backyard. Gabrielle could not see outside as it was dark, and the shade was drawn. In the kitchen, there was a door. Mike opened the door to show her where the washer and dryer were kept in case she needed to do some laundry.

"You can sleep in my room, and I'll crash on the couch."

Gabrielle was not going to have it this way. It was a pointless argument. She did not want to put Mike out in any way, but his stubborn, chivalrous nature won over her fear of inconveniencing him.

It had gotten late, now twenty-three minutes past one. The chaos of the day caught up with her and she could no longer keep her eyes open. Having Mike in the other room while she slept gave her the comfort she needed to ensure a good night's sleep—despite the grim future ahead. While she may have avoided harm in the motel, Peter Lugo would not stop unless Gabrielle backed down. Or worse, until she met the same fate as Rick Evans.

CHAPTER FORTY-TWO

"What's gotten into you? I've never seen you this giddy ... ever." April questioned Gabrielle's sudden change in demeanor.

It was true. Gabrielle could not stop smiling, more likely beaming. Her cheeks hurt from being stretched wide the entire morning. It was the first time in her life Gabrielle ever felt truly happy. She never had this feeling with Hank and certainly had nothing to be cheerful about while Cynthia remained in a coma. On the surface, it would appear this despondent waitress should have nothing to be ecstatic about, but she did, and it was all Officer Mike Thomas's fault. The very thought of him made her glow—radiating like a ball of sunlight. Gabrielle should be upset and, at the very least, scared for her life. Her sense of self had been violated when the intruder destroyed her motel room, but she would be safe in the presence of Mike. He had a gun and was a trained cop. He would know what to do if anything untoward transpired.

Gabrielle awoke this morning from the best sleep in her lifetime. Throughout the night, after being swept away into R.E.M. sleep, she forgot where she was. When she opened her eyes to face the day, she looked around and remembered she was no longer at the motel. She was underneath the soft 300-thread count sheets of Mike Thomas's queen-sized bed. Of course, he was not in bed beside her, but that did not matter. She was still in his home. Being the gentleman he was, he slept on the sofa in the living room. When Gabrielle picked up the phone to call him the night before, she feared for her life but did not expect him to whisk her away to his place to ensure she remained safe. Yet, that morning, there she was, alone with him in his house.

Gabrielle stretched her arms above her head and placed her feet on the floor. She opened the bedroom door quietly and peered into the living room for fear of waking Mike from his deep slumber. To her surprise, he was already wide awake. He had been up to face the morning for quite some time as he was freshly showered and dressed. Gabrielle found him standing at the stove in the kitchen, busy cooking. He turned around to find her, still in her pajamas.

"Good morning," he grinned as he spoke. "How did you sleep?"

It was the most amazing sleep of my life. "Fine, and you?" she replied.

"I slept well." He pointed to a chair at the table next to the kitchen. Gabrielle noticed it had been cleared and set with dishes for breakfast. "Do you drink coffee?"

She was startled at this treatment. "Yes. Can't start the morning without it."

"Great, there is a cup on the table waiting for you. The pancakes are almost done. I was going to make eggs but realized I didn't know how you liked them, so I opted for a sure thing."

This was amazing to Gabrielle. Never in her life had she received treatment like this. Nobody ever made her breakfast or even considered she may like her eggs over-hard rather than scrambled. Officer Thomas brought the frying pan to the table. He flipped two perfectly fluffy pancakes onto the plate in front of Gabrielle. His culinary skills were superb. The pancakes melted in her mouth after each bite.

Mike finished grilling his pancakes and sat at the table across from Gabrielle. His morning perkiness was adorable. Gabrielle was usually a monster in the morning, afraid to face any ray of sunshine. Officer Thomas made this grumpiness fade from her, and she decided she could live like this every morning for the rest of her life.

"Gabrielle, table twenty looks like they're ready to order."

Gabrielle looked up and saw her manager standing before her. She was daydreaming about her morning and had nearly forgotten she was at work. Nothing, not even Sheila, could dull the ecstatic feeling deep inside Gabrielle. She could not wait to finish her shift and return to her new residence to spend more time with her newfound crush. Nothing had happened between them, yet, but there was a definite sexual chemistry that neither party could deny. There was also a comfort level Gabrielle never found with another man. Moments of silence between them did not need to be filled with constant babble. It was just silent, and that was okay. They understood each other.

As the two sat there eating breakfast, they made small talk to get to know one another. The only thing that Officer Thomas knew about Gabrielle was that she had a horrific live-in boyfriend who beat her occasionally and that she had befriended a woman wanted for murder. It was a wonder he even gave her the time of day.

They chatted about life. He asked where she grew up and was fascinated by her answers. He sincerely listened to every word and showed empathy when she described her experiences being shuffled around from foster home to foster home. A life he had not lived, in sharp contrast to his.

Mike grew up with a normal family in the suburbs of New Jersey. He was the youngest of three: an older brother and a middle-child sister. He spoke of his parents with the utmost respect and did not seem to have any regrets about his childhood. Gabrielle was a little jealous of this past normalcy.

It felt like they were only sitting at the table for ten minutes, but it was an hour and a half. Mike had to be at the Precinct by

11 a.m., and Gabrielle's shift started at 2 p.m. He apologized for having to run out, but it was 10:30, and he would be late for work if he did not leave. Gabrielle got up, thanked him for his hospitality, and took the dirty plates to the sink.

"Gabrielle." Her boss, Sheila, was trying to get her attention yet again.

"I already got table twenty's order," she sniped back.

"No, you have a phone call."

A phone call? In all her years working at the diner, she could not remember one single time when she received a personal phone call while on shift.

As she walked across the restaurant, her thoughts moved to who was on the other end of the line. It could not be Hank; she had not had contact with him since leaving the apartment that dreadful night many months prior. Hank knew where she worked, but he was too useless to attempt to look up the phone number to harass her. Plus, that was not his style. If he saw her on the street, he would most certainly approach her, but there is no way he would seek her out. The media portrays batterers as being fierce and harassing. This could not be further from the truth about Hank. He was busy working or getting drunk at the local joint up the street. The caller was not Hank.

As she reached for the phone, a broad grin emerged across Gabrielle's face. It had to be Mike. She must have mentioned the Village Diner during their conversation that morning. He was most likely calling to see when she would be home. Gabrielle quickly placed the earpiece upon her ear to hear him talk.

"Hello," she spoke in a heightened voice, trying to hold back from sounding overly excited.

"Gabrielle...Gabrielle Price." This was not Mike. She recognized the voice, but she could not immediately place it.

Hesitantly, she replied, "Yes, this is her."

"I know where you are. I've been following your every move, and you had better stop, or else your fate will be fatal."

Gabrielle froze.

Before she could respond, the man on the other end was gone. She stood there unable to move, the receiver still in her hand.

It was him.

She recognized the deep, booming voice. It was the same man whose voice terrorized Cynthia Evans in the cabin. It was a voice she would forever recognize as the real killer of Rick Evans.

It was Peter Lugo.

CHAPTER FORTY-THREE

Gabrielle had a hard time finishing her shift. Somehow, Peter Lugo found her.

How does he know where I work? Is he capable of killing me too? All of these thoughts were disturbing Gabrielle. She had gone from thoughts of bliss with Mike to thoughts of terror.

"Are you okay?" April questioned her. "Ever since you got that phone call, you have been acting very strangely." She brought down her voice into a whisper so that only Gabrielle could hear what she had to say next. "Are you involved with drugs or something? Your mood swings today are freaking me out."

If only April knew the truth. Yes, she was involved with drugs, but not in taking them. "I'm okay. It was just bad news I'd rather not discuss." Gabrielle figured a vague answer would make April leave her alone for the last half hour of her shift.

She could not wait to get back to the house with Mike. He could comfort her, and the thought of him wrapping his arms around her made a small smile reappear at the corners of her mouth. She would have to tell him what happened. This was a serious threat, and as innocent as a phone call seemed, she now feared for her life. The voice on the phone sent shivers up and down her spine. She believed the man on the other end would follow through on his threat and must be stopped before she wound up dead in a ditch.

"Gabrielle, you can leave a few minutes early if you like." Sheila hardly ever let her go before her shift ended. Clearly, she noticed the phone call had distressed Gabrielle.

Gabrielle looked at the clock. It was 8:45 p.m., only fifteen minutes early. Her side work was finished. She had gotten the sweeping, refilling of the salt, pepper, and sugar out of the way. She was ready to go. Gabrielle collected her coat and walked through the parking lot to the green Dodge Aries. She wished she could click her heels like Dorothy and be transported into Officer Thomas's home without effort. But reality settled in, she would have to drive twenty minutes to leave behind the haunting phone call from earlier that evening.

Gabrielle put the green Dodge in drive and made a left-hand turn out of the diner's parking lot onto Highway 20. Mike's house was pretty simple to get to, but he lived on the outskirts of town, on the back roads. She hated driving on winding dark roads at night for fear of hitting a wandering deer.

Gabrielle was suddenly blinded. A vehicle barreling down the other side of the road had its bright beams on extra high, causing Gabrielle to lose sight. She quickly flashed her car lights forward, but the light emanating from the other vehicle only appeared to get brighter. They were driving fast, faster than the maximum speed limit. Gabrielle had to ease her foot off the gas pedal to avoid veering off the road. She tried to focus her line of vision but was still blinded. Then, she realized the vehicle coming at her was not on the other side of the road. It was on her side of the road. The wrong side of the road. Taking aim at her car.

As it approached, she realized this vehicle was not a car but rather a huge truck barreling down the highway. The driver had to see her coming. She honked her horn several times to alert the motorist who had veered to the wrong side. The sound of the horn did not appear to affect the truck driver. He was headed right for her without hesitation. The truck did not slow down nor show any intention of getting out of the way. Gabrielle had nowhere to go. She was playing an unwanted game of chicken with a truck three times the size of the Dodge. The truck was moving fast. The impact would crush her. She had to decide quickly: hold her ground or jerk the car out of the way.

Two seconds until death.

Gabrielle's instinct told her it was better to live than risk being crushed by the undercarriage of a semi-trailer truck. Without another thought, she jerked her car as quickly to the right as she could. Gabrielle did not see her car hit the side rail, but she felt it jerk forward. Good thing she formed a habit of wearing her seat belt from a young age. She credited her first foster mother, who was obsessed with the possibility she would hurt herself just by breathing, so she took caution with every little thing she did. Gabrielle was surprised her foster mother would even drive a car at all. She did not drive at night, though; long-distance highway driving caused her to hyperventilate. At any rate, the extreme cautiousness of her former pretend mother was the sole reason Gabrielle was still alive and breathing at this precise moment, rather than ejected through the front windshield and left for roadkill on the side of the road.

Gabrielle had no idea if she had been knocked unconscious for a long time. The truck was nowhere to be found when she came to. Her head struck the steering wheel. Her car was too old to have the mandated airbags of this century. Gabrielle made a mental note for when she purchased a new vehicle, to be sure it was equipped with such amenities.

She lifted her head and tried to look around, but the soreness prevented her from turning her head too far to the right or left. In front of her was the steel beam of the guardrail that stopped her car from rolling any further off the road into the ten-foot-deep ditch behind it. Looking down at the steering wheel, she noticed her blood smeared in a circular pattern. She placed her hand on her forehead and found the blood still flowing from a cut to her head. She peered in the rearview mirror and realized the gushing blood was coming from a slight wound—the blood loss looked worse than the actual injury. She grabbed the apron she threw on the floor of the front passenger seat. That was better than nothing to stop the flow of blood until she could dress and clean her fresh wound properly. As she leaned back in the driver seat, a pain shot out in her shoulder, whiplash from the jerking forward of the seatbelt. The full achiness would take a few days to kick in. The most important thing to Gabrielle was whether or not her car was still drivable. She had to get off the side of the road and back to Mike.

Gabrielle turned the key in the ignition. The engine churned and tried to kick in but stalled. She tried again, and the same thing happened.

"Please, just work," she begged the green Dodge.

Gabrielle tried to turn the car on again, letting it churn for ten seconds while pumping the gas pedal. Finally, the roar of the engine kicked in. Gabrielle screamed with excitement and backed the car away from the guard rail. She heard the crunch of the front hood as it backed away. She winced with fear and wondered what the front of the car must look like. She would have to deal with the damage later as she could not waste another moment getting back to Mike.

She had to tell him about the events of the day. She hoped these were the final events to convince him about Cynthia's inno-cence. The run-in with the big rig was no accident. The events of the last twenty-four hours were too coincidental. First, her motel room was trashed last night, then she got a threatening phone call at work, and now she was nearly killed as she was run off the road. Mike had to believe her. Gabrielle's life depended on it.

CHAPTER FORTY-FOUR

Gabrielle pulled up to the front of the house at about 10:30 p.m. The lights were on. Mike must have been awake awaiting her return. She knew he would question her about what happened as soon as she walked through the door. There was no way she could hide the bruise on her head. It had not fully stopped gushing.

She pulled the car to the curb and made her way up the driveway. She got to the front door, where she paused. Gabrielle considered turning around, returning to her car, and not entering the premises. However, that option did not exist, as she had nowhere else to go. She had to face Mike. She opened the front door and walked inside.

Gabrielle found Officer Thomas on the couch reading the latest edition of *Sports Unlimited*. He did not get up to greet her or put down the magazine he was reading. Gabrielle hoped he would come to the door as he heard her enter. She imagined him running to her side with arms wide open, only to collapse her entire body in a warm, embracing hug.

Her fantasy could not have been further from reality. He did not move off the couch. He did not notice anything unusual had happened. Gabrielle began to get upset. She needed Mike now more than ever, but she was expecting more from the man than he was willing to give. They were not dating. They were barely friends. He liked her, but this was no more than a platonic relationship. Gabrielle stood two feet from the door, unsure what to do next.

Mike noticed she was still standing in the vicinity where she entered and looked up. "Gabrielle is everything alri ..."

He stopped midsentence when he saw the disheveled woman standing in his home. He got off the couch and went over to comfort her with an embrace. It was a start, a little delayed reaction, but it was exactly what she needed at that precise moment.

As soon as she felt the warmth of his body around her, Gabrielle began to cry. The shock from the last twenty-four hours surfaced all at once.

"You're shaking," he told her, leading her to the couch to sit down.

Gabrielle could not respond. The words would not come out. Mike wrapped a warm blanket around her shoulders and headed to the bathroom to get gauze and peroxide to clean out the wound to her head. The peroxide foamed, causing extreme pain to her forehead, but it was a wound that needed to be cleaned. After four separate peroxide applications, the pain started to numb, and Officer Thomas placed a bandage over the opening.

"See, it's not so bad once it gets all cleaned up."

Now that she was medically cleared, it was time to discuss what happened.

"I got run off the road," she told him without any preceding question.

"On purpose?" He seemed shocked by this.

Gabrielle told him about the truck, the blinding lights, the game of chicken, and how she swerved and wound up unconscious at the wheel. As Gabrielle spoke, she was not sure he believed it was intentional.

"I also got a threatening phone call at work."

He looked at her quizzically. "What did they say?"

"Something about they were going to find me and I was going to face my fate." Gabrielle wished she could remember the exact wording, but her thoughts were jumbled after the accident.

"Do you think Hank is capable of really hurting you?" Gabrielle looked at Mike with shock.

Hank? Did he really believe that Hank was capable of this?

True, the Hank Officer Thomas knew was the Hank that beat her. But it was never serious enough to send her to the hospital, never with enough rage to kill her suddenly.

"I mean, first the message on the bathroom mirror in the trashed hotel room, the threatening phone call, and then you are run off the road, though I am not convinced that was as intentional as you think … could have been an accident."

Gabrielle was getting angrier with each word the officer spoke. Hank was not doing this to her; Peter Lugo was, and he could not, would not see that. Hank was too lazy. He would not seek her out. He acted angrily, but Gabrielle never felt that he threatened her life.

"If not Hank, then who?" Officer Thomas asked.

"Peter Lugo." The officer's body language closed off as she spoke those two words. He could not believe Gabrielle would go down that road again. "At least hear me out." Her voice got louder with each word she spoke.

Gabrielle's life was in danger, and without convincing him otherwise, there was no way she would be safe. She explained all the evidence stacked up against Mr. Lugo.

"I went to the cabin with Cynthia. I saw heroin."

"Did you see Mr. Lugo there?"

No, she had not. However, she heard the same voice in the cabin, that had called her on the phone at the restaurant.

"Do you know how to get back to the cabin? We can go and check it out."

No, she did not. She was not the one driving and did not recall the exact location, other than a few minutes of turns off the New York Thruway. She did not even pay attention to the exit number.

"Do you have any pictures or other proof of the heroin?"

No, she did not.

"How did you know it was heroin? Have you seen heroin before?"

Only in the movies.

"Gabrielle, the only evidence you have given me is that he owns a Python 3600. That's hardly enough evidence for me to try and indict Mr. Lugo for murder."

She had to keep trying. "But …."

He interrupted her. "A neighbor saw Cynthia at the crime scene. She witnessed her walking up the driveway into the house shortly before the gunshots rang off, then saw her pulling out of the driveway in her car."

Gabrielle had no response. She knew otherwise, but she did not know how to convince him of that. She just sat there on the couch with nothing else to say, fearful about what would happen next.

The phone in the house started to ring, breaking the awkward silence between them. Mike got up from the couch to answer it. He listened intently to what the person on the other end had to say. Mike appeared to be getting bad news, and Gabrielle sensed she did not want to know what that news was.

"What time did this happen?" Mike questioned the person on the other line. They spoke for a few minutes until he finally hung up. When the call ended, he did not speak right away. He just stared at her. Gabrielle knew he was searching for the right words but could not find them.

Finally, he just said what needed to be said. "Hank is dead."

CHAPTER FORTY-FIVE

Gabrielle had to fight the vomit rising from her stomach and into the back of her throat. Hank was dead, and she was responsible. Her actions, her selfish desire to change her drab existence, had resulted in his demise. Gabrielle did not know the circumstances surrounding his death, but she was sure they were looking for her instead. She was positive that whatever fate landed upon Hank was meant for her. If Officer Thomas could not see it differently, she would have to take matters into her own hands. She would have to kill Peter Lugo herself. It was the only way to stop him.

Mike was still speaking, but she could not hear his words. His mouth was moving, but the audio was muted. Everything appeared in slow motion as if time stood still, and a second took three times as long to complete. The rotation of the earth slowed. Her brain ceased to function. All she could think about was death and murder. He had to die. Peter Lugo had to cease to exist. He was dangerous to society. She was the only person on earth who knew his terror and was willing to take him head-on. She could not waste another moment.

Officer Thomas was midsentence. Gabrielle turned her back to him, grabbed her coat off the couch, and headed out the front door. He looked stunned.

"Gabrielle," he called out to her.

She did not look back. She was in a trance.

"Gabrielle, where are you going?"

Gabrielle got into the green Aries and proceeded down the highway. She had to find Peter Lugo. She was unsure what to do once she found him, but that could be figured out along the way. She glanced at her watch. It was 11:30 p.m. Most likely, he would be at home. That was where she would head, his humble abode. She obtained the address from the DMV list Mr. Crowley provided. Gabrielle intended to visit his home as part of her investigation into the murder of Rick Evans. She stared at that address so many times, she knew where to go without skipping a beat.

Gabrielle had not yet seen the millionaire's home, but she imagined it to be a lavish two-story mansion surrounded by security cameras and vicious guard dogs. She wondered if it were as easy in real life as in the movies to lure off the dogs with a slab of meat from the local butcher shop.

"1422 Pine Creek Road." Gabrielle's keen sense of direction would help her to navigate to this destination. Forty-five minutes later, she drove down the dimly lit suburban road, Pine Creek.

The houses on the block were larger than the neighborhood she lived in when she was younger, but they were nowhere near as extravagant as she expected. There were no pillars, no gates, and no visible security cameras. Gabrielle could have driven her little green car up the front lawn and onto the front stoop. This was probably not the best option if the plan was to be subtle. She pulled the car across the street and turned off the engine and the headlights. She saw a light in front of the home, indicating someone was inside. She sat with her head resting on the back of the front seat and stared at the Lugo residence. It was a big suburban house on about 1.5 acres of property. It sat twenty feet from the road, hidden by numerous birch trees in the front yard. There was a nice wraparound porch and a two-car garage. The house was two stories with a peak and a window above the front door. There were at least four bedrooms on the top floor. Gabrielle was impressed with the home, but not, knowing how much money the man was worth.

"Now what?" Gabrielle thought out loud to herself. She had not thought this through. She needed to catch him by surprise. She decided she would wait there in her car. She would wait there all night, sleep there if she had to. That was the extent of her plan for the moment.

As the thought of an overnight stakeout in her freezing car began to sound like a less-than-appealing plan, there was movement from the Lugo home. The garage door opened, and a red Python 3600 backed down the driveway and onto the street.

Where could he be going after midnight?

She was about to discover the answer as she turned on her engine to follow the red sports car down the road.

CHAPTER FORTY-SIX

It had been a long day for him. While most people are ending their day at the dawn of a new one, his was about to get more hectic. Midnight is the witching hour when the majority lie in slumber underneath the warm sheets of their beds. He, however, had no time for sleep. Sleep would come later, after the shipment. It was the third Wednesday of the month, and time to collect his precious cargo off the pier. He was anxious for what was to come.

Usually, he was not nervous; it was the same operation month after month, but the air this time felt different, thicker. The events that transpired earlier in the day put him on edge. This woman, Gabrielle Price, was getting too close for comfort. Too close for her own good. She needed to be stopped. She was putting her nose into places where it did not belong. He had no idea what she knew, but was quite sure it was minimal, or she would have already gone to the police. He heard a rumor that she was with Cynthia Evans the night of the arrest. If this was true, she was looking for answers. These answers, if revealed, were dangerous to him—a threat to his entire existence.

Jimmy called to tell Peter an unknown woman was poking around his old neighborhood in Connecticut. She pretended to be writing a human-interest piece. Jimmy saw her speaking to the neighbor, then she came over to his house. Little did Miss Price know, Jimmy was his confidant. A boy who has been like a brother to him; the loyalty runs deep between them. Jimmy is the only person he has ever trusted, which is saying a lot. Trust nobody.

The motto he lives by. If she was as dumb as she portrayed to Jimmy, he should have no problem intimidating her.

Jimmy visited the home of her pathetic boyfriend, not knowing she had moved out. Jimmy relayed how aggressive and angry the guy was at the mere mention of Gabrielle's name. The man needed some anger management classes. His temper met a fate of death.

Jimmy did not mean to kill the man, but the angry boyfriend lunged at him and was in attack mode. It was a defensive killing. Jimmy feared for his life. The attacker did not look strong enough to kill a cat, yet he displayed brute force as strong as Mr. Universe. The guy deserved to be shot in the head. There was no remorse to be felt for him. Karma. Whatever vibe you put out in the world returns itself upon you. Those who view the cup as half-empty get just that, a half-empty life. Her boyfriend viewed the world as a hostile, angry place, and that is, in return, what he got out of life.

Luckily, before the fatal shot, the boyfriend revealed Gabrielle was staying at a hotel somewhere. He did not know anything else, and it was apparent he did not care to know. The missing information was easy enough to discover. Preston is a small town, and there are only a handful of places in which travelers can rest. Rarely does a person ever plan a vacation to Preston. It is a town tourists pass through, only stopping to close their eyes before moving along to their targeted destinations.

Peter made three phone calls and found Gabrielle staying at the motel near the edge of town. Peter and Jimmy went there together, but she was not there. They just wanted to scare her. The girl was obsessed with Cynthia Evans. Upon entering the room, they found hundreds of newspaper articles dispersed. There were clippings and pictures taped to the wall. He even found his name circled on a list she seemed to have acquired from the DMV. She knew his name. She possessed a list containing his car registration information. He was unsure what this meant, but it was a bad omen. The two men trashed the room, sending the young girl a message to cease her probing.

They also discovered where she was employed. Peter hoped the phone call placed to Gabrielle at the diner would further convince her to stop. To solidify the seriousness of their threats, a truck intentionally ran her off the road after work. He would kill her if it came down to it.

As he drove down the dark, deserted streets, he spotted the green car in his rearview mirror. It was a far enough distance to try and be hidden, but the engine roared loud like an airplane, so it was impossible to miss. It was her. She was following him. Jimmy had described the car in detail. He had gotten a good glimpse of it when she ventured out to his hometown in Connecticut.

Nothing will convince this woman to stop her meddling.

No choice but to let her follow him. He would deal with Miss Price upon arrival at his destination. She was clearly on a mission to find answers and would not stop until she got them. He would give her the answers she was searching for. Her last dying wish before he pulled the trigger, sending a bullet straight to her heart.

CHAPTER FORTY-SEVEN

Gabrielle had not thought this through. She had to stop Mr. Lugo, but how she would do so remained unclear. She had no plan for when he reached his final destination. She had no cell phone to call for backup, no camera to take pictures for evidence, and no idea what incriminating clues she would unveil.

After a few turns they finally arrived at a pier on the Hudson River, just twenty miles outside Preston. Mr. Lugo pressed an automatic opener and headed through an entrance by the docks. The logo on the gateway belonged to NATCO. A fenced-in gate housed the back end of trucks that carried cargo. The road inside the fenced-in area split off in two directions; the right led to the warehouse's entrance that belonged to NATCO, and the left led down to the water. This place appeared to be a drop-off and pick-up site for goods shipped across the country. The red Python proceeded inside the opening, which automatically shut behind it.

Gabrielle would not dare try to drive her car through the gate, but she could not sit in her car contently. Curiosity got the best of her. She needed to know what was happening in the secure facility. She needed to get a closer look.

She could make out figures in the night from where she parked, but none clear enough to pick out in a police line-up. Mr. Lugo parked his Python and was greeted by a man. The nameless man was of average build and height. He had a clipboard he referred to in his hands. It was time to get out of the car and try to make her way to the other side of the fence. She opened her car door. The crisp breeze made the little hairs on her arms stand upright. Luckily, Gabrielle placed her coat in the back seat. She reached over for it and put it on to keep the frigid air away from her skin. She ventured forward, careful not to be noticed.

Gabrielle was sure there were hidden cameras about the perimeter of the property to detect movement. There was no way to avoid them. She did not want to be caught but did not fear it. There was nothing to lose in her life right now, and facing the heartless man who killed without remorse did not scare her. However, she was not about to alert him to her presence.

She walked as quietly as possible toward the fence. When she got up close, she noticed the impossibility of scaling it as the entire top part was covered with barbwire sharp enough to puncture the skin. If she had some pliers, she could try to cut a hole in the metal barrier and squeeze her way through, but lack of the necessary tools prevented this game plan from coming to fruition. Mr. Lugo entered the building with his associate, and nobody was outside the compound to spy on.

Standing at the fence, gazing at the property, she noticed a cargo ship docked in the water. There was movement from a few people on the vessel and light inside the deck room. Boxes were maneuvered from the boat onto the pier. As she stared at the merchant ship, she became intrigued as to whether those were illegal drugs being hauled off and placed onto the dock. Lost in her thoughts, she felt a startling tap on her shoulder.

"Turn around slowly, and I'll spare you... for now." It was him. It was the same voice that froze Cynthia in the cabin——the same threatening voice that called her at the diner.

She turned around and finally faced the man. She stared him in the eyes and tried to analyze his soul. She never encountered such an evil aura. A soul so filled with self-centeredness it would stop at nothing to achieve all the power and money in the world.

"Mr. Lugo," she stated as she faced him. She looked at him. He was exactly as she pictured he would be, except for the gun in his left hand pointed in her direction.

"How are you, Miss Price?" It was more of a rhetorical question, as it was apparent he did not care how she was doing at that particular moment.

"Nice to put a face to the voice."

"I warned you to stay out of my affairs, but you had to go and disobey my requests, so now you'll be dealt with accordingly."

"Why don't you shoot me here and get it over with?"

"You would like that, wouldn't you? This is too out in the open… too messy. Besides, I have other business that needs my attention. Then I'll deal with you."

He grabbed her right hand and placed it around her back. Then he grabbed her left hand and did the same. He secured both wrists with tight handcuffs, pushing her toward the fence, which was now open.

"You, my persistent friend, will remain here. You should've listened to my warnings. If you had, you would've been alive to see your next birthday. I hope your last one was good because that's the memory you will die with." He was ruthless.

He grabbed Gabrielle by the hair and shoved her into the back of an SUV. The SUV had tinted windows, so people outside could not see what was happening inside. He shut the door and left her there while he went on to complete his midnight affairs.

CHAPTER FORTY-EIGHT

Mike sat on his couch in disbelief. He could not believe she left. She just got up and departed, mid-sentence. She did not listen to the words he said. He told her Hank was dead. That was when she stopped listening. If she paid attention to the rest of the words, she would have heard him explain that something was wrong with his death.

Something was not right with the harassment Gabrielle had been getting. The time frames did not match up. Hank had been declared dead thirty hours prior. Shot with a single bullet through the forehead and discovered dead-on-arrival in his apartment. His boss at the auto shop called the police when Hank failed to show up for work that afternoon. Gabrielle told Mike she received a threatening phone call at work, earlier in the evening. There is no way that Hank placed that call; he was already stiff as a board. It was also unlikely he was the person who trashed the motel room the night before as the time of the break-in was after the approximate time of death determined by the medical examiner's office. It did not add up.

As Mike heard this news, his heart sank. Something very wrong was happening to Gabrielle. He started to doubt his stubborn belief in Cynthia's horrific crimes. Maybe Gabrielle was right and somebody else, ruthless and powerful, was responsible for the death of Rick Evans.

Gabrielle was upset about the news of Hank's death. This set off a spark of jealousy inside the officer. Of course, he understood, they had a history together. They were a long-time couple. Hank was all Gabrielle had. Regardless of the abuse, it is hard to just leave that behind. Mike, however, did not think she would react irrationally. Gabrielle's eyes darkened and she was unable to function. If he did not find her, she might do something regrettable.

Quite some time had passed since Gabrielle left the residence, but Mike had a good idea where she went. He used his detective training to deduce that she was headed to the Lugo household. She was deranged and delirious from the news of Hank's death and likely went to solve this mess herself. Mike needed to find her before she got herself into more trouble. The thought of Gabrielle seeking her just reward by killing Peter Lugo terrified him. If Peter Lugo is the real killer, Gabrielle is incapable of protecting herself. He may never see her alive again, suffering the same fate as Hank Anderson and Rick Evans. The officer was scared and could no longer sit in his house. He had to act now.

Mike headed out the door and got into his Ford F-150. His truck was outfitted with needed police equipment to assist in undercover patrols. Unsure where Mr. Lugo lived, he sent a radio request to the station to obtain the needed details.

"This is Officer Thomas to base, over."

"Hey Mike, you're off duty. What's your business calling the station?" The voice on the other end of the radio receiver crackled.

"Hey Ronnie, I need some information. You think you can look it up for me?"

"Sure, no problem."

Mike asked him for the location of Peter Lugo. The voice on the other end scanned the police records and provided the address requested.

"Thanks for the info. Can you do one more thing for me?"

"For you, anything."

"Can you run an APB on a green Dodge Aries? It is a little beat up in the front. I need to know if anyone in the field has seen it and its location."

"Sure, is everything alright? It's not like you to be running background checks and APBs when you're off duty."

Mike took a moment and paused before answering.

"Yes, everything's fine, though I may need some backup later in the evening. For now, everything is fine." He said it, but deep down, he did not believe it. He did not believe everything was alright. He knew Gabrielle was in serious trouble; every passing second meant more danger. He needed to find her now. Her life depended on it.

Mike pulled up to the corner in front of the Lugo house. It was 2:20 a.m., and all was quiet. It did not appear anybody was home. However, the household members could be sound asleep, tucked nicely into the sheets on their mattresses. Mike looked around. He rolled down the window and listened to the silence of the dark night. The only sound emanating outside was the crickets singing their nightly operas.

He scanned the street. He looked up and down both sides of the block. He did not spot Gabrielle's green Dodge in the neighborhood. She was not present. Mike thought for sure she would be there. He had not considered other options because he was positive this was where he would find her. Either she had been abducted by Lugo himself, or she went someplace quiet to reflect on the events of the day. For her sake, he hoped the latter to be the truth. Mike still needed to find her. He wanted to embrace, comfort, and help her figure out what was happening. He had no clue where to look next.

"Mike, I have status on the green Dodge Aries, over." There was a higher force watching over him.

"I'm here. What's the location, over."

"Down by the Hudson Pier, just outside Preston. The car you're looking for is parked alongside the road, but it's empty, with no passengers. Do you want me to call for backup or run a search for the owner? Over."

Mike did not want to get any other officers involved until he knew what he was dealing with. "No. I'm on my way. I can handle it from here. Thanks for the information, over and out."

Mike knew the officer on the other end of the radio would not like this answer, but he did not want anybody else involved. The more cops involved, the more dangerous for Gabrielle. He needed to find her, but he needed to do it alone.

CHAPTER FORTY-NINE

Gabrielle sat in the back of the gas-guzzling vehicle, helpless. There was nothing she could do. The handcuffs limited her mobility, and the doors were locked. She had been shoved into the back cargo part of the SUV. A wire cage wall separated her from the front of the truck. The apparatus was installed to prevent the contents in the rear from repelling forward in the event of an accident. At this time, it served the purpose of keeping Gabrielle in her place. Her future was looking increasingly dim. She tried to devise a plan, but nothing would help the predicament she got herself into this time.

She waited. That was all she could do. Wait. It was torture. Torture. Impending death, and all she could do was wait. Chinese water torture would have been more humane.

Finally, the driver's side door opened, and a young man entered. Another man entered the vehicle on the passenger side. The two men spoke to each other, barely aware of her presence in the back of the truck. Gabrielle recognized the voice of the driver. It was the neighbor she spoke to in Connecticut. The same man who slammed the door abruptly in her face. She was sure of it. The pieces started to come together.

He works for Lugo.

He must have told Peter Lugo about her visit to Connecticut. Right after she returned home from the New England state the harassment started. She did not get the phone call until afterward, her hotel room was not trashed until afterward, and Hank did not die until afterward. That trip proved to be the deadly turning point in her investigation into the murder of Rick Evans.

The vehicle's engine started, and the SUV backed out of the parking spot.

Gabrielle knew exactly where they were headed without even asking. They were going to the cabin.

CHAPTER FIFTY

Mike drove up to the side of the Dodge Aries parked along the road. Gabrielle was nowhere to be found. He peered inside the driver's side window and looked for clues. It was her car. He recognized it from the few times he had found her sitting in it. As he surveyed the area, he found no unusual damage that would lead him to believe there was a struggle. He saw the dents to the front and the smashed-in headlight, which he assumed were caused by the accident earlier in the evening when Gabrielle had been run off the road.

"Where could she have gone?" he wondered aloud.

He pondered her whereabouts and turned around to face the pier. There on the fence across the street was the NATCO symbol. It was a circular globe emblem with the continent of North America etched out. Inside the continent was the name NATCO. The color scheme for the trucking company was maroon and gold. Mike deduced this was their shipping headquarters. The place their cargo arrived, then packed up to be hauled by one of the company drivers across the various cities of the United States and Canada.

Mike looked at his watch. It was 2:45 a.m. He could not detect any movement inside the shipping port behind the wire chain link fence that guarded the property. Just as Mike was about to make his way across the street to survey the compound at a closer distance, he heard the automatic gate swing open. A black SUV with tinted windows came through, followed by a red Python.

The exact car Gabrielle tried to use to incriminate Peter Lugo for the murder of Rick Evans.

Mike stood in the darkness across the street, far enough in the shadows and out of the way. A passerby in the night would not know he was there. Mike was unsure where they were headed but was sure he should follow them. His gut told him wherever it was, Gabrielle was with them, and she was not an invited guest on their road trip.

He quickly made the way to his truck and followed the caravan. He kept his distance so they would not suspect they were being followed. A skill he was quite good at. He had lots of practice during his first few years on the force. When he first joined the squad, he was placed on overnight duty, which involved many stakeouts and car following. He was now quite skilled at being invisible to the normal eye yet still aware of everything happening around him. The skill would come in handy this evening in his search for Gabrielle.

The cars in front guided the way. They did not appear to pause or even notice the truck following behind them. They made their way out of the suburbs of Preston and onto the New York State Thruway, heading north. Although Gabrielle had only mentioned a cabin in the woods upstate in passing, he was sure that was where they were headed before dawn broke.

Mike needed a plan when he got to the cabin. He would be in unfamiliar territory and out of his element. There was no way of knowing what to expect once they arrived.

Mike began to wonder about Gabrielle. Rage started to build up inside of him. If Peter Lugo laid a hand on her, he would be sure to return the favor and then some. He did not want to see her hurt, or even worse, killed.

He thought about each time he had gone to the apartment where she and Hank lived. The first time he met Gabrielle he was drawn to her. Of course, it is against police honor and ethical codes to show interest in a victim while on duty. Mike, however, was mesmerized by her presence. He clearly recalled the first time he saw her. It was his first month on regular patrol. Before then, he was the stakeout king. He had grown tired of sleeping in his car, consuming only bear claws and coffee. He begged the police sergeant to put him on a regular rotation. Mike had become a policeman to help people and wanted to be out in the war zone. He craved the line of fire, going out in his squad car and answering the 9-1-1 dispatcher calls. He imagined rescuing people from armed robbers and capturing the most heinous criminals.

Life as a cop, however, was not as glamorous as he thought. Most shifts, it was quite boring. One could tell it was a slow night by the number of police who showed up for a routine graffiti complaint. The most common calls for the town of Preston were domestic disputes. Usually, it was a mother and her uncontrollable teenage son who had come home drunk or the neighbor complaining that his fellow yard sharer played music at decibels loud enough to wake the gods in heaven.

The first time Mike got a call about Hank Anderson was different. He drove up the block and saw her sitting on the curb with her face in her hands. Gabrielle did not have to glance up for him to know how beautiful she was. As the cop car parked on the street, she looked up to face the officer. Mike noticed the tears running down her face. She looked so innocent and helpless sitting there.

"Miss, did you place an emergency call about a domestic dispute?" he asked.

Gabrielle did not respond to the inquiry. She simply nodded her head in the affirmative.

Mike looked at her and observed a bloody lip swollen to three times its normal size. "Where's the person who did this to you?"

She pointed toward the apartment where she and Hank resided. Officer Thomas only met Gabrielle for three minutes, but he still felt anger toward whatever criminal would choose to lay a finger on a girl as beautiful as her.

He walked toward the apartment, a fury brewing in his stomach. He tried his best to keep the rage concealed as he was on duty. Mike knocked on the door and found an inebriated Hank. He could barely stand and was slurring his speech into incoherent phrases. Gabrielle let Mike lock up Hank in the precinct. He was released the next morning, and charges were never filed or pursued.

Mike visited the home at least a dozen times over five years. It was always the same. Gabrielle would be out on the corner awaiting the arrival of the police. When he arrived, he went inside and found Hank, who was taken away in handcuffs. Each time, Mike would engage Gabrielle in conversation. He would offer to take her to the hospital, and she would always refuse. Then, he would beg her to leave Hank once and for all. He would tell her she was better than this life and deserved so much more. She would always agree, but she always went back. Mike feared the day when Hank took his beatings one step too far, and Gabrielle would be in the emergency room due to his brutality.

Mike was surprised the night the radio call mentioned Cynthia Evans being at that address. He was sure the 9-1-1 operator had been mistaken. Sure enough, when he responded, he found Gabrielle with Cynthia. There was no way he would allow Gabrielle to be locked up, even if it meant risking his badge. At the scene he made sure to be the officer in charge of investigating her involvement with the Preston Murderer. Police protocols require an interrogation of the suspect at the scene—taking them into custody when warranted. In reality, Mike did not ask Gabrielle any questions about what she was doing with Cynthia. He had already made up his mind that he would let her go. Seeing her bruised and beaten once again by Hank solidified his decision.

When he got back to the station, he told his colleagues Gabrielle had no idea who Cynthia was and had simply offered help when she found Cynthia stranded on the side of the road. Nobody questioned his information as he had an impeccable reputation. Mike knew if Gabrielle laid low until the media frenzy died down, nobody would even notice. Most of the evidence singled Cynthia out as a lone actor, so there was no need to pursue anything further from Gabrielle.

The officer did not want her involved in any of this and told Gabrielle to stay away from Cynthia. When he asked Gabrielle to promise to stay away from Hank, he sensed a difference in her. Mike could feel this time was the last straw and that, this time, she was leaving for good. He remembered looking into her eyes and knowing she felt comforted talking to him. Mike also knew the injuries Hank had caused her that evening were the worst yet, which scared him. He was pleased she had not returned to Hank since that evening.

What he did not expect was her determination to prove Cynthia's innocence. This persistence led to her current situation. A fate of death, a brutal one at that. Not as brutal as one of Hank's outbursts, but a fate far worse and heinous. Mike shuddered at the thought of Gabrielle being tortured by Peter Lugo.

He was angry with himself for not listening to her. She believed Cynthia was innocent, but he did not want to hear it. In hindsight, he wished he had. Then, this whole mess could have been avoided. All he had to do was listen to her, but he was too stubborn, and his cop pride blinded him. He thought he had the killer and was not open to any other interpretation of what happened on that deadly evening. Mike would never be able to forgive himself if Gabrielle died at the hands of Peter Lugo. He had to make sure that did not happen.

Gabrielle did not know how Mike felt about her. He has not stopped thinking about her since the first day he saw her, and now Mike may never get a chance to tell Gabrielle how he feels. It may already be too late.

CHAPTER FIFTY-ONE

Gabrielle sat in the back of the truck and fantasized about her obituary. She wondered what it would read. It would not say 'beloved so and so' of anyone. She had no husband, child, mother, father, or grandparent. There was no beloved anybody of whom they could put. Her boyfriend was dead. He, too, was no longer a 'beloved.' Would they write 'beloved waitress of the Village Diner'? Would she even have a wake or funeral? She could not think of anybody who would arrange it.

This is one thing people take for granted. Next of kin are left to pick up the pieces upon your passing. Wakes and funerals are artificial. They help the grieving process and ease the time to say goodbye to those who have passed. Gabrielle did not need such a period. No person on earth would need time to mourn her death.

She wondered about the John Does of the world who die without any relatives. This happens often. Plenty of people wind up in the morgue without someone to claim and identify the lifeless body.

What happens to these cadavers? Are they donated to science? Are they cut open on the fake operating tables at top-notch medical schools to teach students how to perform surgery? Or do they get cremated by the medical examiner, who then takes the ashes and spreads them out in the wide-open space of the sea?

Gabrielle hoped the latter was true. She envisioned a peaceful serenity as her ashes floated in the wind to lay rest upon the waves of the Atlantic Ocean.

As much as she was coming to terms with her impending death, something deep in her gut told her that this was not the end. This was not how her life would stop. There was still more life to live and more accomplishments to be attained.

One of these tasks was helping Cynthia Evans. The chance meeting had sent her existence into a tailspin. This unexpected turn of events in Gabrielle's life brought her new meaning and fulfillment. She had to bring Peter Lugo to justice for the Evans' murder. However, it was not just the Evans' family members that she was avenging. She was also seeking vengeance for the deaths of the other men who worked for NATCO. She had no concrete proof that Peter Lugo was responsible for Justin Enrel's and Earl Peterman's deaths but his sinister ways were all the evidence she needed.

Gabrielle thought of the three men and their mourning families. Justin Enrel was a young man when he passed away tragically from faulty brakes on the truck he was driving for NATCO. Earl Peterman died an unforeseen death after robbers broke into his home while he was there. Both of these men worked for NATCO and are connected to Peter Lugo.

Once a killer, always a killer. Any man who would have no problem ordering the death of a husband and his two young children must have killed before.

Gabrielle knew she was meant to do bigger and better things with the life she was given. She had not completed the tasks the higher-ups had for her, and she needed more time.

Time, however, was quickly running out.

CHAPTER FIFTY-TWO

ENREL-Justin M., 28, of Cradle Rock, NY, on March 23, 2000. Formerly of Canton, Ohio. Beloved son of Margaret and Stephen Enrel. Survived by his sister, Katelyn. Devoted Grandson of Patricia Devlin. Visiting at Davis Funeral Home, 4598 Mulberry Ave, Cradle Rock. Fri 4-8 PM, Sat & Sun 2-4, 7-9 PM. Funeral Mass at St. Thomas RC Church, Cradle Rock. Mon 10 AM.

It was a warm and breezy day. Justin could smell spring in the air and little flower buds would soon be cropping up all over. It was his favorite time of year––the perfect weather to drive a truck. He could roll down the windows and let the warm breeze whip through his hair as he sped down the highway.

He had been driving a truck for the past eight years, since he was twenty. His parents had always dreamed of their beloved son attending college, Justin did not see the importance of furthering his education. Plenty of his colleagues from his small Ohio high school had gone on to graduate from a university, and either became slaves to the corporate man or had so much revolving debt they could not live. He had a fine career as a truck driver.

Justin got to spend his days on the road traveling the nation. He has been places most Americans had never seen before. People in this country are obsessed with traveling, but their travels take them overseas. The countries of Europe offer magical destinations, but so do places in each of the fifty states. This country has so many hidden treasures most people miss out on.

It amazes him the things people come up with to make money and survive. Justin had seen it all throughout his travels for the past eight years. He witnessed people sitting on the side of the highway with all their possessions holding a trunk garage sale, a homemade beef jerky hut, and even a roadside snake salesman.

Being a truck driver was the perfect job for Justin. He loved to navigate the open roads. It was his chance to get away from his otherwise dull and boring life. His parents did not understand him and disowned him once he decided that college was not his place. School always bored him, and he could not understand why he had to go.

Once Justin was old enough, he cut class as often as possible. At sixteen years of age, he spent more time in the back of the school, behind the football bleachers, smoking cigarettes and blunts, than in the classroom. He was a bright individual, but he thought sitting in class all day was a waste of his time. Justin never did a lick of homework but somehow managed to pass all of his courses, just enough to earn his diploma and graduate.

His sister, Katelyn, on the other hand, was a child protégé. His parents loved her and made it known. She was the head cheerleader, the yearbook editor, and the star of the math team. Everybody loved her. Everybody sang her praises. She went on to graduate magna cum laude from Princeton University and scored a job at a big corporate firm on Wall Street. This was something Justin could not and did not want to do.

He did not have a job or a life path when he graduated from high school. There was no plan of action. His parents were not happy with this decision. He mooched off them for a year, pretending to seek gainful employment and never finding a steady job. He was good at conniving. He was not a liar but rather a deceitful, yet charming, individual capable of gaining the trust of others before they realized they were being taken for a ride.

His parents, however, never fell for his tricks. Having raised him from birth, they knew this side of their son. They knew what he was capable of and were not willing to put up with it past his nineteenth birthday.

Justin remembered the day they kicked him out of the house as if it were yesterday. It was the day after his nineteenth birthday. He came home at 10 a.m. after staying out all night partying with his pals. He walked through the front door of the Victorian home only to find all his precious belongings dispersed among three large black garbage bags, awaiting his arrival in the front foyer.

The air was different that morning, a distinct tension. He stepped over one of the black bags and headed to the living room where he found both of his parents sitting in silence. They were awaiting his arrival and did not look pleased. Justin did not think twice about their sour faces, as it was a common greeting. His parents did not approve of his lifestyle, and quite frankly, Justin did not care.

He still felt a little dizzy from consuming alcohol into the early morning hours. He stopped drinking by 5 a.m., not enough time to completely sober up. Justin hoped to grab a big glass of juice from the fridge and then pass out in his bed, face up, to recover from the festivities of the night before. This plan was not to be executed.

As he walked past the parental units, they called out his name. Justin just proceeded to ignore them and headed to the kitchen.

"Justin, your father and I need to talk to you … now!" His mother's voice was harsh.

He was not in the mood to listen to their nagging. Their constant opinion of his life put a damper on his lifestyle. Justin wished they would let him live and keep their noses out of his personal affairs. He kept walking past them and proceeded to the fridge to get a glass of the juice he was craving. After finishing the beverage, he placed the dirty glass into the sink and returned to the living area.

Something told him he should listen to what the folks had to say. He figured it would be the same speech they gave him at least once a night. They would talk about how they did not approve of his lifestyle of partying all night and underage drinking. They would discuss his future and how he should get a job. He needed to accomplish something, make something of himself. Blah. Blah. Blah. Blah.

Justin would sit there and pretend to listen. He would nod in agreement and promise to make a valiant effort to get a job. He may even get the class registration pamphlet from the local community college to pretend he considered taking some useless courses toward a degree.

As Justin faced his parents, he saw them sitting with their arms crossed across their chests.

"Your mother and I have been doing some thinking." His father always started off this way.

As his old man spoke, he looked at them. Something was very different about this conversation. His mother would not look in his direction. Her eyes were swollen and red.

"We think it's time for you to move out," his dad continued.

"Sure, Dad. As soon as I find a place."

"No, I don't think you understand." His father sounded scared to say these words. "Your mother and I want you to leave now, as in today."

What? Justin did not believe his parents had it in them to kick him out.

"We took the liberty of packing your things for you already." Justin realized those were his personal belongings blocking the front entranceway.

"You want me out now, as in right now?"

"Yes, now," his mother yelped.

"A little warning would have been nice." Justin proceeded to raise his voice in anger. "Fine, I will leave now. But I cannot believe you would kick your only son out on the street without a place to go."

"Justin … your father and I still love you," his mother replied.

"That is bullshit," he yelled. "If you loved me, you would let me stay here."

"Justin, such language is not used in this household," his father yelled back.

"Well, I don't live here anymore, do I? So I can say whatever the fuck I want to say, can't I?"

Justin headed toward his room. He pulled a duffel bag out of the closet. He headed back to the plastic bags strewn about the front entrance. He proceeded to pull out those items that were essential——a few t-shirts, jeans, clean socks, underwear, and his toothbrush. His duffel bag was filled to the brim. He left the other bags, half filled, where he found them. He opened the front door, placed his body on the other side, and slammed the door as hard as possible. It shook the house and bounced back open.

"Assholes!" he yelled in the street, causing an echo into the clear blue sky.

When he reached the driveway's end, he stuck his middle finger up, gesturing violently toward the house. Little did he know it would be the last time he would ever set foot in his childhood home. It would be the last time he would see his folks in person. Over the next nine years, he spoke to his parents a total of fifteen times. Usually, the exchange would be awkward. His mother would ask him where he was, if he was safe, and if he needed anything. The conversation never lasted longer than ten minutes. His father seldom came to the phone.

Justin never forgave his parents for kicking him out that warm spring day. By no means did he deserve that kind of treatment. Your parents were supposed to be there for you unconditionally. Kicking him out was cowardly. His parents did not want to deal with him, so they told him to leave.

Justin did not feel he was worse than his peers. Sure, he went out drinking most evenings until the sun came up. He smoked a few joints on those nights he was not drinking. He never came in before 4 a.m. He slept most of the next day away until it was time for the sun to set and start the party all over again. What did his parents think college students did? They stayed up all night partying four or five times a week. Only they had it worse off because they had to sit through boring classes while nursing hangovers. Even then, half did not bother to make it to the lectures. As long as they got the class notes, usually on file at the campus library, they could prepare for the final exam and ace the course with flying colors. It seemed to Justin the only difference between him and a college grad was a degree earned through their parents' money.

School was not for him, and his parents did not understand. He was doing just fine. Justin did not need a 'real' job. He performed odd tasks to secure enough money for his booze and weed habit. When it ran out, he would work a day or two until he had enough funds to begin the binge drinking once more. He cleaned out schools, worked in construction, landscaping, trash hauling, and even the occasional dishwashing at a local restaurant when the immigrant worker did not show up.

His parents did not find this behavior acceptable. Either they would have a son who was an upstanding citizen, or they would disown him. He had enough of their conservative ways. Justin decided if they did not want him in their home, then he would not return, and this was a promise he kept.

It was fine for a few weeks. At first, Justin stayed with his friend Gary. Gary had his own pad. Justin usually spent most of his time there anyway, but Gary quickly grew tired of Justin's mooching. Justin slept on the couch, did not clean up after himself, and ate most of Gary's food. It did not take long for some hurtful words to be exchanged, and Justin found himself back on the street.

With no place to turn, he knew there was one woman in his life who would not turn him away. He remembers the exact day he called her. Justin had just enough money to make this phone call. If she did not answer or did not want him in her home, he would be no worse off. Justin reached deep down into the pockets of the jeans he was wearing. He brought out a quarter, three nickels, and four dimes. On the corner in front of him was a pay phone. He picked up the receiver, placed the money into the slot provided, and dialed the number he had memorized since he was five. The phone rang four times on the other end before a lady picked up.

"Hello, Nana, it's your grandson Justin." He fought to keep the tears at bay as he spoke to his grandmother.

She sounded surprised to hear his voice and wanted to know where he was. Justin was sure she had a million unanswered questions. There was no time for chit-chat as the money inserted was only enough for a single three-minute phone call. Justin quickly got to the point and asked her if he could come and stay with her until he figured things out. Without even a second of hesitation, she agreed to let him come to her. She told him she would wire him some money through the nearest Western Union, and he could ride the bus to her home outside Suffern, New York.

The bus ride was the longest twelve hours of Justin's life. He was anxious to get there and see Grandma Devlin. He had not seen her since he was thirteen. His mother had a falling out with her. Justin was unsure of the circumstances that led to the feud, but he knew it was bad enough for his mother to disown her——a typical response from his mom. She was a coward——always running from situations and relationships rather than sticking it out to try and mend the not-so-perfect relations.

Grandma Devlin was the person Justin looked up to. She was a strong woman, full of life. She understood him and all the decisions that he made, whether good or bad. She always stood by him. She even continued to send him birthday cards in the mail despite her daughter's disapproval. His mother did not approve of the relationship between them, but then again, his mother approved of nothing he did in life.

As the bus pulled into the depot, he saw Nana standing by the curb, awaiting his arrival. She beamed as she saw him step off the bus and onto the sidewalk. Justin walked over toward her and embraced her in his arms. It felt nice to be in the company of someone who appreciated him.

The drive to her home was about twenty minutes. When they arrived, he found a quaint ranch set in a suburban neighborhood. Nana made up the guest room for him to stay. Justin dropped his bag on the bed and tried to make himself comfortable. She resided in a one-story, three-bedroom home. His grandmother used to live with her husband, the man she married after divorcing his grandfather. They were only married three years before he suffered a heart attack and passed away suddenly. Since that time, Nana lived alone in this quiet residential neighborhood. Justin imagined she must be lonely living in this town without family or friends. He smiled at the thought that he could provide companionship for his beloved Nana.

As he showered, his grandmother prepared a glorious meal for dinner. That night, Justin ate the greatest meal ever served. She outdid herself. There was turkey, yams, string beans, mashed potatoes, carrots, salad, and homemade tapioca pudding for dessert. Justin knew he made the right decision by calling her for help.

Several weeks passed, three months to be exact. Justin settled right into the home of Nana. Justin did not have a job, though he did not make much effort to secure one. He would sleep until 2 p.m., wake up, turn on the television, and waste the day away until it was time to eat dinner. Justin missed having friends he could party with all night until the wee hours of the next morning. This made his life very boring. He craved drinking. He craved staying up all night. He craved companionship with people his age. Sure, he loved his grandma, but did not have much in common with a woman in her late sixties.

As the time passed, he felt he was overstaying his welcome. Nana would start to leave hints around the house. She would buy the daily newspaper and slide the 'Help Wanted' section underneath his bedroom door while he slept. Occasionally, she would even circle some of the jobs with a red marker. Justin never called those places.

On the contrary, he never even looked through the section for a job. Why would he need a job? He was living a free ride. His grandmother footed the bills, did his laundry, cooked his meals, and made his bed. There was no reason for him to overexert himself any more than he had to. He did not feel the least bit guilty about this at all.

Then, one evening, things changed. Nana had cooked another one of her glorious meals for dinner. As Justin sat across from her at the table in the kitchen, she peered across at him and laid down an ultimatum.

"Justin, darling." This would not be a conversation he wanted to hear. "You're going to have to start contributing to this household."

He did not know what to say in response to her, so he placed his fork down on the side of his plate and stared back at her, speechless.

"I'm a retired lady. You know I'd do anything for you, but I can't financially support the both of us at this stage in my life. If you want to stay here any longer, which I am more than happy to have you do, you must find a job and help out."

It was nothing new and shocking to him. He knew that, eventually, his welcome would be overstayed. Justin had two options. First, either get a job or, second, move out and find a new person to mooch off of. Unlike his parents, he valued Nana's opinion of him. He did not want to let her down. The more he thought about it, the more he thought he could get a job. At least it would give him something to do during the day and provide him with some contacts his age.

"Sure, Nana. I'll look for a job."

Maybe the months of sobriety led him to agree to this. Grandma Devlin was the one person in his life he did not want to disappoint.

As agonizing as it was, Justin headed out to begin the search for gainful employment the next morning. He never had to do this once in his entire lifespan of nineteen years. Justin had no idea how hard it would be. He thought he could walk into the first place he found, and they would hire him immediately. He could not be more wrong. Justin went to ten different places that first day and was shunned by all of them. It was not looking good. He was disappointed. His whole life, things came easy, and people were willing to give him anything he wanted without much of a struggle. This was not the life he was used to.

Several weeks went by, and still, there was no employment to be found. He was letting Nana down and was scared she would not put up with his shenanigans much longer. For the first time in his life, he was trying to do something. For the first time in his life, he was failing. It did not feel good. Justin felt shameful as he sat across from Nana at the dinner table.

"Honey, I ran into Ms. Patterson at the market this morning. She indicated that her son … you know Brad? Anyways, he got a job driving one of those big trucks you see on the highway."

Nana meant well, but Justin could not see himself as a truck driver. As she spoke, Nana slid a piece of paper across the table in his direction. It was the phone number of a contact at a company called NATCO. All he had to do was call the number, and then an interview would be set up for him.

"Just think about it," she said as she saw the disdainful look across his face.

That is exactly what Justin did. He thought about it. He thought about it for days and weeks. The number sat there on the table next to his bed. He wanted to call it, but something deep in his stomach held him back.

Then, one day, his life changed with a single phone call. The phone in the house rang. Nana had run out to the store, and Justin was the only one home. After weeks of disappointment, he had fallen back into his old habits. He would stay up all night and sleep all day. Justin groggily got out of bed to answer the phone as it was 11 a.m., and he still had at least three more hours of slumber before him.

"Hello," he said in a groggy morning voice.

"Justin Enrel, please." He tried to think who would call him on the home line as he never gave the number to anyone.

"This is Deborah Meyers from the NATCO Corporation, and we wanted to know if you had some time today to come down to our headquarters in Suffern for an interview."

Justin was shocked. It was the company Nana had given him the number to, but never called. She went behind his back and told them to call. This enraged Justin. He could feel the anger fermenting in his stomach. He did not want to be a truck driver.

"Today?" It was all he could think of in response.

"Any time this afternoon would be great. Just ask for me when you get here; thanks."

Before Justin could say anything else, the woman on the other end of the phone was gone, and all he could hear was the recorded operator's voice telling him to 'check the number and dial again.' The lady hung up.

"Great," Justin thought out loud.

Although he did not want to attend the interview, he felt he had to. Sure, Justin could ignore the phone call, go back to sleep, and move along with his life. There was something, however, holding him back from doing so. He could not pinpoint exactly why he felt the need to go for the interview, but decided it was in his best interest.

At 3 p.m., Justin arrived at the NATCO headquarters. He met with a man whose name slipped right over his head. Justin could not recall his name for the entire interview. His charm worked, and the interviewer liked what he heard and saw because he was offered a job as a truck driver right on the spot. Justin could not believe his ears. He had a job offer as a truck driver, and the benefits were amazing.

Justin enjoyed the life of a trucker. This shocked him more than anybody else. For once in his life, he had gainful employment, which he enjoyed. It was a job he would keep for the next nine years. Little did he know how life-altering this job would be.

There was a rigorous six-week-long training session. He obtained his commercial driver's license from the department of motor vehicles and started working short shifts. They started all the newbies on the shorter rides to get them used to the hauling, gradually easing them into the longer hours on the road. Soon enough, he was driving longer distances. Justin loved the drive. It enabled him to think about his life, the course it had taken, and all that had gotten him to that very point. He started on smaller routes. That lasted for three months, during which he learned how to log his work hours, and his miles, keep track of his cargo, and most importantly, how to handle the eighteen-wheeler.

There were nine other men in his class of truck drivers. Justin got to know the group rather well. For the first time since he arrived at Nana's house, he felt a part of a crowd. Justin was the youngest driver by five years, but he enjoyed their company. There was one woman, but she tended to keep to herself during the classes. Some of the men were single, and some had families to go back home to. Justin could not imagine choosing a career as a truck driver and then leaving his family alone for weeks at a time while he traveled the highways alone.

Before the end of the training course, each of them was given a radio handle. This was the name that they would use as they traveled along the roads. The basic rule of thumb: never use your real name. Justin decided his handle would be 'Raging Bull.' It fit him well. A man by the name of Rick came up with it. He always told Justin that he knew Justin was quiet on the outside, but deep down inside, a fiery pit of anger awaited. Justin was not quite sure what he was angry at. He knew he was still angry at his parents, but that was not the full source of all his anger. Some days, he was angry just to be angry.

In total, there were about one hundred and fifty employees at NATCO. Justin genuinely enjoyed being a part of this group. Each night, after a long day of lectures and notes on rules and regulations, they would meet at the bar around the corner to throw back a few drinks. These bonds of friendship were important in the industry. As he traveled the interstates of the United States, he would come across the drivers. They would chat on the radio, meet at the truck stops, and even plan gambling excursions in Reno, Deadwood, or Vegas.

It was the perfect life of debauchery Justin craved. Plus, he was making money, which made him and his grandmother happy. However, Justin had no idea what was happening behind the scenes at this company. He did not suspect a thing. He stumbled upon it one day by accident. It proved to be a fatal accident.

As Justin obtained a consistent income stream, he realized the power of money. The more he earned, the more powerful he felt. He would show his parents, support his grandmother, and financially be more successful than his corporate sister.

Justin did not meet Peter Lugo until he worked at the company for three years. He spent those three years driving the truck back and forth from Suffern to Los Angeles. It was Justin's main route, and he had the landscape for the 3,000-mile drive memorized. The number of miles logged was too numerous to count, though if they had frequent travel miles for truckers, he would have three free trips around the world and back.

It was a crisp fall day, and Justin had just returned from the West Coast. He checked his truck into the main cargo lot and logged the miles and gas used. Peter Lugo was inspecting the truck in the hanger next to his. Although Justin had never met him, he knew exactly who he was. After all, Peter Lugo was the most powerful person at NATCO. He was the owner, the man who made the company what it was. He built the company up from bankruptcy to the million-dollar corporation it is today. His picture was hanging in the main lobby of the corporate headquarters and was on the front of every manual provided to all truck drivers.

"How are you today, Mr. Enrel?" Mr. Lugo addressed Justin as he walked past him.

Justin froze in his tracks. Peter Lugo was speaking to him. Not only was he speaking to him, but he also addressed him by name. Then again, that is smart business. Justin was sure Peter Lugo made it a point to memorize what his drivers looked like and their full, middle, and last names. Just in case he ran across them during the course of his day.

"How was the trip this week?"

Justin liked this man more and more. There was a unique, likable quality about him. Be it schmoozing or not, Justin appreciated the attention.

"The weather on I-80 was good this week, though I am sure the winter weather will be here sooner than anticipated."

Peter Lugo grinned. "I like you, Mr. Enrel. Keep your head up. You'll go far in this company."

Peter patted Justin on the back and walked out of the truck garage. It was a brief encounter with the CEO, but it was a memorable one.

That night, Justin could not wait to discuss his meeting with some of the boys over drinks at Dirty Sally's, the local pub around the corner from the NATCO headquarters. A local bar—dirty and dingy inside, a total dive, but every NATCO driver frequented it. An unwritten rule after your return shift, you had to stop in the bar for at least one drink. There was a hundred percent probability you would run into a colleague who just got back in town.

Sure enough, when Justin walked into the bar, there, sitting on a stool talking to the bartender was Earl Peterman, handle name 'Dirty Vegas.' Earl was an older gentleman, on the hefty side, roundly built, with a smile that lit up the room. His handle was a perfect match. Peterman was a loner, lived by himself, and whenever his truck route took him anywhere near a casino, there was always a lost day due to some unforeseen event. However, every trucker knew that unforeseen event was an extra few hours at the craps table.

"Raging Bull, how was your latest trip?" He placed his hand in the air, and they slapped palms in a gesture of hello.

"It was pretty uneventful," Justin stated as he nodded to the bartender that he wanted a beer from the tap. Justin sat down next to Vegas, and they engaged in unimportant conversation. They talked about the California coast, the weather, the prostitute at the rest stop on I-80, and why they were glad to be back in New York.

"Vegas, have you ever met Lugo?" Justin inquired.

"Yeah, several times." Earl looked uncomfortable talking about his encounters with Mr. Lugo to Justin. "Why do you ask?"

"Well, I met him for the first time before coming here. I was quite shocked that he knew who I was. I mean, he knew my name and everything."

"Peter Lugo is a dangerous man." Justin was shocked by this response. "He is powerful, more powerful than you know. Did he ask you to do any special assignments for him?"

"Assignments?" The more they spoke, the more intrigued Justin became.

"There is an exclusive team that runs special cargo."

Justin did not understand. "How do you know this? Are you on the exclusive team?"

Peterman did not answer. He hung his head low over his beer and just stared into his glass. Justin would not let the conversation end here.

"You are. You're on the exclusive team. How'd you get to be on one of these special teams? Do you get paid more? What's the cargo?" Justin's eyes widened with each word spoken.

"STOP!" Vegas yelled loudly. The other patrons in the bar were staring at them. "Stop," he stated in a lower, calmer voice. "You need to stop. It's not something we should discuss or that anybody should know exists. Just drop it. It's not something that you want to be a part of."

Justin let it go——for the moment.

It was obvious Earl did not want to discuss the secretive operation. There was no way, however, Justin was going to drop it. He would do his best to discover who else was involved with the exclusive cargo. Who else knew about it, and how could he become a part of it? If it meant more pay, power, and a closer relationship to Mr. Lugo, then Justin needed it.

Justin spent the next part of his career trying to find out about the secret operatives. This stubborn persistence led to his demise.

It would be another four years before Justin discovered the special cargo. Sometimes, he was obvious with his questions; other times, he was not. Justin would work Peter Lugo into his conversations with other truckers any which way he could. He knew enough never to bring it up in front of Dirty Vegas.

Then, one day, Justin discovered the truth, all on his own. There was another man who worked for NATCO named Henry Wasserman. He was a loner and did not make friends with any of the other employees. He never came to office holiday parties or happy hours at the end of a shift. Henry made it a point not to speak one word to any of his colleagues. His handle was 'Silent Mule,' though <u>Justin</u> was unsure Henry was even aware this was his handle as the man never once spoken on the radio during his travels. There was an air of mystery surrounding Henry Wasserman.

It was a sunny Thursday morning. Justin was checking in to gather his cargo for the next trip, this time out to Utah. Henry was there loading the truck next to his. Not as much as a 'good morning' exchanged between them. Henry headed inside, and Justin could not help himself. As Henry headed inside the headquarters, Justin climbed into the back of the truck bed and snooped around. Not certain what it was he was looking for, but certain he would know what it was once he found it.

He did not hear Henry walk into the truck. Justin was too busy staring at what he found. There in front of him was a box full of rectangular aluminum-wrapped packages. They were not marked, but Justin had enough crackhead friends to know this was heroin. He grabbed one and touched it. It was as if he would not believe it was there unless he could feel the aluminum texture on his fingertips.

"What do you think you are doing?"

Although Justin had never heard the man's voice before, he was certain it was Henry Wasserman. Looking up, Justin found an incredibly angry and irate Henry Wasserman standing before him. Justin could not even think. He could not speak a word. He simply placed the package down where he found it and made his way out of the back of the truck.

Justin tried to process what just happened. Did he stumble upon heroin drug smuggling? Was NATCO trafficking drugs? He had a hunch his company participated in secretive transporting, but he had no idea it was narcotics. He thought it was a specialized class of truck drivers authorized to transport such hazmat as liquid nitrogen. He had no idea it was an illegal operation. Justin was dumbfounded. He did not know what to do. He decided his best option was to continue the job as if nothing had ever happened, as if he had never snooped around the back of Henry Wasserman's truck. It was too risky. He did not want anyone to know what he knew.

Justin headed into the central office to collect his checklist and be cleared to head out on the road. Jimmy, second in command to Lugo, was in charge of clearing all the drivers before they went out with a new shipment. Jimmy must have noticed Justin appeared a little spacey because he stared at him uncomfortably. All Justin wanted to do was to get out on the road as quickly as possible. He needed to get away from the Suffern headquarters. The fresh air of the road would help him clear his head and decipher his newfound knowledge.

Jimmy checked the list and made Justin run to the back store-room to get a new fire extinguisher. The location of the back warehouse could not be further, but the quicker he got the new fire extinguisher, the faster he could get on the road.

Finally, he was ready to leave. Justin sat in the driver's seat and headed onto the highway, west toward Pennsylvania. He merged into the oncoming traffic and pushed the gas to the floor to get the truck to highway speed.

Justin must have been engrossed in his thoughts about drugs and NATCO because he did not see the silver Mazda cut him off. As he tried to stop from rear-ending into the back of the car, the brakes failed. He pressed down, but there was no deceleration of his current speed. On the contrary, he was gaining speed in defiance of Newton's law of physics. To avoid a messy back-end collision with the car before him, Justin instinctively veered to the right. The truck jerked and slammed head-on into the cement overpass as the back end swerved to the left behind it. It came to a rest on its side, twisted about the four-lane highway. The front end compacted like an accordion waiting to be pulled out for the next chord.

It was a miracle there was only one fatality. The police reported no other injuries.

CHAPTER FIFTY-THREE

PETERMAN-Earl, 56, of Watertown, NY, on September 4, 2002. Formerly of San Francisco, CA. Survived by his sister, Margaret Stevens. Funeral Mass at St. Paul Episcopal Church on River Avenue in Yorktown Heights 10 am Fri.

Earl never imagined he would be affected this way. He never thought about what he agreed to do. It was harmless, really. It is not like he was forcing the drugs down the throats of the young children of the world. He was simply transporting them. He was not making the drugs, nor selling them. He was just driving them from point A to point B.

In his mind, Earl rationalized away the potential danger he placed upon society. He never thought about it, for if he had, he would not have been able to do it. He would be too guilt-ridden, and he needed the money more than he needed the guilt. Perhaps if he had been raised as an Irish Catholic, the guilt would not have seemed as bad, as they are born filled with a guilty conscious about everything they do in life. Earl, however, did not want any remorse. It was not until one morning in August that his guilt kicked in, and he did not see it coming.

Earl had been driving the same route for fifteen years. He would go from Suffern to San Francisco. A route he travelled twice a month. He was a familiar face to all the stops along the way. People generally liked him, and some even looked forward to his presence.

The waitress at the Truck Stop Diner off Route 80 in Iowa had become fond of Earl. He was fond of her, too. He even developed a schoolboy crush on her. She was the first and last person he saw on his trips west with a truck full of cargo. Her name was Josephine, Josie for short. She was not beautiful in the traditional sense, but still, there was an undeniable chemistry between them. She had messy, dirty brown hair and a thick Midwestern drawl. She was polite and vibrant. Earl looked forward to each of their meetings.

"Hiya, Earl."

Before he could even take his coat off to sit at the counter, she had a mug filled with coffee waiting for him. They would strike up casual conversation for the next two hours. She was the only person he ever opened up to about his life. Josie was kind and nonjudgmental. For some reason unknown to Earl, he could talk to her freely. Maybe it was because there was a sense of detachment with her. He knew he only saw her twice a month, and she did not know anyone he spoke about. She never met any other truckers, his sister, or his nephew in San Francisco and had never been to the small town where he resided.

"You got any special side trips planned for this outing?"

"Gonna stop for two days in Deadwood. There's a Wheel of Fortune slot machine calling my name."

She just smiled at his remarks. Josie knew he loved to gamble. She just had no idea how much he loved to gamble. So much so that he was thousands of dollars in debt. It was an addiction. He knew he should not continue to bet the money, but it was all he looked forward to. He never married in life and never had any children of his own. Earl knew this was partly due to his uncontrollable gambling problem. He was on a first-name basis with the bookies and was always in debt to them. No matter how much money he won, he would always be in debt. With the money he wasted in casinos, he would have been better off just setting a pile of hundred-dollar bills up in flames.

This addiction was why he agreed to join the HOT Team at NATCO that day Peter Lugo asked.

"Earl, you're the longest-standing employee at this company. Your loyalty is unbeatable, and I'd love to reward you for your dedication. I want to present you with an opportunity to make it further in this company and make some extra cash. However, I have to tell you it may not be an easy decision for you to make, and before I tell you what it involves, you have to take an oath of secrecy, for once you know about this special operation team, there is no turning back."

The initial statement intrigued him. Earl did not have to think twice about it. All Mr. Lugo had to say was there was an opportunity to make some extra cash, and he knew he wanted to be a part of it. If Earl could score some extra income, he would be able to pay off his debt and live comfortably. Only that was a dream. The extra money did not bring happiness, just more debt.

At first, Earl did not want to traffic heroin. But once he agreed, he could not turn his back on the invite. Earl was mad at himself for agreeing to truck the forbidden shipment, but after the first payment of fifty thousand dollars cash, it was all worth it. He used the funds to pay off his bookie. For the first time in twenty years, Earl was debt-free. This lack of money owed only lasted a few days——eight to be exact. As soon as he was sent back to San Francisco, he was in the casino. With this new amount of money, Earl could make higher bets, which meant higher losses. He quickly found himself in insurmountable debt again——a debt he would never be able to repay no matter how much money he earned.

Earl sat in the diner sipping his coffee. He thought about his debt, the mess he had gotten into, and how it would be this way for the rest of his life. He would live like this with a black cloud hanging over his head until his last dying day.

"Earl, you're always at the casino. You got any other plans on the road other than listening to the chiming of the slot machines?"

"I plan to stop in the Bay Area to see my sister and her son Christopher."

Josie smiled. She knew that Earl was excited to see them. Christopher was his godson, the closest thing to having his own offspring. Earl thought of him as his own kin and would do anything for that child.

"How old is Christopher these days?"

"He's just nineteen. I remember when he was ten years old. I tell you, they grow up so fast."

"They sure do, they sure do." She spoke as if she remembered children of her own who used to be young.

Earl had no idea if Josie had any children. He had no idea if she was married. He never got into the personal details of Josie's existence. He made it a point to remain detached from her personal life. Earl did not want to be involved. Knowing about her life made her a person worth knowing, and Earl did not want to know anybody.

That was one of the last normal conversations Earl had before his life was altered forever. If he had known Josie would be the last person he would converse with, he would have put in more effort. Earl had no idea his life would perpetually change once he got to San Francisco.

Five days later, he arrived in the Bay Area. Earl spent two nights in Deadwood and then drove through the wee hours of the morning to make up for lost time and ensure the secret shipment arrived in Wyoming on time. He knew the men with whom he dropped off the aluminum packages but did not feel anything toward them one way or the other. It was not his job to judge. They were businessmen. Most citizens would view these men's morals as corrupt and evil. But those same people would view the process of transporting the drugs to be just as evil. Earl did not see it that way. He was detached from most of the process. He did not know what happened to the heroin before it got into his truck. Earl also did not know what happened to the heroin when it got to Wyoming. He preferred it that way. The less he knew, the better.

"Hi bro, how was the trip?"

Earl was close with his sister. She was three years younger and always looked up to him. He enjoyed seeing her and her son. They were the only family he had left. Their mother passed when they were in their early twenties, and neither remembered their father, as he had walked out on them when Margaret was just a few months old.

His sister did not have the easiest life. Margaret grew up with only her brother and their mom. She was devastated when their mother died. Margaret became depressed and dropped out of college in her sophomore year, unable to deal with her grief and the pressure of classes. Margaret never made it back to finish her degree. Then, at the young age of twenty-one, she met the love of her life, Brian Stevens. The two quickly grew fond of each other and were married within a year and a half after meeting. They moved to a nice suburban household in the Bay Area, where she now resided.

As if her life had not been hard enough, the unthinkable happened. One night, fourteen years into their marriage, Brian was murdered. He was in the wrong place at the wrong time. Brian stopped at a convenience store on his way home for a quick snack and a lotto ticket. A strung-out druggy walked into the store right after him, with a gun and a desire for whatever cash was in the register. The cashier behind the counter was unwilling to relinquish the funds without a fight. There was a struggle for the gun between them, only neither of them faced the bullet when it went off. Brian took a direct hit to the heart and was killed instantaneously.

Earl remembered the night he got the phone call from his sister. He thought of his nephew Christopher, who was eleven years old then. Earl knew he would have to be there for both of them. It was the only time he took off during his entire employment at

NATCO. Earl flew to San Francisco for three weeks and stayed by their side.

The funeral was sad. It was packed with friends and family. Brian was young, merely thirty-six years old. A pure tragedy. Nobody should have to face such events in their lifetime. Again, Margaret was left alone, only this time she had a son to raise. Earl knew she would need the help. He made a pact to be there for her and stopped off every time his job took him to San Francisco. This was at least once a month.

He looked forward to seeing them each time. They were his family. They were all he had. Earl loved Christopher as if he was his own son. He watched him grow from a little boy into a young man. Earl was the prominent male figure in his nephew's life. He wanted to be a positive role model in Christopher's development.

Over the past few months, he had seen a change in his nephew's demeanor. He did not think it was anything serious. Adolescents are occasionally moody and grumpy. Still, it was disheartening to see Christopher change from the young boy who would run out of the front door to greet him, running wide-armed into his uncle's arms. Now Earl barely got a 'hello' from the boy. Half the time, he did not even come forward when Earl was there. And, if he was there, he spent the biggest part of the visit watching television or locked away in his room.

One night, on his last trip to San Francisco, Earl discovered the root of his nephew's problem. He stumbled upon it accidentally.

The weather that evening was unseasonably cool. The clock next to the nightstand read 3:37 a.m. It had been a restless night; Earl had been tossing and turning and was struggling to sleep. This was not unusual, as frequently Earl faced bouts of insomnia. He often sat up late at night on the couch watching mindless television, unable to close his eyes and rest. Insomnia did not bother him; it was the perfect disease for a truck driver. His job required him to remain wide awake for prolonged periods, so the inability to sleep was almost a blessing to get him through his long travels on the interstates. He was happy not to have the opposite problem, for narcolepsy would be disastrous to his career.

That night, he was not worried about his inability to sleep as it was part of his routine. Earl was tired of tossing and turning, pretending slumber was around the corner. He pulled back the covers to the bed and placed both feet on the ground. It was time to entertain himself with some mindless television watching. He would watch the tube, but at three in the morning, there was little programming. Most of it was infomercials and really bad C-list movies. If Earl were lucky, he could catch a re-run of some of his favorite sitcoms from the 1950s.

Earl slowly opened the door to his guest bedroom and headed into the hallway. He tiptoed past his sister's room, careful not to wake her. Earl proceeded past the bedroom door to his nephew's room. It was wide open, and his nephew was not sleeping in his bed. This alarmed Earl, but he figured his nephew would return soon. Who knew what he was doing gallivanting about the town in the wee hours of the morning?

True, he was not Christopher's father, but he still felt concern for his nephew's well-being. Earl figured Christopher would be home any minute, and he would be fine. He would see him walk through the door, trying to be all sneaky and quiet. Earl would be sitting in the living room watching television. From the couch placement in the room, Earl would have a full view of the front door when his nephew arrived. Christopher would not be able to avoid him. He would see Earl as soon as he opened the front door.

Earl would not lecture the boy, but he would be sure to make him feel guilty for staying out all hours of the night. The boy, after all, was nineteen and able to handle himself. Still, a young man under twenty-one had nowhere to be this late at night. Anyplace he remained was sure to bring trouble.

Earl turned on the television and turned the volume to a whisper so as to not disturb his sleeping sister. He was in luck, the episode presenting itself to Earl was a classic. The main character had gotten herself into some shenanigans with her best friend, and her husband was going to have to bail them out. Earl had to try to remember to contain his laughter inside.

CLANK!

Earl's amusement was interrupted by a loud crash emanating from the house. Earl was not sure if he was imagining the noise or if it was real. He muted the television and sat still on the couch. His ears perked up, listening intently for any noise to follow.

There was nothing but silence.

Even though all was quiet in the house, Earl felt uneasy. The little hairs on his arms were standing upright. Something was not right. Bravery was not something Earl prided himself on having. Society had made it the man's job to kill the spiders, catch the mice, and search the house with a baseball bat for intruders late at night. As much as Earl wanted to run screaming into the back of the house toward his sister Margaret's room, he had no choice but to investigate the mysterious sound himself.

"It's nothing. Probably just a squirrel." Earl spoke out loud in a calm voice to convince himself everything would be alright.

Earl turned off the television and sat on the couch in the dark. It took a minute for his eyes to adjust to the darkness. There in the room across from him was the fireplace. Earl noticed an array of tools on a stand, designed to help with the fire. He walked over and grabbed one that had a sharp, pointed end. It was made of iron and would provide enough weighted force if swung in the direction of an unwanted intruder.

Then he heard another sound. This one was not as loud and was more of a human whimper than the crash that previously resonated through the room.

Earl stood in front of the fireplace and tried to decipher the location of the sound. It appeared to be coming from the bathroom off the kitchen. He grabbed the fire tool in a position over his left shoulder to swing it if needed and quietly approached the noise. When he got near the bathroom, the door was closed. He slowly turned the knob, but it was locked. Earl pressed his left ear to the door and strained to listen for another sound to come from behind it. There was muffled movement coming from the other side. Earl tried to turn the doorknob once more. It was definitely locked.

Earl knocked calmly as if it was normal for a complete stranger to have locked himself in the bathroom. "Is everything alright in there?"

No response.

Again, he knocked, more forcefully the second time around. "Are you alright?"

No answer.

Earl was positive it was not his imagination. The sound was coming from the other side of the locked door. Whoever was in the bathroom did not belong there and needed some help. Earl had no choice but to try and knock down the door.

Noise was no longer an issue. Earl forgot about his sleeping sister. Adrenaline fed his actions. Earl placed the fire tool he acquired onto the floor. He took his left shoulder and charged the door, trying to bust it off its hinges. The force was not great enough. It took at least six tries. Finally, the door caved in. Earl was not prepared for what he found on the other side.

He stood there on the door threshold, paralyzed, unsure what to do next. Seconds flew by without any action. He was so stunned he did not hear his sister come up behind him.

"Is everything alright? What's all the commotion? Earl, what is goi..." she stopped midsentence——shocked by the image presented.

"Call an ambulance, Margaret ... CALL AN AMBULANCE." Without uttering another word, she ran to the kitchen and dialed 9-1-1.

Earl suddenly snapped out of his trance and ran into the bathroom. There before him was his nephew Christopher. He was lying on the cold tiles of the bathroom floor, surrounded by a pool of blood, his head cracked open. From how his body was positioned, it was obvious his skull had hit the porcelain toilet bowl on its way down to the ground, knocking him unconscious. Christopher's body was shaking and convulsing in spasmatic twitches, his mouth foaming as if he were a rabid-infested dog.

In the sink was the culprit of Christopher's condition. There was a spoon, a needle, and a bag of white powder, which Earl recognized immediately as heroin. A thick rubber band was placed tightly around Christopher's left forearm, cutting off circulation and causing pronounced veins.

Earl ran toward his nephew's lifeless body and cradled his head in his lap. The blood was still gushing from his skull. Without thinking, Earl removed his shirt and wrapped it around his nephew's head to try and stop the bleeding. It did not take long for the shirt to be soaked through. Earl knelt on the floor, trying to make Christopher aware of his surroundings.

"Stay with us, Christopher. Help is on the way. They'll be here shortly."

His nephew's eyes rolled into the back of his brain. He was not able to speak or communicate. Earl just held the young man and prayed for help to arrive quickly.

It took fifteen minutes for the paramedics to arrive. The emergency workers rushed to the door and tried their best to resuscitate Christopher. They performed CPR and lifted his body onto a stretcher into the back of the ambulance. Earl and Margaret followed the flashing vehicle to Metropolitan Hospital and waited patiently in the Emergency Room's waiting area. They waited, embracing each other, while the doctors tried to work their magic.

Four hours passed, and the doctor came to tell them the unwelcome news. All he had to say was, "I am so sorry."

They knew the worst had come true. Margaret burst out in hysterics, and Earl stood there in the middle of the hospital hallway, embracing his sister. He, too, had tears streaming down his cheeks, but he had to be strong for her.

Earl called Peter Lugo to let him know he would not return to New York anytime soon due to a death in the family, though he dared not tell his boss the death was due to an overdose. He was understanding. Peter Lugo told him to take as much time as he needed.

The funeral was harder than Earl anticipated. The wake was packed——typical when such a young life is taken away so tragically. Margaret did her best to maintain a smile and shook every hand that walked through the funeral parlor doors. Earl was amazed at her strength.

The real test for Earl and Margaret would be in the weeks after the chaos of the wake and burial. Earl stayed in town for fourteen days following the death. He wished he could stay longer. He hated leaving his sister alone. She was strong and resilient. He knew she would be all right for the time being. Earl was going to figure out a way to make this all okay.

Leaving California, that last time, was the hardest trip home Earl ever had to take. It was the longest drive of his life. He did not stop except to go to the bathroom and grab a quick sandwich at the convenience stores along the route. He did not want to be on the road any longer.

Earl could not shake the sight of his nephew lying on the bathroom floor, convulsing. Christopher overdosed on heroin. Earl felt responsible. He was responsible for giving his nephew the drugs. He trafficked the drugs to the West Coast. Somehow, those drugs made their way into the hands of his nephew. Earl had no way of knowing if they were the same drugs he shipped in his truck, but he blamed himself. He blamed himself for shipping the drugs, blamed himself for not seeing the warning signs of his withdrawn nephew, and blamed himself for not getting into the bathroom sooner to help him. It was all his fault. Earl would never be the same.

At that precise moment, Earl wanted out of the HOT team at NATCO. He would no longer be willing and able to transport the illegal narcotics. Earl was responsible for his nephew's death, which he would have to live with for the rest of his life. No amount of money was worth that cross he bore.

Earl knew Peter Lugo would not take his renouncement of trafficking drugs lightly, but he naively wished there would be some understanding. Peter Lugo was a charismatic boss with a soulless heart. If you crossed him in any way, he would ensure your demise. When Earl accepted his position on the HOT team, he had been warned there was no leaving. Once he made the decision to know about the smuggling, he was in it for life.

At the time, his decision was an easy one, based solely on monetary greed. Earl never imagined a scenario that could convince him otherwise. Never say never, as not an ounce of his being would ever partake in the drug operation again. The guilt and remorse he felt for his nephew's death would not allow it. Earl would try to plead with his boss to let him return to his regular truck route, without the sidebar stops in Wyoming. It was worth the ask, but he knew it would not go anywhere.

Earl knew what Peter Lugo was capable of. Peter did not know it, but Earl overheard him on the phone, two years prior, devising a plan to get rid of Justin Enrel. Earl was filling a gas container near the fuel tanks on the NATCO property when his boss walked into the garage. He knew Peter did not see him behind the various machines and thought he was alone. Peter's phone rang and Earl could hear the tension in his voice.

"Slow down, Henry. What do you mean Justin discovered the goods?"

Earl knew right away Raging Bull found someone's heroin stash. Although Justin only questioned Earl once about the secret operation, he kept pressing all of the other employees for information.

Without skipping a beat, Peter promptly hung up and dialed another number. "Jimmy, it's time to execute the plan we discussed. Send Justin to get some additional supplies for his route to buy you some time to cut his brake lines."

Earl was shocked at the ease with which Peter spoke those words. When the news broke that Justin lost control of his truck while driving down the interstate, Earl knew what really happened, and that it had been no accident.

Earl agonized over how to tell Peter Lugo of his decision. He waited three days upon returning to New York before approaching his boss. Peter reminded him of the agreement when he joined the HOT Team and that there was no backing out.

"Besides, we'll miss you at NATCO because you're one of the best drivers in the company," Lugo said, sitting back in his chair.

Earl thought this was a strange comment. He did not tell his boss he was quitting. He just did not want to be part of the secret operative team any longer.

"Take as much time as you need. Sit home and relax. It'll all be resolved soon," Mr. Lugo told Earl.

With those words, Earl knew he would face the same fate as Justin Enrel. Peter Lugo was no fool and despite any tragedy that befallen Earl, he was still a liability.

Four days later, in the afternoon, a knock came at the door of his apartment. Earl was sitting on the couch watching mindless television. He was depressed, and it was all he could bring himself to do. Television allowed him to escape the reality of his life and forget all the horrific tragedies that had recently transpired. Enough time had passed since his meeting with the boss, he started to think his life would be spared.

Earl got off the couch and went to the front door to find Jimmy standing before him.

"Mr. Lugo wanted me to see if you were okay."

"I am fine."

Never before in all his years working at NATCO did Earl know any of the bosses to make a house call. They stood there in silence in the doorway.

"Aren't you going to invite me in?"

Jimmy forced his way past Earl into the apartment and made himself comfortable on the ottoman across from the couch. Earl reluctantly sat on the couch across from his visitor.

"Jimmy, tell me why you're really here." Earl did not want to waste any time playing games.

"I wanted to change your mind about NATCO. Peter really would like you to reconsider your position on the special team. You know, it's not something easy to get out of." Earl did not like what he was hearing.

"There is no physical or emotional way I can continue. I have shown nothing but loyalty to NATCO but I can no longer be a part of the team." He was to continue with the drug trafficking or meet the fate of death for fear of leaking information. Earl knew this.

"I am sorry to hear that." Jimmy had a blank look as he spoke those six words.

Earl did not respond. He knew what was to come. Peter made it very clear once you agreed to be a part of the team, there was no way out.

As he prepared to face his death, Jimmy sat across from him with a gun drawn.

"I guess this is it then," Earl stated.

"I guess so," Jimmy stated back. "I am sorry it has to come to this."

"Were you sorry when you cut the brakes on Justin's truck?"

Earl did not fear his death. He knew he would be reunited with his nephew and mother in the afterlife. He did not want to leave his poor sister alone, but she was strong and resilient. She would survive.

Earl did not flinch when Jimmy pulled the trigger. It was a straight, painless shot, right to the head.

CHAPTER FIFTY-FOUR

Mike knew exactly where they were headed. It was the infamous cabin Gabrielle spoke about. Although he shut her down when she spoke about Cynthia's innocence, he still listened to every word she said. He loved to hear her voice. She had such passion and conviction behind her words. It was sexy seeing how passionate Gabrielle was about Cynthia's innocence.

The day she came to the Precinct threw Mike off guard, but he was happy to see her. Sure, he was upset she would not drop the private investigation, but it provided another opportunity for them to converse. Mike was hurt the day Gabrielle turned down his invite while at the bookstore. He was certain he had blown it and there was no way that a woman like Gabrielle Price could ever be interested in a bachelor like Mike Thomas. She liked bad boys—the ones with a harsh side, tattoos, and a wild edge. Mike had none of those things. He was a police officer and carried a gun on his left hip daily, but if Gabrielle knew how afraid he was of his gun, she would probably laugh in his face. Every morning, he would pray this would not be a day he needed to use his weapon.

Mike became a police officer to help people. He had a bleeding heart. He wanted to help those less fortunate than him and keep society safe from those who deviate from social norms. He had been on the job for eight years and never once drawn his weapon. Mike knew the day would come, and he was ready for it, but the thought of aiming at another human being did not thrill him.

As he followed the Python and the SUV onto the thruway, Mike tried to devise a strategic plan. He was sure they were headed to the secluded cabin. The cabin where Gabrielle allegedly saw stacks of heroin. Any doubt about the veracity of her story now subsided, and if true, then Mike needed backup.

The cabin was out of his jurisdiction. Preston is a different city, heck, a different county. There was no way any of his colleagues would travel two hours north on the thruway to assist. Mike could not radio for reinforcements; he did not even know the exact location where they were headed. This was a task, a dangerous one at that, he would have to face alone. No turning back. That was not an option. If he did not continue the pursuit, then Gabrielle would be killed. A plan of action was needed, and fast, to save Gabrielle from a fatal bullet.

CHAPTER FIFTY-FIVE

Gabrielle was uncertain what would happen when they got to the cabin, but she knew they were prolonging the inevitable: her death.

I wish they killed me while at the pier.

If only she heeded the warnings to stop her investigation.

I should have let Cynthia take the fall for the murders.

Gabrielle thought this as she sat in the back of the SUV, helpless, but she did not believe her thoughts. She would not have been able to live with herself letting an innocent woman remain in prison. Gabrielle's conscience would not let her ignore the truth, and it would eventually kill her. Either decision in life led her down the same road, impending death.

This can't be the end. This can't be the way this scenario plays out.

Gabrielle was determined to fight. She needed to know what happened that night in the Evans' household. Even if she did not live to tell another soul, she had to know the full truth before passing on.

As she thought these thoughts, the SUV slowed down and stopped completely. They had arrived at the cabin. Gabrielle's time was decreasing faster than anticipated. The driver and the passenger of the vehicle got out of the car. They did not say a word to her. They had not spoken to her the entire ride on the thruway. From the moment they got into the vehicle, they did not acknowledge Gabrielle's presence in the back of the SUV. They had to know she was there in the cargo section. She was not hiding. The driver knew of her presence as he had to stare at her every time he looked in the rearview mirror.

At any moment now, they would open the back hatch and remove her from the rear of the SUV. Gabrielle waited, but nobody came. The vehicle was parked to the side of the cabin, in seclusion, far enough away from the main operations. From her location, she could not see what was happening outside. Gabrielle could see if a person walked toward the car to retrieve her, but she could not see anything beyond, just trees.

Waiting alone in the car, not knowing what was happening, was terrifying.

CHAPTER FIFTY-SIX

He dodged a bullet. Gabrielle had gotten too close. Peter did not know the exact information she knew, but it was clear she suspected him to be, somehow, involved in the death of Rick Evans. Lucky for him, she was not all that bright. She thought she could just walk onto the pier and see whatever she wanted. Her car alone gave her away. The girl would never make it as a private investigator. Even so, he had to be more careful. He had no idea this woman was investigating him. If not for the chance of her stumbling upon Jimmy in Connecticut, Peter may have found out too late.

Now, here she was, awaiting her fate in the back of the SUV. He wished he could have gotten rid of Gabrielle while at the pier, but that was too spontaneous. Each of his killings involved copious planning. Every detail thought out before executed, careful not to leave a trace of evidence behind. When Miss Price followed him to the NATCO headquarters it threw him off his game. Peter did not know what to do with her, so he threw her in the back of the truck and continued with the shipment, buying time to devise a plan to get rid of the snoop once and for all.

Right now, there were more important matters to tend to. His monthly delivery had arrived via cargo ship. It needed to be sorted and divided among the assigned truckers. Peter did not trust just any of his employees with this precious cargo shipment. He was not one to fully trust anyone. He had been this way his entire life. There was a monster lurking within, a devious side that made him the power mogul he is today. If someone were to crawl inside his head and read his thoughts, they would be astonished. They would not believe that a man so nice and calm on the exterior could have such horrific, murderous thoughts on the inside. Peter was selfish, and he knew it. He did not care. He was put on this earth for himself and nobody else. Peter would stop at nothing to protect himself, and anybody who attempted to thwart him would be shut down.

He had a plan to be rich and powerful. From the age of nine, he knew this was his mission in life, and he would stop at nothing to get there. Today, he had achieved that goal. Granted, he had to ensure a few people were put in their place along the way, but it was worth every moment.

Drug trafficking was not an original part of his plan. Initially, he bought the trucking company hoping to turn it into the profitable enterprise it has become today. The previous owner, who was seventy-five, had nothing left to give. The owner had only five trucks in his fleet and was exhausted. The old trucking company stopped yielding a profit and was on the verge of bankruptcy. Lugo knew an opportunity when he saw it and jumped at the chance to invest in the business and make it his own. Within five years, the company turned a surplus of a couple million dollars, had sixty employees, and trucked all different types of cargo throughout North America.

Then, one day, while visiting his mother in the retirement community where she lived in Wethersfield, Peter ran into an old buddy from high school. When they were fifteen, they were inseparable. They had gotten into a lot of trouble at that age. His mother knew his old friend Sean was no good and eventually forbade them from hanging out.

But at that point, the bond of friendship had formed, and the damage had already been done. They spent a lot of time stealing cars, graffitiing buildings, and robbing innocent children on their way to school. The two boys spent a few months together in juvie. Eventually, they graduated high school and moved in separate directions. They lost touch like most good friends did, not because they had a falling out but because their lives took opposite paths.

When he saw Sean that day, it brought back a flood of great memories of the past. Lugo remembered the rush he got from disobeying the law and the resulting money he obtained. He would not trade that feeling for any other, and the risk outweighed any time spent behind bars. The resulting riches were worth the cost of protecting his freedom.

Sean told Peter he wrote for a freelance newspaper circulating throughout Connecticut. They talked briefly and agreed to meet for lunch a day later. Unlike most disingenuous offers of 'we should get together' that never wind up in a reunion, the two men met for lunch. They discussed their lives, their jobs, and their dreams. The conversation flowed as if they never missed a day——a testament to true friendship. Then it came out. Peter had a hunch his friend did more than a little freelance writing as his extravagance did not match his job. Most freelance writers were starving and struggling to pay rent. Sean, however, was driving the latest Hummer and wearing Hugo Boss designer clothes.

"Remember the good times we had stealing those cars? Don't you miss the adrenaline rush we got from jacking them?" Sean asked innocently of Peter, who knew there was a hidden agenda behind the statement.

"I do. I'm not afraid of the law," Peter stated purposely to incite further conversation.

"Do you want to know what I do in truth?" Sean motioned his index finger for Peter to lean in closer to him and looked around to ascertain there was nobody close enough in the restaurant to hear what was about to be said.

"Drugs."

"You do drugs?" Peter answered in disbelief. His friend did not appear to be strung out at the present moment.

"No, I traffic them." He was not a hundred percent clear why Sean was telling him this. "I think with your trucking company, we could yield a profit margin greater than I can make on my own."

Peter did not agree to this business merger right then and there. Although intrigued, he knew it was a risky enterprise and would take some serious consideration before agreeing. He thought about it for a couple of weeks, twenty days to be exact. Peter lost a lot of sleep in those weeks. The phone call he made to Sean would be one that would change the course of his life forever. Only, Peter was too greedy to agree to a merger. There was no way he would risk being in a partnership with Sean. Sean could never be trusted. He was just as sinister and ruthless as Peter, each of them unable to trust the other.

Sean had gotten involved with drug trafficking through a Mexican he met while traveling to Cabo. His trafficking involved monitoring parcels from ships into various ports in New York and Miami. With the addition of NATCO, the shipment could extend further into the landlocked parts of the United States and Canada.

Peter went straight to the source to foster a deal. Lugo and his trucking company were invaluable to the cartel. An insider with the ability to maneuver goods undetected was priceless to their mission. Peter did not directly tell the narcotics organization to get rid of Sean, but he had not heard from his high school buddy since the date an agreement was reached. No further discussions about Sean were ever had.

Initially, Peter was nervous, but after the first two shipments went smoothly, he became very calm about the entire operation. He dubbed it the Heroin Operational Truckers (HOT) Team and selected only a handful of his drivers to be in the know about the drugs. Among them was Rick Evans. Peter knew he would have to be extremely careful about whom he chose to be on this team. Lugo would have to give them a cut of the profit to make it worthwhile for them to risk their freedom by breaking the law. He also had to ensure these men knew this was a lifetime commitment. Once they knew about the drug trafficking, they could never turn back from the unit.

Peter knew the day would come when he would have to deal with a person wanting out of the illegal activity. He was not as prepared as he thought he would be when that day came. This reached a boiling point only twice in the past twenty years of NATCO operations. The second man to meet this fate was Rick Evans. The first was Earl Peterman.

Earl had been a truck driver his entire adult life. He was good at what he did and found immense joy through his travels. It was no secret the man loved to gamble. Most bosses would be annoyed at the loss of time spent in casinos rather than delivering cargo on time to the consignees. But the man was good at what he did, so Peter was sure to allow extra time on Earl's travels to shoot some craps.

Earl lost a ton of money in his lifetime. He never married or owned much property. Peter assumed this was due to Earl's gambling addiction. The evident greed was a perfect reason to let Mr. Peterman in on the opportunity of a lifetime. It was a no-brainer decision for Earl when presented with the ability to make more income. Shipping drugs meant more cash, a significant amount of more money. It was a way out of his cycle of debt. Peter knew he had made the right decision in enlisting Earl as a member of the HOT Team. Then, one day, something changed.

Earl had gone to San Francisco to deliver a truckload of goods to a client he worked with for the past five years. The client knew Earl well and developed a relationship with him. Along the route was a stop in Wyoming, where the drugs were dropped off. They, too, knew Earl. The client in Wyoming enjoyed seeing Earl, not because they particularly liked him, but because it meant their shipment had arrived.

Something on that last trip changed Earl. When he arrived back at the NATCO headquarters, he looked frazzled. Earl appeared disheveled and unshaven. Something had spooked him more than just a family death. He told Peter he no longer wanted to be on the operation team. He was no longer willing to ship the heroin. There was no persuading him otherwise. Earl would not go into details with Peter, but he was adamant about ending the route.

It was a decision that Peter was not ready for. Earl knew there was no other option. This was the first thing told to those who joined the secretive operation. It was the number one rule: there was no way out. Peter did not feel the least bit remorseful about the fate that came upon Earl. It was his own fault. Earl made a choice, a bad choice, and he had to face the consequences.

Peter sent Jimmy to Earl's apartment that dreadful day. He should have gone himself, but Peter was better off if he could avoid the actual pulling of the trigger. Jimmy did a terrible job of killing Earl Peterman. He botched the job horribly, and for months afterward, Peter feared it was the end of NATCO.

When Jimmy arrived at Earl's home, Earl knew exactly why Jimmy was there. He sat in his armchair calmly waiting for Jimmy to complete his assigned task. So, Jimmy did just that. He shot Earl——a single bullet right through the forehead. This is not the part of the job that was botched.

Jimmy then proceeded to trash the apartment. It had to look like a robbery. Only Jimmy is not the sharpest knife in the drawer. He trashed the television, ransacked all the dressers and cabinets, and cut through the mattress. Jimmy took an hour to complete the scene, yet he did not take a thing. What robber would spend an hour ransacking an apartment and not take anything? Also, there was no evidence of a forced entry. The lock was not jimmied, and the door latched when he left. Peter was furious at Jimmy for his stupidity. Peter, however, only had himself to blame. He should have completed the job himself.

But there was another thing——something that kept eating away at Peter. According to Jimmy, Earl knew Justin's death was no accident. Earl knew Jimmy cut the brakes on Justin Enrel's truck. Peter could not fathom how Earl obtained this information. They had been so careful. Peter obsessed over every detail in his mind. He never figured out how this information leaked. It gnawed at him. From that day forward, there was no room for error. He could never again leave any trace of evidence behind.

Lucky for Lugo, Earl had no family and a few enemies. He owed a hundred thousand dollars to a bookie for a bet he made in Reno on his last road trip. The police deduced that this debt was why Earl faced the fate he did. A shoddy police investigation, but there was no evidence to lead them to believe that NATCO was in any way involved with the death.

Peter thought about Justin Enrel and his last day working for NATCO. Justin was an ambitious young man. When Peter met him, he could see the greed in his eyes. Justin craved power. This was a dangerous mindset, and Peter knew that if he gave the boy too much power, he would want more—never fulfilled. For that reason, he decided Justin was not a suitable candidate for the special operations team. Justin, however, felt differently.

Somehow, the young boy got insider information that there was a special operation team. It was not clear he knew what that entailed, but it was clear he wanted to know more. Justin started snooping around and asking questions. He wanted to know who was on the team, what they knew, how much money they made, and how he could be a member. He would stop at nothing until he found out. Peter was sure once he discovered the information sought, he would use blackmail to get on the special team. Peter did not take kindly to extortion.

Justin was a snoop, and Jimmy kept close tabs on him. They tracked each person he spoke to and what information he knew. Justin was a good employee. He managed the trucks well, got to every delivery on time, if not early, and never missed a shift. Regarding the NATCO shipping industry, the boy was a valuable asset. If only he had kept his nose where it belonged, Peter would not have had to do what he did.

Jimmy provided a full account of the events that transpired the morning that Justin stepped out of line. He was in the yard checking to ensure all his cargo was in place for his next trip.

Along came Henry Wasserman. Henry is a man who keeps to himself, and every employee at NATCO knows to let him be. He never socializes at the obligatory happy hour upon returning to headquarters. He stands six feet tall with a muscular build. Not the inviting type. Henry was, and still is, part of the operational team. He loves the money he gets from illegal trafficking and would not risk losing his life or money for any reason.

Henry was about to leave for his trip up to Canada. He checked his cargo and headed inside the central office to go to the bathroom and complete some last-minute paperwork. Justin was there that morning as well. He saw Henry go inside and took the opportunity to snoop around the back of his truck. Justin entered the trailer and searched around the boxes. He was so involved in checking out the shipment that he did not hear Henry return. Justin found one shiny aluminum package. He was holding it in his hands when Henry came upon him. Henry was visibly angry.

"Just what in the hell do you think you are doing?"

Justin froze. He had no answer. He would not say what or why he was snooping in the back of the truck. Not one word came out of his mouth. All he could do was stand there and show Henry the package that he found.

This only incited further anger inside Henry. He walked toward the back of the truck where Justin stood. He grabbed the package out of his hand and snarled at the trespasser, "Get out!"

Justin did not have to be told twice. Without a word, he squirmed toward the exit and left the truck. He, too, had to ascertain whether his cargo was ready to go.

Henry watched him leave. He flipped open his cell and made a phone call to Peter.

Peter knew right away what to do as he had been closely monitoring Justin Enrel for the past several months. It was only a matter of time before Justin learned about the secret operations of the company he worked for. Not only did Justin find out about the drug trafficking, but he also now had hardcore proof. This information was deadly to both the organization and to Justin. He needed to be stopped from inquiring further and telling anyone about his discovery. Not a second more could pass while Justin retained this critical information.

Peter got off the phone with Henry and immediately called Jimmy. In anticipation of any potential breach, Jimmy and Peter had developed strategic actions to take should anybody ever discover the HOT Team. Jimmy was working at the headquarters checking the cargo and logbooks on all the trucker routes that morning. It was time to execute that plan.

As Jimmy hung up his cell phone, Justin Enrel approached him. He had his cargo list in his hand and awaited approval to start his route. Jimmy took the clipboard and headed to the truck with Justin for the final inspection. Justin appeared eager to get out of there. His mind was notably elsewhere and not on the actual task of getting the cargo to its specified location. Jimmy knew this was because of Justin's newfound knowledge about NATCO, but he dared not ask him about it.

Jimmy looked down on the checklist and sent Justin to the supply room on the farthest side of the headquarters to get a new fire extinguisher for underneath the truck dashboard, as the current one had passed expiration.

As Justin left to ensure his big rig complied with the federal regulations, Jimmy put his plan into action. It would take Justin at least ten minutes to get to the warehouse where the equipment was stored, about two or three minutes to locate a new extinguisher, and then about ten minutes to return to the truck. In total, Jimmy had twenty-three minutes to finish his plan.

He walked over to the garage about one hundred feet away. There on the metal bench were a pair of pliers and a pair of electrical scissors. Jimmy grabbed them and placed them into his front right pocket. He returned to the truck and scooted face-up underneath the front end.

Jimmy had some experience in car mechanics. His first job upon graduation was with a local auto body shop in Wethersfield.

He was also a Connecticut Technical Education and Career System (CTECS) high school student. This meant that he got to take vocational classes over academic ones. So, while most of his peers studied useless things like the French Revolution and complex algebra, Jimmy took auto shop. He learned to change oil, repair flat tires, and check brake pads. These were his most useful skills when Jimmy left high school. Skills he still uses to this day.

Jimmy knew exactly what he was doing as he lay with his back on the floor underneath the truck bed. He took a pocket flashlight out of his front left pocket and placed it between his teeth to illuminate the area above him. Then he took out the scissors and pliers. Jimmy scanned the bottom of the engine and found the cable for the brakes. He took one of the wires into his hand and snipped it with the scissors in his other hand. No one would be the wiser about the brake failure. The accident would prove to be fatal.

Peter shook his head at the thoughts of those who had gotten in his way. Soon, Gabrielle would be facing the same fate. He stood in the cabin with a clipboard. The last shipment was picked up and placed on the truck parked outside the front of the log home. Peter watched the truck pull down the driveway to leave toward the thruway. Now, Peter had to complete one last item—the task he was dreading.

It was not as if he enjoyed the death of those who got in his way. He felt that they deserved the fate they sought. People were nosy creatures in general. If they learned to keep their noses out of other people's business, there would be no problems. Gabrielle was not one of those people who could exercise this self-control. She could not stop herself from meddling in other people's affairs. She would be penalized for this with her life.

Now, he was standing in the empty cabin. The shipment this month had gone smoothly. There was nothing left to do except dispose of the girl. Jimmy was in the back bedroom, tracking the shipment onto the laptop. It was routine for them to track the shipment data into a chart showing exactly how much was received, whom it was given to, where it was going, and how much money there was to be collected upon the return. This usually took about twenty minutes. Peter decided to use the downtime to get rid of Gabrielle.

He wanted the killing to be glamorous. All morning long, he had been unable to devise a method for the murder. He decided it was just going to have to be simple. He would take her out of the truck, stand her near the woods, and take aim. Shooting her while she sat in the truck would be easier. The shot would be cleaner, and there would be less room for her to squirm. Peter, however, was worried about the blood splatter. It would ruin the leather upholstery of the truck, and he would be unable to clean it up without suspicion.

The body would be easy to get rid of. He would take it down to the lake, a mere five minutes down the road. The body could be weighted with cinder blocks. It would sink straight down to the bottom of the fifty-foot human-made sinkhole. Nobody would find her there. If they did, they would also find Brandon and Billy, the real trigger pullers of the bullets that killed the Evans' household.

Peter walked out of the cabin and down the gravel driveway toward the parked SUV. He had his gun easily accessible on his left hip. He got to the back of the truck and found Gabrielle silently waiting. He lifted the back door above his head and came face-to-face with his next victim.

"Hello, sweetheart." He took one look at her before removing her from the truck. She was an attractive lady. Peter thought if he had passed her on the street, he would certainly be one to turn his head and sneak a second look. Still, her beauty was no excuse for probing into the NATCO operations.

Gabrielle did not say anything in response to his presence. She snarled back at him, only making her more attractive. However, it would not stop his current mission.

Peter grabbed her by the hair on the back of her head and dragged her out of the truck. She fell to the ground with her hair hanging over her face. She screamed as she fell and sat on the ground, huffing heavily to catch her breath.

"Get up, you bitch," he yelled at her. Peter wanted her to look him in the eye as he pulled the trigger. He wanted her to see it coming.

She did not respond to his commands.

Peter did not take this lightly. He took his right leg and kicked her in the left thigh, repeating his demand, "Get up!"

"You are a ruthless bastard," she yelled back. This made Peter chuckle. "You think this is funny. I'm about to die, and all you can do is laugh."

This made Peter laugh more. It became one of those uncontrollable laughs where he could not stop. Only nobody else was laughing with him. It was a deep, sinister laugh. It was not contagious. It was mentally unstable.

Finally, Peter regained control of his outburst and, again, demanded Gabrielle rise to her feet. For whatever reason, whether it was the third time was a charm or she was simply tired of sitting, she rose to her feet. It took a few tries, as her hands were still locked behind her back in the handcuffs placed there at the pier.

"Are you going to kill me now?" Gabrielle inquired innocently.

This question puzzled Lugo. He had never been asked that question before and was unsure how to answer it. He was let off the hook, as Gabrielle did not wait for an answer and continued talking.

"You are a coward. Killing me is cowardly."

He was not pleased with her accusations. He wanted to pull the trigger right then and there, but something held him back from doing so at that exact point. He did, however, take the gun from its holster, place it in his right hand, and point it in her direction.

"Such strong words for a woman with a gun in her face."

"I don't fear death."

"Well, that's good, as it is inevitable." He pulled the trigger back on the gun and aimed it toward her.

"Wait!" she screamed.

For some unknown reason, Lugo hesitated. He did not pull the trigger but pointed the gun toward the ground. He himself could not say why he hesitated or did not pull the trigger and end it immediately. But for some reason, he did not. She was the enemy, but he let her have the last word.

"Before you kill me, I need to know the truth," she pleaded with him. He did not answer. He was intrigued but said nothing. "I need to know what happened to Rick Evans."

"You mean you don't know, you haven't figured that out already?" he asked, partially serious, partially sarcastic.

"Well, I know Cynthia loved her husband. I know she was not the killer. I know he worked for NATCO, and I know that, somehow, this all involves heroin."

"You know a lot," he sneered at her.

"I need to know what happened. You owe it to me."

"I do not owe you a thing!" he yelled back. This bitch was aggravating him. She was the one investigating him and his business, and now she thought he owed her something. This pissed him off. He raised his right arm and re-pointed the gun barrel in her direction.

"I know you killed Justin Enrel."

He remained stoic. *Is she trying to make me release the trigger?*

"I know you killed Earl Peterman."

He chuckled.

This was not the reaction she expected. "You find the death of Earl Peterman humorous?" she snapped.

"That man knew the rules when he agreed to this." Suppressed anger was making its way out.

Then, in a moment of clarity, it was as if Peter suddenly remembered why he was there. He remembered what he had walked outside to do before he was distracted with questions and incessant babble.

"This conversation is over."

He took the gun back to its target position. This time, he did not hesitate. Gabrielle closed her eyes in anticipation of what was to come. She did not want to see the bullet coming in her direction. A gun went off, and the bullet was released from its shaft at the speed of sound. The bullet hit its victim, knocking him to the ground with force.

CHAPTER FIFTY-SEVEN

Gabrielle opened her eyes. She was still standing. She did not feel any pain. She looked down, expecting to find blood smeared about the front of her clothes. Her body was clean. Her shirt was not red or stained.

How was this possible?

She was sure she heard a gun go off. She heard the sound of a bullet being shot, but she was still standing there, breathing in air and life. Gabrielle looked forward and noticed Peter Lugo no longer standing before her. He was lying face up in front of her, knocked unconscious to the ground.

Was this divine intervention?

At first, she thought he had turned the gun toward himself in a desperate act of suicide. A shocking turn of events in her favor as he did not seem remorseful for his actions during their brief conversation right before the gun went off.

"Gabrielle!" a familiar voice called out her name. She was not expecting the utterance and, at first, did not hear it or respond. "Gabrielle, are you alright?"

She turned to look in the direction the sound was coming from. There to her right, about two hundred feet away, stood Officer Thomas—Mike Thomas, whom she had left standing in his home the previous evening. She had so many questions. If her hands were not cuffed behind her back, she would have pinched herself to confirm that she was not dreaming. Gabrielle had no idea how the man found her, but he saved her life. He was still wearing the same clothes he had on when he told her Hank was dead——blue track pants and a gray hooded sweatshirt. In his hand hung a small revolver. Gabrielle knew, as soon as she saw the gun, that Mike was the one who shot Lugo.

Mike made his way over to Gabrielle. He fished in his pocket, searching for something small.

"Turn around," he motioned to Gabrielle. He fiddled with the handcuffs and was able to set her hands free.

Her wrists ached from the metal, which had secured her hands in an uncomfortable position for several hours. When free, she turned to face the man before her and swung both arms around his neck.

"Thank you," she whispered in his ear. It was all the energy she could muster to say at that moment.

Gabrielle looked toward Lugo and wondered if he was dead. She had forgotten Peter was not the only person at the cabin. She heard another voice.

"What's going on out here?" It was the voice of the SUV driver.

The man was walking from inside the cabin, now down the length of the gravel driveway, to the spot where Lugo lay unconscious. Mike and Gabrielle froze. They had let their guard down and were unprepared for another person to see them. The man saw the body lying on the ground and turned toward the two strangers standing nearby.

"You killed him," he exclaimed, in great wrath. "You killed him." He said it again as if the reiteration of those words might bring his friend back to life.

The body of Peter Lugo remained motionless on the ground. The man reached behind himself, into the waistband of his jeans, where he stored his gun. He pulled out a pistol and waved it frantically toward Mike and Gabrielle——visibly emotional over the loss of his friend.

Gabrielle and Mike backed away from the truck and the lifeless body on the ground. They moved cautiously, not wanting to startle the man before them into a shooting frenzy.

"Shoot them." It was the voice of Peter Lugo. The voice did not sound full and vibrant. It was weak and limp. Still, it was his voice giving instructions. "Jimmy, take your gun and kill them both."

Jimmy did not do as he was instructed. Instead, he headed closer to the body of his friend lying on the ground.

"Boss are you okay?" he asked, surveying the damage to his friend.

The shot must have knocked Lugo out. He was clearly hurt badly and unable to gather himself off the ground, but some life still allowed him to remain in this realm.

"Jimmy, you're not listening to me. Kill them. Kill them both."

At that moment, sirens could be heard. The backup officers Mike radioed before shooting Peter Lugo had found their way to the cabin. Three squad cars approached and surrounded the people standing outside. The cars came to a screeching halt, and four officers got out with their guns pointed toward Jimmy, who was still holding his weapon. Jimmy had no choice but to place his gun on the ground before him and place his hands high above his head in surrender.

One officer made his way to Jimmy to place handcuffs on him. Another officer radioed an ambulance and headed to Lugo to assess the damage. The third officer went into the cabin to uncover any evidence lingering inside. A fourth officer spoke briefly to Mike and Gabrielle about what had happened. He examined them to make sure they were okay and went into the cabin to help his colleague in the investigation.

The nightmare was over. Gabrielle had been saved.

After the investigating officer left, Mike made his way to Gabrielle. He grabbed her hand and squeezed it. "Are you okay?"

She nodded. She was fine, just fine. Even after all she had been through, this was the best she had been in years. She had found life. She had found not only her life but the life of her friend Cynthia.

Mike started to tell her he was sorry——sorry she was involved in all of this, sorry he did not believe her, sorry for most things.

Gabrielle stopped him from speaking. She knew how he felt. They were words that did not need to be said. Once the police gathered all the evidence, they would find out what happened that night in Preston, and Cynthia Evans would be a free woman. There was no need for words.

Mike pulled her close to him and kissed her on the lips. Gabrielle was not expecting this. She was pleasantly surprised. She pulled back to look into his eyes and smiled.

"Let's go home."

CHAPTER FIFTY-EIGHT

My eyes are open, and I can see clearly. The roof is covered with white drop ceiling tiles that push up when pressed. I am not at home. I hear a beeping noise to my left. I turn sideways to see what is making the constant pinging sounds and observe medical equipment, an intravenous line, and tubes. The soft flexible tubes are connected to both my right arm and my nose.

I am in a hospital; hooked to machines.

Suddenly, a tidal wave of memories overpower me. The last thing I recall is eating oatmeal—flavorless, mushy, inedible oatmeal. I was in jail; framed for murder. My husband was killed. My two children are dead. Everything I have left to live for is gone. Tears stream down the side of my face. This is reality, my horrific reality.

"She's awake." I recognize that voice. It is familiar. "Mike, go get the nurse. She is awake."

It is Gabrielle. The one person who believed me. I turn to my right and see her standing at the edge of my hospital bed. She looks put together. Her hair is blown out straight, and her face has a rosy glow. She is staring at me, smiling from cheek to cheek.

"Cynthia, can you hear me?" I am not sure how to respond. "Cynthia, if you can hear me, just nod."

This I can do.

This response makes Gabrielle giddier. It is time to break the silence. Her happiness is not helping my sullen mood.

"Gabrielle …" That is all I can manage to say.

I start sobbing. I cannot formulate any more words. I do not want to be alive.

Gabrielle does not say anything in response to my tears. She walks closer and grabs my hand in hers. She squeezes it gently. This simple act of consolation calms me down. Something about her presence here at my bedside gives me hope.

As she stands there in silence, I realize it was her voice I heard in my dreams——her voice talked to me.

"I heard you speaking." Gabrielle looks at me, puzzled. "I don't recall what exactly you were saying, but I distinctly remember hearing your voice."

She smiles softly. "I've been here every day, at your bedside, for the last four months, reading you my favorite novel."

"Four months?" *Have I been here that long?*

"Yes, you have been in a coma." I have no response, but I know she will keep explaining. "The police believe the man who killed your husband had a drug slipped into your food, making you unconscious."

My heart sinks to the bottom of my body as she speaks about Rick. I know it will be hard, but it is something that I have to hear. While I listen to Gabrielle speaking, something she says strikes a chord.

"You said *the man*. Did I hear you correctly? You said *the man that killed my husband?* Does that mean I'm no longer the number one suspect?"

"Yes." She smiles even more.

"How long have I been in this hospital?"

"Perhaps I should start from the beginning. There's a lot to explain."

She speaks, and I listen. She tells me about her investigation and her discovery of the Python belonging to Peter Lugo. She talks about her trip to Connecticut, being run off the road, kidnapped, and taken back to the cabin where the two of us had our last adventures together.

"That all sounds so awful. I can't even imagine what you have gone through." I pause. "You did that for me; why?" *You barely know me.*

"I don't know. Something deep down in my gut told me it was something that I had to do. I had no choice."

Truth be told, I feel that connection between us too. We had one of those meetings in which you immediately feel comfortable in the presence of the other person, as if cosmic forces brought us together. If I believed in reincarnation, I was sure we were friends, perhaps even star-crossed lovers, in a past life.

"The nurse will be in here in a minute or two." It is a man's voice, one I recognize.

I look up and see him standing there. He is the police officer who arrested me. The officer who would not believe my story, the man who questioned my innocence.

"What's *he* doing here?" It is a question not directed at anybody in particular.

Gabrielle senses my disapproval and tries her best to smooth over the situation.

"Cynthia Evans, this is Mike Thomas."

"I know who he is," I say in a condemning tone.

There is an uncomfortable silence in the hospital room.

"I think I'll just wait outside," Mike says as he turns around and leaves the room.

"He's not a bad guy. You just don't know him."

"He arrested me. He yelled at me. He branded me a murderer. The only other thing he could have done to me was spit in my face."

Gabrielle remains quiet. The look on her face reveals sadness. I know that I have hurt her feelings.

"Are you two an item?" I ask, though it is clear what the answer is before any response. "What happened to Hank?" Not that I wanted Gabrielle to remain in a relationship with that volatile man. He was a testosterone-filled filthy pig. If I never saw Hank again, my life would be better off.

"Hank is dead."

Be careful what you wish for.

Gabrielle continues the story she was busy telling. It all seems unreal.

"You know Mike was just doing his job." Advocating on his behalf makes it clear she is in love. We are barely friends, but it is obvious my opinion matters to her.

"I'm willing to keep an open mind."

Despite his initial treatment of me, the officer has gone out of his way to visit the hospital. Gabrielle states he has been here countless times with her. I am willing to give him a chance to redeem himself.

"We have a live one here," says the nurse as she walks into the hospital room. She is a hefty woman with short black hair. "Gabrielle, I know you two have much to catch up on, but I must ask you to leave for now as we need to run some tests. Mrs. Evans needs her rest."

Gabrielle picks up her purse beside the bed and slings it over her left shoulder.

"Is it alright if I come to see you tomorrow?"

"I would like that," I respond.

She grins and turns toward the doorway to leave.

"Hey, Gabrielle… so that you know, I've always preferred Cindy." She looks at me quizzically. "Cindy. My friends call me Cindy, not Cynthia."

She smiles brightly and nods her head. "I'll see you tomorrow, Cindy."

As she leaves, I feel a calmness in the universe. Gabrielle risked everything for me. Because of her bravery and persistence, I am given a second chance at life. At this moment, despite the tragedies that have befallen me, a glimmer of hope remains.

AUTHOR NOTE

Thank you for purchasing and reading my book. I am extremely grateful and hope you found joy in reading it. Please consider sharing it with friends or family and leaving a review online. Your feedback and support are always welcomed and allow me to only get better with each new manuscript.

I have dreamed of being an author since the age of ten. This is the first book I have been brave enough to publish. I have been writing and crafting this story for the last twenty years, mostly because, well you know, life... and I got in my own way. After finishing law school, graduate school, travelling the world, getting married and starting a family I figured now was the time.

I was born and raised on Long Island, New York and spent ten years in my early adulthood living carefree in New York City. I currently reside with my husband and two beautiful children in the western suburbs of Chicago, Illinois, where I am a practicing attorney.

I hope to continue to publish many more novels that entertain and thrill readers.

ACKNOWLEDGEMENTS

I want to thank my husband, Rob, and my children, Lillian and Jackson, for believing in me. I also want to thank the wonderful team at Word-2-Kindle.com, especially Marin Lewis and Izelle Theunissen, who provided great insights into my story and excellent feedback on editing and formatting. The amazing cover design would not exist without their creativity. Thank you also to Angela Pruden, who did an excellent job proofreading my final draft and spotting all the errors that I was blind to. Your work is appreciated much more than you will ever know. Lastly, thanks to my beta reader Caly James for some good insights into things I overlooked. These skillful people helped me to present a polished story.

I appreciate every reader who took an interest in this book. I hope you enjoyed the ride. If you are reading this, I appreciate you more than words can express.

www.ingramcontent.com/pod-product-compliance
Lightning Source LLC
Chambersburg PA
CBHW061225310726
48971CB00007B/1942